THE DRAGON'S LADY

THE DRAGON'S LADY

JOANNE PENCE

QUAIL HILL PUBLISHING

First e-book edition: December 2011

Second e-book edition (Quail Hill Publishing): September 2012

[Early editions published under the title *Gold Mountain*]

Third e-book edition (Quail Hill Publishing): November 2014

First Quail Hill Publishing Print: November 2014

Second Quail Hill Publishing Print: August 2018

© Roys | Dreamstime.com - Fire In The City Photo

ISBN: 978-1-949566-15-4

THE DRAGON'S LADY

To be a stranger in a strange land:
Whenever one feasts, one thinks of one's brother
twice as much as before.
There where my brother far away is ascending,
The dogwood is flowering, and a man is missed.
---Wang Wei (699-759)

The highbinder tongs hold secret sessions, the business of which is to arrange
for the collection of tribute. Each tong has its regularly appointed 'soldiers'
who are commonly known as 'Hatchet Men.' It is the sworn duty of these
Hatchet Men to murder all those who have invoked the displeasure of
the tong.
---Thomas F. Turner, Investigator, U.S. Industrial Commission, 1901

San Francisco Chinatown 1900

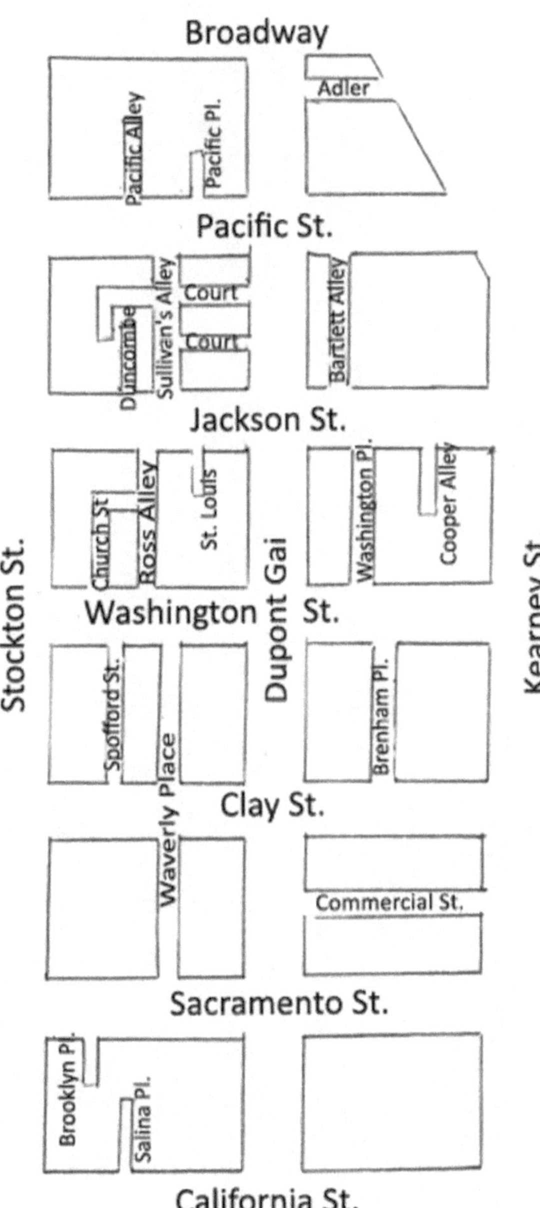

CHAPTER 1

San Francisco, Summer 1905

THE CARRIAGE STOPPED in front of a mansion in San Francisco's fashionable Pacific Heights. Ruth Greer, daughter of one of the city's prominent shipping magnates, emerged juggling purchases from her latest shopping spree. As she passed through the open gate in the wrought iron fence surrounding the home, she stopped, astonished.

A small, sad Chinese boy sat on the bottom step leading up to the front door. Not only were Chinese rarely seen outside of Chinatown, but their children never wandered around alone.

Ruth approached the child, determined to send him on his way. He looked about six or seven years old, and wore the dark gray pajama-like clothing common in Chinatown. His little face clouded over with apprehension as he watched her come closer.

"Who are you, boy?" she demanded.

No answer.

"Do you understand English?" Her green eyes flashed with irritation.

Slowly, he gazed up at her. He seemed to have no idea what to say, and was most likely too scared to answer anyway.

"It will be dark soon," she said sternly, not caring if he understood her or not. "You had better run along home right now!" So saying, she walked past him up the stairs.

Ruth came from one of the wealthiest of the hill-dwelling families of San Francisco. Her father, Winston Greer, was a self-made man whose fortune was in shipping. He owned one of the largest fleets to sail the Pacific, bringing goods from the Far Eastern markets into San Francisco. Ruth was the heiress apparent, the eventual sole owner and directress of a multi-million dollar international business, and no one was more aware of it than she.

The young boy watched her for a moment, and then lowered his head. As Ruth swung around to shut the door, she noticed the bowed head and glimmer of a tear on the child's cheek. Something stirred within her at the sight, but she had no idea what to do, having had no experience whatsoever with children, and regarding them as basically pesky creatures.

But then, she couldn't simply leave him there. As she looked at him, so small and afraid, the frown cleared from her brow. She left her purchases in the house, and went back outside.

"There, now," she said softly as she walked back down to where he sat.

He jumped to his feet.

"What's wrong, child?" she asked.

More silence.

"Do you understand anything I'm saying?" She gently placed a hand on his shoulder.

Very hesitantly, he gave a slight affirmative nod.

"Good. Now tell me what's the matter? Why are you crying?"

He softly murmured, "I can't find my house."

So that was it. The child was lost. "Well, I should say, you are a long way from Chinatown. Do you know your address?"

"My house is in Lungfun," he said.

"Lungfun? I've never heard of that, but then I'm not exactly on familiar terms with Chinatown," she replied.

"It is in China," he said. "I'm going to China, but I can't find the way."

"China?" She gave a small smile. "I'm afraid you're hardly likely to be successful. China is a long way from here, not to mention that an ocean lies between our countries. Did you know that?"

"No." The tears came more heavily now.

Ruth took his hand. "You live here in San Francisco, right?"

He nodded affirmatively.

"Do you know how to find your San Francisco home?"

He thought a moment, then replied, "It's near Dupont Gai."

Dupont Gai, the name the Chinese used for the main street in Chinatown, had become what all San Franciscans called it. The words conjured up exotic images and visions of intrigue for Ruth.

She had never been to Dupont Gai, had never even seen it, and thought it ominous, mysterious and more than a little exciting. And now, here was a little child who actually lived near that infamous street.

She looked down at the boy, fascinated and curious, yet a little appalled by him and all he represented to her.

"I can tell you how to get back home. All right?"

She looked at the boy, but he remained silent. She spoke again. "Do you have any money for the cable car fare? Do you know how to ride a cable car by yourself?"

With each question the tears, which had stopped, began again. He looked at the ground and shook his head.

She could send him home with the coachman, but then she would be asking an employee to ride into that notorious area, something she had no right to do for an unimportant stranger.

The only alternative was ... *No, I can't do that.*

Even before she completed her thought, a hundred reasons against it flooded into her mind.

But on the other hand ...

She didn't see how she could do anything but to take the child home herself. That would mean, however, that she would face the dangers of Chinatown—a place with fierce hatchet men who belonged to infamous tongs, opium dens, prostitutes known as "sing-song" girls, and a place where people vanished right off the streets and were forced into slavery or worse in China – being "Shanghaied" they called it ...

"Stuff and nonsense!" she said aloud to the child's surprise. The area couldn't be as dangerous as all that.

In fact, she suspected that Chinatown wasn't dangerous at all, and that its whole wild reputation was a ruse devised by men so they could have a place to go without wives and lady friends tagging along. A place for wild, scandalous fun. Ruth heard that despite all the so-called dangers, many white men were frequent visitors there, and gladly took part in gambling, dining, opium smoking—and possibly more—and returned home safely, the worse only for the wear they inflicted upon themselves.

The more she thought about it, the more she liked the idea of having a first-hand glimpse of what all the fuss was about. The child offered the perfect excuse. Besides, nothing would happen to her. She was Ruth Greer.

With the self-assurance that drove all who knew her to distraction, she took the boy's hand and together they began the short walk along Pacific Heights to the Jackson Street cable car. Ruth passed a couple of her neighbors' servants along the way and was quite bemused by their gaping expressions of shock and disbelief as they watched Ruth Greer, her red hair elaborately combed in the latest fashion and wearing a Paris original, not only walking along the street like a commoner, but holding hands with a little Chinese boy.

Ruth and the boy soon reached Jackson Street and after a short wait a cable car came by. With speeding glides, head-snapping jerks, and raucous clanging of bells, the cable car carried them from the hilltops where the richest of California's new gentry lived, down the streets towards Chinatown. They rode along in silence. Ruth had not even thought to ask the boy his name, much as one did not inquire about the children of servants.

The cable car conductor turned towards Ruth. "You'll have to get off here for Chinatown, Ma'am," he said. "We turn and don't go all the way to Dupont Gai."

When the car came to its lurching halt, Ruth and the boy stepped off it. She saw nothing to indicate that this sector of San Francisco was different from any other. On the next block, however, things began to change. The first change was the smell—an aroma of cooked food with spices and flavorings that Ruth had never tasted. The smell was pungent, and became slightly unpleasant as they walked further along. They passed a shop with dried meats and fish hanging from the ceiling, and sacks of food marked with the strange Chinese characters Ruth found so attractive, yet so impossible to regard as writing. She assumed the sacks must contain rice or wheat from the size of them.

At the next shop she stopped and stared at the goods again, until she noticed that the shopkeeper stared at her with every bit as much surprise and curiosity as she felt towards him and his shop. She turned with a flourish and continued down the street.

At the end of the block she came to an intersection, and there it was—Dupont Gai.

Excitement pulsated through her. The street was at once much more and much less than she had expected. For one thing, she felt as if she was no longer in San Francisco. It was another country, just minutes from her home, and felt more foreign to her than the many European cities she had visited.

"All this is incredible!" she exclaimed. Everything seemed profoundly and shockingly colorful, noisy and smelly. Signs in red and gold with big, black Chinese characters on them hung in windows; wind-chimes and banner-type signs dangled from roofs and over doorways of shops. Shopkeepers displayed goods on tables, in carts or barrels placed on the sidewalk. Between the signs Ruth didn't understand, the goods and foodstuffs she had never seen before, and the crowds of people bustling up and down the street, she felt both dazed and exhilarated. How had she missed all this?

"I know how to find my house," the child said. "I go now."

She could let him go ahead alone, and then turn around and head back home herself. No harm done; no danger. But when she looked at the intriguing sights around her …

"No. I said I'd see you home, and so I will! Which way do we go?" Ruth took his hand again and walked with the boy along Dupont Gai, taking in everything she could. People who looked, dressed and spoke in a way that seemed quite odd, went about their business and hardly paid any attention to her, but spent far more time staring at the boy. She was used to being the center of attention, and decided they must have been looking at the child because of their surprise to see him with a prominent white woman.

Before setting out on this little adventure, she thought all she wanted was a glimpse of Dupont Gai. Now that she was here, however, she didn't want to tear herself away. With the child, she headed deeper and deeper into the area white San Franciscans referred to as Chinatown.

Eventually the boy turned off of Dupont Gai, continued up a steep street for about a half block, turned again and headed down a small, narrow side street. A hand-painted sign announced the name as "Waverly Place."

A door to a house in the middle of the block opened, and an elderly Chinese woman stepped onto the stoop, faced the boy, and seemed to give him a piece of her mind in a high screechy voice at the same time as her eyes betrayed her joy at seeing him. She was dressed in a black sheath that covered her from neck to floor, and she had long gray hair pulled straight back off her face into a tight bun at the base of her neck. She looked agitated, angry, yet intensely relieved to see the boy again. The child hurried to her without saying a word, and put his arms around her. She gave him a quick hug before he stepped back, pointed at Ruth and spoke quickly in Chinese.

"I was trying to help him home," Ruth attempted to explain, but quickly realized that her words were lost on the woman.

The woman bowed deeply to Ruth then spoke to the boy who hurried inside calling out to someone in the house.

The woman again smiled and nodded as she held the front door open and beckoned Ruth inside.

"Thank you," Ruth said automatically. She didn't hesitate, but entered a short hallway that led to a narrow staircase. The old woman gestured for Ruth to follow her up the stairs. The steps and walls were bare except for a slap-dash coat of whitewash on the walls. The staircase was quite long, and when Ruth reached the top she found a starkly empty hall with a several doors along both sides.

The old woman went to the first door on the right and opened it, then bowed and nodded for Ruth to enter.

As Ruth stepped from the barren hallway into the room she felt as if she had entered another world. The door shut silently behind her.

The large room had creamy white walls and a floor of dark polished wood that shone like glass. In the center stood a low, square table of ebony elaborately inlaid with mother of pearl. A high cabinet of black lacquer with intricate gold leaf design stood against one wall, and on the wall opposite, a silk tapestry hung An incense burner languorously smoked in the corner, filling the air with a musky, sweet aroma.

Ruth wondered if she should stand there or sit on the chaise upholstered with a bright orange and gold brocade in a Chinese star motif, or perhaps on one of the three high-backed chairs with simi-larly colorful upholstery in a mandala design. Everything about the room and its furnishings was alien to her. The realization struck that no one knew where she was. But as quickly as the thought arose, she tamped it down. Fear was a thing unknown to Ruth Greer, and she wasn't about to let it enter her life now.

She heard a footstep behind her and turned. A tall, lithe man entered the room and walked, sleek and panther-like, towards her. He did not wear the braid, or queue, that was often seen in Chinatown. Instead, his straight, blue-black hair was cut Western style, and was only slightly longer than fashionable. His clothing was anything but Western, however. He wore a black tunic and slacks. The yoke and sleeves of the tunic had been lavishly embroidered with silk thread in red and gold that shimmered as he walked. He was of proud, handsome demeanor even as he eyed her with a look filled with both suspicion and curiosity.

Ruth stared back with equal boldness, and maintained unwavering eye contact as he approached.

He stopped and bowed slightly, jet black eyes locked with hers. "My name is Li Han-lin. I understand you have returned my son to my household." The words were stilted and carefully pronounced.

Ruth was relieved that he knew English. "It was the least I could do. The boy seemed lost, and he's far too young to be alone on the streets of this city."

"Yes, very young, indeed. I want to thank you."

"You are most welcome," she replied. She could almost see grammar rules being called forth as he spoke, and smiled at both his attempt and his success. For a moment, his eyes smiled too, but then it seemed as if a veil to mask his expression descended. He bowed again, and to her surprise, openly studied her. His gaze swept over her lavish day gown and jacket, leather walking shoes with small heels, and then up to her red hair and large green eyes—eyes that regarded him with equally frank curiosity.

Rush found the penetrating intensity of his gaze, mixed with his exotic good-looks, surprisingly disturbing. The coy charm and teasing flirtatiousness she always used with American men seemed out of place, and she realized she had no idea how to deal with this man. She drew in her breath, then gravely stated, "It appears he may have been running away."

"Running away?" Han-lin sounded surprised.

"Yes. He said he wanted to go to China."

Han-lin's eyebrows rose at this news. "Please, won't you join me in some tea? I would like to teach about this."

"To learn?" she asked, confused.

"Yes, to learn about my son." He motioned his hand towards a chair for her to sit. He went to the door and, opening it slightly, softly speaking Chinese to someone standing nearby.

He returned to Ruth and sat on the chaise opposite her. "I'm afraid I was not told your name," he said.

"Ruth Greer," she replied, expecting some reaction, but getting none. "And yours was...let me see, *'Lee Hahn-lin'* did you say?" She pronounced the name slowly and phonetically.

"Yes, that is a good pronunciation." Now, his expression turned both curious and bemused. "You must be very brave, I think, Ruth Greer. Is it not a fearful thing to come to Chinatown—especially for a woman?"

Oddly, with that question, Ruth's discomfort began to dissipate. "I'm not brave. Perhaps I have too much curiosity, but I didn't even think of being afraid." That bent the truth only slightly. Why had she really come here, she wondered, and why, for heaven's sake, didn't she hurry home now instead of accepting tea?

"Good, very good." He nodded his head in honest approval.

Just then the door opened and the same old woman who had greeted Ruth earlier came in carrying a tray with tea and sweetmeats.

As the woman poured the tea, and Han-lin explained the flavors and fruits that made up the small cakes, Ruth decided he must be thirty at most, no more than five or six years older than her. She perused his face—the deep black of his hair, brows and lashes, his dark brown eyes, and the warm ivory color of his skin. His nose was straight and small compared to the large, bent or bulbous noses of many of the men who came to call on her. His mouth was also nicely shaped, not protruding, or worse, spittle-laden. She had never been close to a Chinese man before, and she was surprised that his looks were—to her eye—refined and exquisite, a reaction that both confused and troubled her.

He stopped talking and waited for her to respond. It took a moment for her to recall his question about the desserts her family served. She hoped he didn't realized how intently she had been studying him. They continued to talk about food—likes, dislikes, and interesting concoctions they had eaten. It was an inane conversation, she had to admit, but for some reason, she enjoyed it, and Han-lin seemed to as well. She had never before talked to or laughed so readily with someone from a culture so foreign to her.

He asked about his son, if the boy had given her any indication of why he was heading for China. She didn't know, and Han-lin said he would talk to the child, and try to learn what had upset him so badly that he'd want to go so far from his family.

As they discussed the boy, the door opened again and a beautiful young Chinese woman entered. She was exceptionally petite and exquisitely dressed in a silk and satin dark blue dress with a high collar and slanted cut of the bodice. From the waist, where Western clothes flare out in bustles and petticoats, this dress hung straight and smooth over her hips and along her legs. A slit along the seam from the floor to her knee gave Ruth a start.

The woman nodded towards Han-lin first, and then stepped up to Ruth and bowed deeply.

"This is my wife," Han-lin said. "She would like to thank you for returning our son, Pao-yang, but she does not speak English."

"She is very beautiful," Ruth said softly. "Please tell her I was glad to be able to help the boy, and that I am delighted to be here."

Han-lin translated, and then asked his wife to join them in their tea.

Ruth turned to Han-lin. "I was wondering how you learned such fluent English. Have you been here long?"

"You are kind, but I find my English very poor. I have been in this country about five years. I learned English in China from American missionaries. We have many. Did you know that?"

"I didn't," Ruth admitted.

"My wife was not allowed to leave her father's house, so she was never taught to speak English. It makes it difficult for her now. I'm afraid I have no patience to teach her."

"There must be classes here that she can take, aren't there?"

"The adult classes are only for men. Chinese women are supposed to stay in the home," he explained.

"That's a pity," Ruth said, her mind racing. Was that an invitation? Dare she take it? Ever since she entered this house, ever since she turned the corner on Dupont Gai, in fact, she had been fascinated by everything she saw and heard. Her own life suddenly seemed boring, dull, and hideously self-centered. She wanted to learn more about Chinatown and the people in it. She glanced at Han-lin. She wanted to be able to come back to this house. Here was an opportunity, and if she didn't take it, would she regret it? Regret was something Ruth Greer had never experienced, and she decided that this wasn't the time to start.

"I was just thinking," she began cautiously, "I could teach your wife English. I would love to, in fact. It would be fun, and I could learn some Chinese in return."

"That is true," Han-lin said seriously, but almost too quickly as if he had somehow anticipated Ruth's offer. He added, "Then you could both benefit." He turned and spoke rapidly to his wife. They talked only a brief while when Han-lin turned back to Ruth and said, "My wife would be honored for you to teach her as long as you so desire."

"Wonderful," Ruth said smiling at the woman.

"Would you mind also if the children sat in on the lessons with you?" Han-lin asked. "They would be no trouble."

"How many children do you have?" she asked.

"Two boys and one girl."

"I'd love to help them," Ruth said. "I'll get books and supplies together and then come back on Thursday morning, about ten o'clock, if that would be all right? But now, I must be going. It's getting late." She stood.

"I shall call for my carriage to take you home." Han-lin jumped up and went to the door to speak to the ever-present servant just outside it.

His carriage? For some reason, that surprised her. She hadn't thought of Chinese people as having carriages. How unobservant and small-minded had she been? "Well then, until Thursday, Mr. Han-lin, Mrs. Han-lin, it was a pleasure meeting you."

"A real pleasure for us too, Miss Greer," said Han-lin. "One thing, though, I should explain. My name, Li Han-lin—Li is my family name and Han-lin is my given name. In Chinese my 'last' name comes first. So I am Mr. Li and my wife is Mrs. Li."

Ruth looked momentarily puzzled, but then she smiled. "I do have a lot to learn from you."

"Then, it is good we shall meet again," he said, his voice soft and low as their eyes met and held a moment before Ruth dropped hers, flustered without knowing why. Men never flustered her; she was the one who caused them to act awkwardly, and this turnabout bothered her.

"Until next time, then," she said, hurriedly and breathlessly, then added, "Good day."

The wife bowed.

Han-lin murmured good-bye as he watched Ruth follow his servant down the steps and out the door to the waiting carriage.

CHAPTER 2

T'ANG TSU-SHAO ENTERED his room and tore off his clothing. He had to get the stench of cigars and the Americans' food and drink from his nostrils. Wrapping himself in a robe, he reached for his opium stash, and meticulously prepared a pipe. He lit the opium lamp, filled the ceramic bowl with opium powder, and then attached the bamboo stem to it. The lamp channeled the amount of heat needed for the opium to vaporize.

T'ang lay back on his bed and inhaled the rich smoke. The sweet aroma enveloped him as he tried to forget the experience he had just had. That he, leader of the Wang Shao tong, would have to enter an agreement with a round-eyed barbarian was more than despicable. He hated it, yet it was necessary. The terms had been agreed upon. T'ang offered Winston Greer a great deal of money for a pittance of space on his cargo vessels; too much money for Greer to refuse. The space would be used for opium. The San Francisco port authorities would not check on the cargo Greer carried, thanks to the man's reputation ... and the bribes he paid out.

It was interesting, T'ang thought, that even a man as rich as Greer, was ultimately greedy.

Their deal should make T'ang wealthy. Soon, he would be the biggest and the best among the tong leaders. Bigger even than the husband of his half-sister, the man he despised over all others, Li Han-lin. Their rivalry was long and bitter. He was amazed neither had killed the other yet. Once, Li had smote T'ang down as if he were a fly, but did not kill him for his wife's sake. That had been his fatal mistake.

Soon, this rivalry would be over. The opium would bring T'ang enough money and power to be rid of Li Han-lin forever.

T'ang drifted into an opium induced stupor filled with dreams of wealth and revenge ... and his half-sister. They shared a father, a dissolute man, who knew how to enjoy life. T'ang had been a shy, awkward boy of fourteen, when his eight-year old half-sister discovered how different his body was from hers. She explored him, and taught him to crave her touch. As she grew older, she taught him to touch her in special ways, ways he knew were lewd and indecent, and all the more seductive and erotic because of that. She was bold and beautiful, and enjoyed the control she had over him. She ruined him for all other women, and much as he tried to find a replacement, he could not. Fortunately, she was clever, and to this day managed to sneak away from the Li household from time to time, claiming her husband could not pleasure her the way T'ang did. As his lips turned into a grimace-like smile at the memories she evoked, they exposed blackened, snarled teeth that gave his small, thin frame a more skeletal look than usual.

A smart rap on the door awakened him with a jolt. T'ang shook the drowsiness from his head and slowly rose to open the door.

A lovely girl of about fourteen or fifteen was pushed inside T'ang's room by an officer of his tong.

"This is the woman the fuss was about," the officer said. "She was a gift to our tong from Dee Bao, the peddler. He got tired of all the trouble she caused him. He wanted her and took her, but she kept running away. She's smarter than she looks!" Both men chuckled at that. "Dee Bao gave her to us to keep with the others. He just asked free use."

T'ang snorted. "The man's a pig." He eyed the girl. "But he does have a good eye for women. Who is she? Do you know?"

"Her name is Soo Mai-ching. Her father is first cousin to Soo Chen-gai of the Yuen-li tong."

At the news, T'ang roared with laughter. The girl raised her eyes and looked with fear at the creature that could have such a maniacal ring to his mirth.

"Yuen-li! My brother-in-law's tong! That is wonderful." He

stepped closer to the woman and placed his hand about her throat and chin, forcing her face upward towards his. "Ah yes, this is very good indeed." His other hand roamed elsewhere over her body, admiring the beauty before him. The girl shuddered under his touch, which caused him to laugh again.

He dropped his hands, and ran them over his own eyes, heavy with opium. "Keep her. But don't let anyone have her. If she truly is the cousin of Li Han-lin's friend, I may have a very personal interest in this one." He all but dropped onto his bed. "Go now."

The two left the room quietly as not to disturb T'ang further.

CHAPTER 3

RUTH SETTLED BACK into the coach, alternately shaken yet excited about her Chinatown adventure. Not even her coming-out party and being named debutante of the year had matched this day. Everything before was known and, frankly, expected by her. Now, she had met the unexpected, and she loved it.

As Ruth stepped inside her home her mother, Blanche Greer, stormed towards her. Blanche had been drinking, as usual. "Where have you been?" she cried. "You were supposed to get home hours ago. I've been frantic!"

"No need to be. I'm quite all right. I went to Chinatown."

"What!"

"I was in Chinatown visiting a Chinese family."

"I don't believe it; I can't believe it!" Blanche decided it would be proper to faint over such news; first, however, she rushed to the parlor to find a soft chair to collapse into, crying out about a flurry of heart palpitations. "I don't want you to ever go to such a place again!"

"I'll be fine, mother," Ruth said as she climbed the stairs to her room.

"We'll see about that!" Blanche called. "I'll tell your father and he'll decide!"

Ruth didn't bother to answer. Winston Greer never came between Ruth and her wishes. He doted on her, and often said she was the one good thing to come out of his domestic life, which was otherwise a complete failure.

It was ironic that despite being so shrewd, careful and able in his business dealings, his choice of a wife had been such a disaster. He really had no excuse for it, either, having married at the relatively mature age of thirty-five. Nevertheless, the big bear of a man melted over a pretty young thing named Blanche Eugenie Champlain, and had regretted it ever since. He had thought she was everything he was not—beautiful, elegant and innocent. Over the years he found to his dismay that the beauty faded, the elegance could be learned by himself as much as by anyone else, and the innocence stemmed from a total lack of cleverness or sophistication. Winston Greer's child bride never did grow up but simply went from being "child-like" to "child-ish," and it hadn't been a pretty thing to watch.

Ruth's birth had been difficult for Blanche and the doctor announced that no more children would be possible. Not being able to produce sons to leave his empire to was a bitter pill for Greer, but as soon as she began to talk, Ruth devoted her energies to proving to her father that since he had her, he didn't need sons. He learned the lesson well. Ruth Greer was "daddy's little girl" and everyone soon discovered exactly what that meant. She could do no wrong—she knew it, and her nannies and governesses soon either discovered it or were dismissed.

From the time she turned eighteen, Ruth rather than Blanche was the real hostess at Greer's social as well as business gatherings. He groomed her to learn to run the business with as strong a hand as he wielded.

As she grew older, she came to be considered one of the great beauties of the West Coast, having inherited Blanche's good looks. But she went through suitors with casual abandon, coldly grinding them up and spitting them out without a thought for their devastated male pride. She enjoyed proving she was better than them, and if that caused her to be alone, she didn't mind in the slightest.

The family shipping business provided an outlet for her energies. She thought about it and worked at it constantly. She did find time, however, over the next two days, between luncheons and various other social and business events, to also give thought to the Li family. She tried to figure out how to best teach a language to people who could not understand the explanations, and finally decided to start with a set of nouns that could be sketched or pointed at, and hoped to come up with something better later on.

On the day of Ruth's first English lesson, she left the house without saying a word about where she was going, and took the Jackson Street cable car to Chinatown.

Along Dupont Gai, most of the buildings were small and shabby, not at all like the fine structures going up elsewhere in San Francisco, and nothing like the Nob Hill and Pacific Heights mansions that made up her world. Here, many were unpainted, and the wood looked like tinder waiting for a flame. As she turned onto Waverly Place, and spotted the Li house, she realized that it, too, though beautiful once inside, on the outside appeared ugly. Ruth's anxiety and anticipation grew geometrically with each step that brought her closer to the house. At the door, she knocked. Almost instantly, the same old woman Ruth had seen before opened it. She greeted Ruth and led her up the narrow flight of stairs. This time, however, instead of entering the first door on the right, she led Ruth to a large sunny room where she found Mrs. Li and three children, Pao-yang, a girl about age six, and a boy who looked hardly four years old.

Pao-yang jumped to his feet and gave a bow. With a huge smile he said, "Good morning, teacher."

Ruth smiled back. "Good morning, Pao-yang. Are you my translator?"

"Yes, teacher. Please let me introduce my little brother, Chan-hun, and my sister Ai-yeong."

After some time spent on introductions and in trying to get the shy Mrs. Li to say "hello" as her first English word, the lesson commenced.

It continued for about an hour when suddenly the three children jumped to their feet while staring at the doorway behind Ruth, and then they bowed. Ruth turned quickly and felt the color rise to her cheeks as she beheld Han-lin standing in the doorway watching her. She thought she remembered how he looked over these days since she had seen him last. But seeing him now made her realize she had "Westernized" his features. The sunny morning light caused him to look younger than she remembered, and, in fact, handsomer. This time he wore no embellishments on his blue tunic, and she saw that fine embroideries weren't necessary for him.

"Good morning," she said, and knew she was doing a poor job of hiding her pleasure at seeing him. But then, why should she hide it? He needed to know she was enjoying being here with his family.

"I am sorry to have interrupted your lesson," Han-lin said. "But I had to see why such strange, foreign noises were coming from my children's mouths." He fought to keep a grin from his face.

"Oh, very funny!" she laughed. "They're doing nicely. You have a lovely family and they are a pleasure to work with."

"Thank you."

"Anyway, it's good you came in. I've been here over an hour, and that's more than enough time for any language lesson." Ruth felt as awkward as a schoolgirl as she quickly gathered up the books and papers she had brought. She turned from Han-lin and explained to Pao-yang that the lesson was over for the day, but that she would be back the next day and they must all practice until then.

As she was about to take her leave, Han-lin said, "Miss Greer, I am wondering if you would be interested in a brief tour of Chinatown with me this afternoon? We could have some lunch first, and then see some of the less notorious sights."

Ruth was momentarily speechless. Tour Chinatown? Did she dare to believe what she had heard? She thought of stories she had heard of the place, and suddenly imagined herself sneaking around it—climbing over rooftops, hiding in back alleys, scurrying through the supposed underground tunnels, all to avoid being caught by the dreaded tong hatchet men. It was a girlish, romanticized, adventurous daydream, right alongside being carried off on a pirate ship or joining a nomadic band of gypsies. Yet here she was being asked to tour Chinatown in broad daylight, obviously quite safely, with this interesting man. She was elated. "That would be wonderful! Yes, thank you!" she said, and realizing her voice had betrayed too much pleasure in the afternoon's prospects she felt her cheeks redden in embarrassment. She quickly turned and said good-bye to Mrs. Li and the children.

oOo

Han-lin watched Ruth as he silently waited at the door to the classroom. He felt bemused but strangely pleased at her reaction to his suggestion that she spend the day with him. No, not with him—he cautioned himself against such thoughts—but rather her joy was at seeing Chinatown and satisfying the obvious curiosity she had about it. He stood back as she went before him out the classroom door. Her skirts brushed against his legs and his nostrils filled with the scent of roses and musk from her perfume. As she approached the steep staircase, he reached out and took her arm. She started at the feel of his hand, but then smiled as she realized he was trying to help her.

When she reached the doorway, Han-lin let her go.

His wife, like most Chinese women, was small and fragile. Ruth Greer was much taller, almost as tall as he was, and her body lush with womanly curves. Her arm felt solid under his hand, and he had been loath to let her go. She walked ahead of him through the door and onto the street, something a woman from his country would never dream of doing. He smiled at her boldness—and at his own, since he never intended to ask her to lunch when he entered the classroom. He simply wanted to see her once more, assuming she wasn't nearly as beautiful or interesting as he kept imagining since the day he met her.

He had been wrong about that—she was even more so.

The day was bright and sunny, the air brisk. Summer days were rarely hot in San Francisco. The thick morning fog burned off about nine or ten o'clock, leaving a dampness over the city, and rolled in again at sunset from the ocean through the magnificent Golden Gate. The days were warm yet breezy, the air clean and pure. It was a perfect day for a walk.

Han-lin turned left and Ruth quickly followed along, rushing to keep up with him. He stopped abruptly and turned to her. "I am so sorry. I must remember that when walking with a Western woman one does not walk ahead, as with a Chinese woman. I will proceed more slowly."

Ruth laughed somewhat breathlessly. "I would appreciate that."

On Washington Street, Han-lin explained that they would be having lunch at a restaurant owned by a friend of his.

As they stepped inside the front door a waiter rushed up and bowed low to Han-lin. He gave Ruth a peculiar look as he led them to a small table in the corner. There were only two other tables with customers and as they passed, the men at the other tables rose to greet Han-lin.

Han-lin held the chair for Ruth to sit, and he spoke rapidly to the waiter before sitting across from her.

"This seems to be a lovely restaurant," Ruth said.

"The food here is quite good," Han-lin replied. "Have you ever had Chinese food before?"

"Only at your house the other day."

"That was but the merest hint of what can be served."

"I am looking forward even more to this meal, then."

"Good. I ordered some of our simplest dishes. Sometime later I'll order you a meal that is truly 'exotic.'"

Han-lin wanted to take back his words as soon as he said them. How could he have assumed she would want to share another meal with him? And then to announce such an assumption? To his relief, Ruth not only looked pleased by his words, but nodded as if she agreed with them. Just then the waiter approached with the first dishes. As he placed each item on the table, Han-lin explained what it was. The waiter then placed a pair of chopsticks beside Ruth's dish, bowed to Han-lin and walked away.

"Oh, my." Ruth turned the chopsticks over and over in her hands. "I have no idea how to use these!"

"It's not hard," Han-lin assured her. "It just takes a bit of practice." He showed her how to hold the chopsticks in one hand, keeping one stick stationary while being able to move the other up and down. Ruth reached the conclusion that her fingers would not bend in the right directions until Han-lin took hold of her hand and properly placed the chopsticks in it. He didn't know where he found the boldness to touch her. Her hand seemed large to him, and her fingers long, yet it was a soft, feminine hand. He noticed her eyes widen at his touch, but she didn't pull away, and he didn't let go.

He tried to ignore the quickening of his pulse as scooted his chair closer and concentrated on helping her learn to hold the chopsticks. When he lifted his gaze from her hand to her face, he saw that her eyes were on him. He scarcely breathed, but held her gaze a long moment—eating implements the farthest thing from his mind— before she shifted slightly, and he let go of her.

She smiled, and then plunged the chopsticks into the plate of noodles, squeezed her fingers together the way Han-lin showed her to grip the food, and raised up her hand. One lone noodle had been captured, and then it slowly slithered off the chopsticks and fell back onto the plate.

Ruth looked crestfallen. She tried again, but overshot the mark and the chopsticks twisted past each other like scissors. She tried again. This time she got two short pieces of noodle trapped. She squeezed the sticks, as if daring the noodles to slip from her grasp, then she leaned forward, opened her mouth wide, and shoved the end of the chopsticks in it.

Han-lin felt ready to burst from wanting to laugh, but constrained himself so as not to embarrass Ruth or stop her attempts. She caught his eye, and as if realizing how amused he was, she laughed aloud, covering her mouth with her hand. Han-lin couldn't hold back any longer, and joined her.

He noticed the other men in the restaurant gawking at him, and he could well imagine what was going through their minds, but he at that moment, he didn't care.

With a bit more practice, plus the aid of a soup spoon, Ruth managed to eat. As she concentrated on the chopsticks, he studied her. From the time he heard her name and watched her poise and bearing he knew who she was. In Chinatown the name of Winston Greer was well known as the Chinese were very involved in shipping and merchandizing between the mainland and the east Asian ports. Greer did not control the China trade, but he was the most influential person involved in it.

Han-lin had heard that Greer had a daughter that he idolized, and who was reputed to be merciless and tough. She was said to be one who would go anywhere, do anything and be afraid of nothing. Marching into a stranger's home in Chinatown was a good indication of that boldness. Han-lin had to admit, however, that Ruth was far more feminine than he imagined from the stories told about her. She was far more pleasant, open, and willing to laugh.

He couldn't help but think he shouldn't have anything to do with Winston Greer's daughter, and suspected he would be much better off if he asked her never to cross his threshold again, yet watching her sit at his side in a beautiful green dress that enhanced the emerald color of her eyes, while regarding him with such keen interest, he knew he could not—would not—put her out of his life if he could help it.

And the realization scared him.

After the meal the waiter brought some fresh tea.

Han-lin rolled himself a cigarette, and the waiter ran out from the back room with a footstool for him; none for Ruth. Han-lin put his feet up, leaned back in his chair and closed his eyes while puffing dreamily on the rich tobacco.

He watched Ruth checking out the other customers in the restaurant. He suspected she recognized how curious they were about her. The room fairly rang with their questions—who was she? Why was she there?

Han-lin ignored the others. He wanted to learn more about English, and asked many questions about usage and idiomatic expressions. As they spoke, he realized words and expressions he had learned long ago were coming back to him much quicker than he ever thought they would.

Ruth, in turn, asked him about the Chinese language. She found its tonality particularly interesting, the aspect that gave Chinese its peculiar "sing-song" quality. He hadn't even realized it had a tonal sound to American ears.

They even discussed literature, and Han-lin told tales of reading Nathaniel Hawthorne with the missionaries back in China. She seemed to enjoy his stories, and he discovered she had a quick wit. He soon learned that his slightest exaggerations caused her to laugh. She seemed to enjoy laughing, and he found her a complete delight.

What am I doing, he thought, sitting in a restaurant I've come to many times, but today I'm with a beautiful white woman, a rich woman I hardly know, laughing over missionaries, old Hawthorne stories, and giving her lessons on eating with chopsticks, while men I know well can scarcely finish a meal they're so busy gaping at me?

Suddenly, he wanted to get away from them. He dropped a wad of money on the table and, as he rose to leave, nodded good-day to the others in the restaurant. They all stood and bowed as he marched out the door with Ruth following close behind him.

Ruth found herself much more amused than irritated by Han-lin's lapse into Oriental "male-first" manners after his little speech in front of his house, but somehow in the very masculine world of the restaurant they just left, she could understand his position. Once outside the restaurant, he did stop and wait for her, they then continued down the street, walking side-by-side.

The first stop in Ruth's tour was a joss house. "It looks like a tiny church," she exclaimed.

"It almost is," Han-lin said. "It's a small temple where people perform devotions to honor their dead ancestors."

Ruth looked askance.

"They do not worship their ancestors, just honor them." Han-lin said.

Ruth found the distinction nebulous, but she said nothing.

Next they visited a number of small shops on Dupont Gai. Ruth was shown beautiful silks, lacquer, porcelain and jade from China. They spent an exorbitant amount of time in the shops, and Ruth kept buying objects that intrigued her, until soon, she had to stop because she couldn't carry any more.

Almost magically, a "friend" of Han-lin's appeared and offered to deliver the packages to Ruth's home so she wouldn't be burdened with them any longer. She was surprised, but grateful.

Bric-a-brac and foodstuffs she had never seen before filled the stores, and Han-lin spent a lot of time giving her explanations. When they reached an herb doctor's store Han-lin kept on going, which made Ruth curious. He hesitated to enter, which made her eager to see what was there. Finally he acquiesced.

Rows and rows of jars with strange black, brown or gray, dried and shriveled objects lined the shelves. When Han-lin attempted to explain what they were, Ruth decided he was joking—eye of giant lizard, gill of shark, bone marrow of Siberian tiger and so forth. Some things were beyond Han-lin's knowledge of English to describe, and others were apparently not the type of thing one should describe to a young, unmarried lady. All in all, when Ruth asked him to take her out of the shop, he gladly did so.

Walking through the shops tired them both. The sun was setting, but neither was hungry enough yet for dinner, so Han-lin asked Ruth if she would be interested in seeing a Chinese opera.

"I am interested in anything where I can sit for a while," she replied. "And I am highly fond of opera."

"I should warn you that this will have little resemblance to the operas you know. For one thing, Chinese opera is an all-day affair. It begins about noon, and runs continuously until midnight. It involves singing, dancing, acrobatics and elaborate costumes and sets, all special and stylized. The singing is in a high falsetto, and the accompaniment is mostly drums and gongs."

From the moment Ruth stepped into the theater, the crush of

people overwhelmed her. They seemed to all be far more interested in talking, eating and smoking, than in the performance on stage. Han-lin pushed through the crowd as if it barely existed and Ruth took his arm to make sure she didn't get left behind. He somehow managed to find two unoccupied seats.

On stage, the opera consisted of a loud clanging din of drums and wails from mysterious instruments. The incredibly high falsetto of the lead male singer who wore a head piece that looked like a massive lion's mane, had a tone to it that Ruth would never have imagined could be sustained by a human. Every beat of the large, loud gong thumped in the pit of her stomach. Still, the costumes were beautiful and the performers were skilled acrobatics who leapt about the stage twirling swords and poles with great skill and flourish.

Han-lin appeared to be enjoying the performance tremendously. The incense-laden air, cloudy with cigar and cigarette smoke filled air, didn't seem to bother him at all, but Ruth soon found the thick air, combined with the throng of people, to be oppressive.

She wanted to ask some questions about what was happening on stage, but the high noise level made it impossible. The never-ending drums caused her head to throb. The strange smells from foods, perfumes, and so many bodies, soon made her head spin. When she tried to breathe deeper, she felt faint. She shut her eyes briefly.

When she reopened them, she tried focus on the stage, hoping the dizziness would pass. It didn't. Instead, she became all but mesmerized by the color and movement that were there. The rest of the theater seemed to turn all black and purple, until only center stage was visible at all. Ruth continued to stare at it, her eyes getting wider, and all thought vanishing from her being.

The stage seemed to come closer and closer. Soon it surrounded her. The room began to swirl. Only the head of the lion, singing in the high wail, remained fixed. Everything whirled faster and faster, while the lion came closer to her.

She felt she could reach out and touch it. She tried to fight the feeling, but could not. She had no strength left. It came closer.

"Han-lin," she whispered.

He seemed not to hear her in the din. A panicky feeling enveloped her, but she felt physically incapable of protecting herself. All the stories of strange dope dealings, opium dens, Shanghai-ings and slavery flashed and mocked at her.

And Han-lin—he had been beside her, but now where was he? Did he leave her? She thought she could trust him, but could she? Where was he? Who was he? Or was this his fault...his fault...his fault...

She leaned forward, shutting her eyes.

"Miss Greer?"

A voice called from far, far away, then swirled about her head with the lion, the drums and the heavy, acrid smoke in the air.

Suddenly, faces seemed to flash in front of her, laughing faces with large black eyes. They came and went quickly, ever-changing as she was swept along with hardly any will of her own. She squeezed her eyes shut.

When the sense of movement stopped, she felt a refreshing coolness and breeze. Clean, smoke-free air filled her lungs. Nearby, she heard Han-lin's voice, pleasant and safe. She wanted to see him. He would help her, she could trust him, but somehow she couldn't find him. He was too far away. She tried to reach him, but could not yet quite manage to.

"Miss Greer, are you all right?" he asked. "Can you hear me?"

Slowly, Ruth opened her eyes. She blinked, then closed them again. She put her hand to her head as consciousness slowly returned. She seemed to be in an alley, her back against a building, with Han-lin standing between her and people gawking at them.

"What happened?" she whispered.

"I'm afraid you nearly passed out in there. I got you out while you could still walk. I believe the room had too many people and not enough ventilation. How do you feel now?"

She breathed deeply a few times. "Better, I think." As she said this, she realized her arm circled his back, her hand clutching the material of his tunic. She became aware of his nearness, his chest, his hips, mere inches from hers. A sudden desire to move even closer almost made her light headed once again. Whatever was wrong with her?

"My goodness!" she said as she pushed herself away from him, stiffly smoothing her dress. "What must you think of me!" Her face flushed with embarrassment, and she tried to still the pounding of her heart by breathing deeply. She quickly patted her hair, wondering if she looked as bad as she felt at the moment.

Han-lin smiled. "I'm glad to see the color coming back to your face so nicely."

She didn't know what to say or do. She felt like a complete ninny and wished she could disappear on the spot. "I am much better already, thank you," she said firmly.

"I know the thing that will make you one-hundred percent okay."

Ruth smiled at his slang expression. "How can I resist?"

He possessively took her arm and folded it securely in his as they started walking. Ruth held onto him for support at first, but before long the fresh air revived her and her dizziness was gone. Still, she chose to do nothing about letting go of him.

The sun had set while they were in the theater, and Ruth was again surprised by Chinatown. Many more people, and not only Chinese, walked around by night than during the day. The streets were brightly lit and many of the shops remained open.

Han-lin turned down a dark, empty-looking alley and stepped up to the door of a forlorn, forbidding building that might have been an abandoned warehouse.

"Here we are," he said.

"Here?" The trepidation in Ruth's voice rang clear. The uneasiness she felt in the theater rushed over her once more.

"You'll see." He entered the small wooden door and started down a narrow hallway. Not willing to stand alone in the dark, Ruth followed him. They arrived at another door. Han-lin opened it and stepped back, gesturing for Ruth to go first.

She peeked through the doorway. Then, astonished, she walked through. She had entered a plush and elegant restaurant.

Each table was surrounded by beautiful silk screens to provide privacy to the diners.

"I don't believe it," was all Ruth could murmur.

"Wait until you taste the food. It's even more unbelievable."

He was right. Han-lin ordered in Chinese, and assured her he only ordered foods she normally ate. She was taken aback to hear that, wondering what else could possibly be on the menu, but she had to admit that she never had anything approaching the perfection of the meal or the service, not even in Europe's finest.

When the meal ended, the waiter brought them each a demitasse of thick, black, Turkish coffee.

"I didn't know Chinese people drank coffee," Ruth observed.

"One of your Western corruptions, I'm afraid, Miss Greer," Han-lin said. He took out his tobacco and proceeded to roll a cigarette that vied with the coffee as to which was the stronger.

After watching him for a while, Ruth said, "By the way, I would like you to call me Ruth."

"Ruth it is then. And you may call me Li."

"Li? But isn't that your family name? To a Western ear, that sounds so cold—sort of like I speak to my servants. I'm sorry," Ruth added, afraid she had offended him. "What I mean is, doesn't anyone call you Han-lin?"

"In China, the given name is used only in families and intimate situations. Sometimes it seems the only one close enough, or caring enough, to use the given name is one's own mother. Do you like the name Han-lin?"

"Oh yes, I think it has a lovely sound. In fact, I must confess, I think of you as Han-lin, not as Li at all. It's too bad it isn't used."

"Since that is how you feel, I would like you to call me Han-lin."

"May I? But won't that sound funny to your friends?" She decided to joke. "They won't think I'm your mother, will they?" she asked with a smile.

He didn't smile; in fact, his face took on a strange expression as he said softly, knowingly, "No, that's not what they'll think. Not at all."

Something about the way he said it, the way he looked at her, caused her breath to quicken, and also made her strangely elated.

"I'm afraid it is getting rather late," Han-lin said. "But if you don't need to return home yet, there is one last place I would like to show you."

She had no desire to leave. "Don't worry about the time, I'm fine." She wondered if her words sounded too personal, so she added, "I would never forgive myself if I missed a single thing!"

"Ah! In that case, we cannot leave you unforgiven," he said with a slight smile. Han-lin spoke for some time to the maître d' and then they left the restaurant.

Outside, Ruth stopped and queried him. "This time, won't you tell me where we're going before we get there?"

"If you wish. We're going to a gaming parlor."

"Gaming? As in gambling? You're joking with me."

"Not at all. Don't worry. This one is perfectly safe. I guarantee it."

Ruth was thrilled. "A gaming parlor! How exciting! Yes, let's go. I wonder if I'll see any of father's friends there."

"Your father?"

"Winston Greer. You may have heard his name."

"I believe I have," Han-lin said dryly as the two walked along, arm-in-arm, with a smile over what had been said, and in the pleasure each was finding in being with the other.

In the time they were in the restaurant the streets went from extremely busy to almost barren. Lights out, shop doors closed and barred.

Only small groups of men stood on street corners.

Han-lin led Ruth to a wooden staircase. They went up one flight, which Ruth thought would lead to a house, but instead brought her to a walkway across a roof top. Finally they reached a door. Han-lin gave a coded knock. The door opened slowly and a large Asian man peered outside. When he saw Han-lin he quickly opened the door all the way, stepped back, and bowed deeply. He remained bent as Han-lin entered. As he started to rise Ruth stepped out of the darkness to where he could see her, and he nearly toppled over.

Again, as Ruth discovered to be the norm in Chinatown, the outer appearance of the building was deceptive. They walked through a small dark room, and out the door on the other side. They crossed another rooftop garden, and came to another door. Again, a coded knock, different from the last, was given. When this door opened, Ruth saw that it was guarded by two men who made the guard at the first door seem tiny by comparison. Like the first man, when they saw Han-lin they bowed low and let him pass. He crossed the foyer, and opened one last door.

As Ruth stepped into the room, she saw that it was enormous and filled with people, whites as well as Chinese, women as well as men. All seemed to be engrossed in various games, none of which Ruth had seen before. There was a bar on one wall of the room, and drinks were plentiful. Smoke from cigarettes, pipes, cigars, and other smokables hung in the air like a heavy blanket.

A number of people came up to Han-lin to greet him. A waiter appeared with small glasses of Chinese white wine for both Han-lin and Ruth. Han-lin cautioned Ruth about the potency of it, Chinese wine being more like a strong liqueur than a dinner drink.

Placing his arm about Ruth's waist, he took her on a tour around the room to explain what the various games were. Fan-tan, mah-jongg, and the card game twenty-one were popular, as was one similar to roulette.

Ruth found herself most intrigued by the mah-jongg which was played with ivory tiles engraved with Chinese characters. As players tossed tiles onto the tabletop, they made a loud clatter. Seeing her interest in the game, Han-lin sat down to play a round with Ruth standing behind him, explaining what he could to her as the game progressed. "Hey! I just won!" Han-lin exclaimed, much to his surprise.

"Congratulations," Ruth added.

"You must be my lucky charm." So saying, he took her hand and placed it on his shoulder as he began to play another round. His tunic's material was fine, and she could feel under the material his collarbone and shoulder, surprisingly thin and delicate for a man, but also the strength in the muscles and tendons as he moved. Most men she knew were heavy-boned, large, rather hulking creatures like her father. The slender but supple feel of Han-lin was a new experience for her. It made him seem vulnerable, almost as if she needed to protect him—an absurd idea, she knew, yet it warmed her heart in a way that was new to her.

When he noticed that she was becoming increasingly interested the more she learned about the game, he asked for a chair for Ruth, and had her sit beside him as he played. He won a couple more rounds, but also lost several. "So much for your lucky charm," she said.

"You're wrong," he murmured. "To have you here beside me, I feel lucky indeed."

She felt surprisingly pleased to hear that.

The waiter brought them another glass of wine, and then another after that.

The interest Ruth generated as she entered the room with Han-lin eventually subsided. She enjoyed the complicated game, particularly as she grew able to distinguish between the different characters and the patterns in them, which she considered a remarkable accomplishment in itself.

When the waiter brought the fourth glass of wine, Han-lin stood up. He took a careful look at Ruth as she took a large sip, murmuring about how tasty it was, and promptly took the glass out of her hand and set it on a table. "What are you doing?" she asked curtly, her eyes blazing at his audacity.

"I do not wish to personally add to the scandals of Chinatown by having it also known as a place that plies young English teachers with alcohol and leads them to evil ways." He gave her a look of defiant mockery.

"How can you ..." Ruth stood up as well, angry at his presumption until she realized how strong the wine was. Standing, it hit like a sledge hammer. "Oh, my," she whispered as its warmth stole over her. "Maybe I should have listened when you said it was strong. It seemed so smooth and mild, though." She looked up at him, her eyes heavy and almost dreamy as the liquid took effect.

"Hmm." One eyebrow went up slightly as he looked at her.

She stepped closer to him, and her pulse raced even more—not because of the wine, but from his nearness. The wine, however, allowed her tongue to loosen, and allowed her to admit, "It's too late now, isn't it?" Her voice sounded low and husky as her thoughts turned to something far deeper than a few glasses of wine. "There's no going back now, is there?"

"Ruth," he said softly. He placed his hands on her shoulders. She knew, by the expression on his face, he planned to turn her around and march her out of the room, but she was a woman used to getting her way in everything, without concern for convention. And so, she stepped closer to him, her face upwards, her lips slightly parted.

Han-lin quickly dropped his hands. He didn't step back, but his posture stiffened. With hardly any movement at all, he could have wrapped her in his arms. Other men had, with far less provocation—men she had chastised and scorned for their boldness. But he didn't. Had she misread him?

Her mind spun back to the way she felt as he held her after her faint at the opera, the way he had looked at her. She found herself drawn to him like a moth to a flame—a mysterious, intriguing flame. If she took one step closer, just one step, every fiber told her he felt the same as she did ....

Han-lin's face suddenly became devoid of expression, almost mask-like, as he brusquely, almost cruelly, took her arm and guided her towards the door. "I think it is time for a certain young lady to head for home if her parents are ever to let her venture out of the house again."

Ruth was not one to be ordered, or to be treated like a child. "I'll have you know I do quite as I please!"

"Of that, I have no doubt." A slight smile cracked the veneer of his stoical expression. Then without giving her time to say another word he led her out of the building, across the rooftop gardens, and down the stairs onto the street.

Ruth could hardly believe it when she realized that the carriage that stood nearby was Han-lin's. She looked at it and stammered, "Where did that come from? How did he know we were here?" To which she received only a smile in reply. One smile, and the irritation she felt in the gaming parlor at his perceived rejection of her advances suddenly vanished.

They boarded the carriage, and rode in silence. As the fresh air cleared her head, she became appalled at the way she had acted. He was a married man; she was his wife and children's English teacher. What strange delusion had she been under? Why, in Heaven's name, had she acted so shamelessly? She didn't know if she could ever face him or his family again.

Too quickly, the carriage stopped in front of the familiar gray house with its massive iron gate. It was a sight that on every other occasion when a gentleman she had been with brought her home, she welcomed more than the entire previous parts of the evening. She had always said a rushed good-bye and almost ran to the house, welcoming being there.

She was tempted to do the same, but knew that would have been wrong of her. She squared her shoulders. "I'm sorry I didn't listen to your warning about the wine. I seem to have made a bit of a fool of myself. I assure you, I'm as appalled by my behavior as you must be."

With that, she turned the handle to open the door. He placed his hand on hers, stopping her.

"Don't part with such words between us, please," he murmured.

She pulled her hand away, placing it on her lap, her heart pounding.

"I enjoyed today and tonight," he said, "more than any day I can remember. Because of you, Ruth Greer. I'll never forget it. Never."

She looked up at him, astonished at how heartfelt he sounded, and found that she liked him even more for being both kind and honest with her. "I feel the same," she admitted. "Thank you for showing me so much of your world."

"I'm glad you found it of some interest," he replied.

"Of some interest! It was all quite fascinating," she said.

"Will you come again to my house?" he asked. "To teach my children and my wife?"

Wife ... She drew in her breath at his subtle reminder. She had already promised Pao-yang and the others she would return. "I told them I would return tomorrow. I'll keep my word."

He nodded.

"Will you be there?" she asked.

She watched his dark eyes turn smoky and clouded before he averted them to look at the darkened street. "I don't think so. I have some business to attend."

She nodded, lifting her chin. She understood. This whatever-it-was between them could not be allowed to continue or, heaven forbid, to grow any stronger. "I understand," she said.

His face fell. "Perhaps I will be able to return before you leave."

She shook her head. "No, it's all right." She quickly opened the carriage door and stepped out. "Good-night."

"Ruth, wait," he called.

She stopped and faced him.

He looked at her a long moment before he murmured, simply, "Good-night, Ruth."

She turned and walked up the long path to her house, her heart growing heavier and her confusion greater with every step she took. Not until she closed the front door behind her did she hear the sound of the carriage driving off.

CHAPTER 4

$\mathcal{M}$AI-CHING WAS BORED, but she preferred that to facing her captors. Over a week had passed since she was brought to the house where the Wang Shao tong's "sing-song" girls were kept—the prostitutes of Chinatown. The Wang Shao made their money on sing-song girls and opium dens.

Mai had been locked in a room that was about three feet by six feet with a single mattress and a bucket. Mai sat on the mattress and waited, not wanting to think about what was to come.

Her troubles began on the infamous day that Dee Bao entered her house while her parents were away. The daughter of a wealthy merchant, she had been pampered, coddled, and educated well for a female, even to the point of learning some rudimentary English. She lived a soft and untroubled life. She had stared at the big, dirty peddler with surprise, but no fear.

"What are you doing in this house?" she asked. "We ordered nothing from you and no one is here to receive you."

"I have come to see you." He had a strange catch in his voice and a wild look about him.

Her eyes widened as he approached. "I have told you no one is here and I have no wish to speak to you. Now, I ask you to leave."

"I'll not go," he said huskily. Her body was small and delicate as she only recently had moved from a child to becoming a woman; her black hair gleamed and had been twisted into a long braid that fell far down her back. He reached for her arm.

"No!" She jumped back, but he was quick for such a large man, and grabbed her in a vice-like grip.

"Stop, please," she cried. She fought him, struggling furiously when his hand reared back and formed into a fist. She turned her face, but the blow struck the side of her head. A sharp, blinding pain gripped her, and then all went black.

When she awoke she was in his room. Her clothes had been ripped and strewn about. As she tried to rise up from a blanket on the floor, her body ached everywhere, inside as well as out, and the full horror of what he had done filled her.

"You have awakened finally! I thought you were dead." From the shadows of the room Dee Bao walked towards her.

She clutched her garments, trying to cover herself. "Let me go home," she whispered, her tears flowed harshly.

"Home? This is your home, with me. What a happy couple we are!" He laughed again.

She turned her head, tears of anger, fear and loathing fell. In disgust Dee Bao walked back to his shadows.

The following days were a nightmare. Dee Bao was alternately a kind and a brutal lover. Professing his love, yet doing everything to assure Mai's complete and total hatred of him, he would tie and gag her whenever he left his room to prevent her running away. She quickly learned that he grew excited when she fought him, and angry and frustrated when she lay like a corpse beneath him. She said and did nothing beyond trying to escape, and in less than a month, he found keeping her was more difficult than even his lust made worthwhile. She wouldn't cook, clean or do anything but lie on the mattress, professing she would rather starve to death than lift one finger for him. The other men in the house didn't interfere with what was going on; they just stayed out of the way, and smirked at Dee Bao behind his back.

Unable to put up with her insolence and rag doll demeanor any longer, Dee Bao took Mai to the "sing-song" house of T'ang.

Before leaving Mai there, Dee Bao turned on her with a look of rage and disgust. "After being used by the men in this place, you'll appreciate me. You'll beg me to take you back. You'll want me. Just wait."

Deep inside, she trembled at the image his words brought to her, but she didn't make any move, gave no reaction at all that he could see.

He waited, but when she did nothing, he stormed out, slamming the door.

When she heard the lock click into place, she knew that this place, too, offered no hope of escape.

Time passed slowly. There were no windows in the cell of a room, no way to tell if it were day or night. Except for the one time she was brought to the room of T'ang Tsu-shao, leader of the Wang Shao tong, the door opened only for meals.

A meal, such as it was, had been delivered only a short time earlier when the door opened again. Mai-ching shrank back in fear. A man stood with a candle and beckoned the girl to follow him; she did so.

He led her to a large room filled with food and several men sitting around the table. She immediately recognized one as the man she had been taken to previously. Noticing her, he gestured to the others.

"Here she is," he said. "My prize, placed in my hand with a stroke of luck. She belongs to people under protection of the Yuen-li tong. When they find out that she's here with me, the battle will be struck. We'll get it over with, and I'll be rid of Li Han-lin at last."

"You can't write him off that fast," warned one at the table.

"That's true," said another. "The Yuen-li aren't to be played with. Is a mere woman worth the risk?"

"She is not the reason for the fight, you fools. She is but an excuse. I want Li out of the way. I want his tong out of the way. They control gambling in the whole north side of Chinatown. I'm tired of Li's interference in whatever I do. His gambling clubs are rich. Richer even than opium. Why? Because the whites go to his clubs. He's made them safe for the so-called good citizens to go to without fear of police raids or other troubles. That's the key to wealth. The Chinese alone don't control enough money."

He continued. "To make it big we need to branch out. We need the Yuen-li wealth. I'll get it and Li will be dead, if it is the last thing I do. I must finish what was started long ago!"

"Li dead? Hah!" said one of T'ang's companions. "He's too well protected. You'd need to get through a barrage of bodyguards to get at him. Even when he walks the streets, you can see his men, like so many ants, moving ahead and behind him."

"They won't be able to protect him in a formal battle. That's what we have to do—a vendetta of the old type, with hatchets. We just need a good excuse. Then, we'll figure out a fail-proof plan. No one questions the winner, after all."

They all laughed at that.

T'ang's eye suddenly fell upon Mai and he slipped his arm around her waist and headed towards the door. Looking over his shoulder at his friends, he called out, "It'll be just like sticking it to Li!" Laughter and knee-slapping flooded the room as T'ang and Mai left.

CHAPTER 5

RUTH KNEW THERE was going to be a problem as soon as she headed up the walk to her parents' home and saw that all the lights were still lit. Sure enough, her mother was sitting in the parlor waiting for her. As Ruth shut the front door, Blanche stood and walked towards her, a smirk covering her face. "Well, it's about time you got home. It's nearly midnight! Your father's back from his business trip." She folded her arms. "He wishes to speak to you."

The last thing Ruth wanted was a confrontation. She wanted to go to her room and savor her evening, and she also wanted to ponder the strange feelings she experienced around Li Han-lin. He wasn't rich, he was married, and he was a heathen Chinese, for pity's sake. Why she should feel anything whatsoever towards him was a mystery to her. The drinks he had given her had surely affected her judgment and common sense.

Ruth marched directly to her father's study, wanting to get any lectures over with. Although called a study, the room was one of the largest in the house, so completely equipped that Winston Greer had to leave it only to sleep. He was sitting in his favorite overstuffed chair, a mammoth figure in a maroon velvet smoking jacket, when Ruth entered. His bald pate glistened as usual. He was alone in the room, which was rare, as his business associates—or "goons" as the local press called them—nearly always surrounded him.

A whisper of pleasure flitted across the hard, rigid lines of his face as he watched his daughter enter the room. She kissed his cheek and asked about his trip.

"It was fine—everything went just as planned. Lathum agreed to sell after hearing our second offer." Greer sneered with disdain. "We were willing to double the price he took. He was too greedy—couldn't wait for a better deal. He had no timing, no class. Anyway, I'll tell you about it later. Right now, I want to talk about some distressing news your mother has given me."

"Oh, Daddy!" Ruth decided to play the innocent little girl role that enabled her to easily wrap Greer around her little finger. "You know how she exaggerates every little thing."

Greer laughed. "She made it sound like someone's out to make a 'sing-song' girl out of you!"

"You know that's absurd!" She pouted at Greer as she sat at his side and toyed with the cuff of his sleeve.

"Maybe you've developed a fascination for a dragon," he said with a snort. "Like in those Chinese parades."

"A dragon?" She laughed, but then she thought about it. As she and Han-lin went through shops where dragons were often on display, he told her the dragon was a symbol of power and strength in Chinese culture, and good luck for people who were worthy of it. She smiled. She would always treasure her good luck at meeting him, so she guessed that meant he was her dragon.

Her dragon.

Yes, she liked that.

"Well?" Greer asked when she said nothing.

She shrugged. "Don't be silly. I just happened to meet a very nice, well-to-do Chinese family. The father and only one boy speak English, the mother and two other children do not. I thought it would be very humanitarian, not to mention Christian, of me to volunteer to teach them a little bit. That's all there is to it. I plan to go in the morning, two or three times a week, and to teach about one hour. They even have a carriage to see me home if I wish to use it. As I said, they're well off for Chinese, and I'm sure they have no designs on becoming white slavers."

oOo

Winston Greer's eyes narrowed as he pondered what to make of his daughter's words about her day and evening, especially in light of his own recent Chinatown adventure with the leader of one of the biggest tongs in the area, an adventure he had taken extraordinary pains to be sure Ruth did not learn about. He planned to extricate himself from having anything more to do with the Chinese after this one, quick, profitable opium deal was completed, but all in all, it would be best if Ruth and Chinatown stayed separated.

He was suspicious of her story. Ruth had never taken any action in her life for "humanitarian" reasons. Not that she was a bad person—just a selfish one. Her father's daughter, he liked to say. "If you only teach one hour," he said, "why are you getting home at midnight tonight?"

"My, aren't we suspicious!" Ruth folded her arms and glared at him. "I haven't been quizzed like this since I was twelve years old! You want to know? I was off with my lovers—all three of them. They're all Chinese. Oh, I forgot the fourth—he's Indian. Geronimo's brother. We had a totally debauched time and I loved every minute of it."

Greer frowned. "You do not need to be sarcastic. Your mother is concerned. I told her you were all right. But it *is* late, you do realize. If you choose not to tell me where you were, I can't make you." His expression was that of a puppy who had been whipped.

Ruth gave him a forgiving smile. "I just met some friends and we went out to dinner and a show."

Greer looked at her quizzically, stroking his chin, and suspected she was bending the truth. But how bad could it be? The subject bored him. "By the way, how's your new love?"

"My what?" Ruth looked at him in surprise.

"Young Harrison. My friend Joe's boy. What's his name? I thought you two would have announced your banns by now."

Ruth smirked. "Me marry him? Are you joking?"

"I thought you liked him. He's nice looking, and his father has money. What's wrong with him?"

"He's a goose."

"Ruth, you really must—"

"Besides," she interrupted, placing her hand on his forearm, "he just doesn't measure up when I compare him to you. As I've told you many times, I simply will not settle for anything less."

Greer laughed with pleasure. "Well then, you'll just have to become an old maid. Give young Harrison a chance, for your father's sake. I think it would be a good match, if ever he could learn to handle you, that is, like I can."

"That would be quite impossible." With that, she stood and gave him a kiss on the cheek. "I'm going to bed. I'm exhausted."

"I can see that. Good-night, dear." What, he wondered again, was she not telling him?

oOo

Ruth went up to her room. Her mind was swimming from the peculiar discussion with her father on top of the extraordinary day with Han-lin. She hated having to lie to Greer, but she knew he would be furious over the truth. A chuckle came over her as she thought of Han-lin or his wife being described as "little old" anything. His wife's delicate and exquisite beauty came rushing back at her.

Ruth studied her own features in her mirror. She had always been thought of as a beauty, and had seen herself that way. Suddenly all she saw in the reflection was someone overly large, with grotesquely huge and colorful features, when what she hoped to see was an equal rival to the lovely and delicate features of Mrs. Li.

How absurd I am, Ruth thought. She abruptly turned from the mirror and flung herself into bed. If she could fall in love with someone like Mike Harrison, life would be much simpler. But experience taught her that men paid attention to her first as Winston Greer's daughter, second as an attractive woman, and only third as an interesting and intelligent person—the exact opposite of what she wanted. She tried to fall in love with several of her suitors, but each experience increased her bitterness and cynicism about their motives until she had built a barrier around her emotions that she thought no man could scale.

She could barely sleep, and was awake to watch the sun come up. A short while later, she got up, dressed, and left the house before her parents or even their servants began to stir.

It was too early for lessons as the cable car carried her down the hill to Chinatown, so she retraced her steps to many of the shops Han-lin had taken her to the prior day. She went into a restaurant for what Han-lin had explained was a Chinese-style breakfast of tea and pork buns.

Ruth took a seat by a window and watched people as they walked about, opening their places of business and beginning their day's work.

As the time approached for her to go to Han-lin's house, she left the tea room and took the short walk there, not going directly, but instead exploring alleyways and side streets, which, she had already learned, was the real Chinatown.

Upon her arrival, Ruth began the lesson almost immediately. It dragged on for almost two hours as she was reluctant to end it. She gladly accepted an invitation to stay for lunch, but Han-lin did not join them.

Finally, having run out of any reason to prolong the visit further, she left for home, deeply disappointed, and made arrangements to return the following week. She didn't return home immediately, however. Remembering her conversation with her father, she stopped at the shop she had visited the day before with Han-lin, and bought a beautiful carved wooden figure of a dragon.

On Saturday night, she was scheduled to attend a party with "young Harrison" as Greer called Mike, but at the last minute she pleaded a headache and stayed home. On Sunday there was church, followed in the afternoon by tea with some lady friends.

The following week found Ruth at the Li household Monday, Wednesday and Friday. By Friday she could no long bear not knowing Han-lin's whereabouts and asked Pao-yang if his father was out working somewhere. "No," the boy replied. "He goes in and out. He sees many people, has much business."

CHAPTER 6

MAI-CHING AWAKENED FROM her uneasy slumber by noise in the outer hallway. There was a ruckus as a number of loud, drunken men entered the house looking for women. She froze listening to heavy footsteps stop outside her door. "Not there, fool," the guard's voice called. "She's T'ang's. Better leave her alone."

The steps shuffled away and continued down the hall. Mai let out a deep sigh of relief. Other footsteps, light and heavy, ran up and down the halls; men and women laughed and joked loudly, and generally seemed to be having a good time. Mai tried to blot out the sound. Could she ever accept her lot as completely, and presumably happily, as these women, she wondered.

Suddenly, the house grew still.

Mai stepped back, as far from the door as she could, wondering what the ominous silence meant. A key entered the lock to her door. Her breathing all but stopped and she put her hand over her mouth in fear. Not T'ang, please, she thought. The man was debauched, disgusting and sadistic. Dee Bao had been right. She would crawl back to him if it meant never having T'ang touch her again. After that first night with him she could not eat for two days, the waves of revulsion and horror that swept over her were so great, and she was tempted by the idea of starvation. But then, he called for her again, and again soon after that. Eventually, she realized that her will to live was greater than even T'ang's cruelties could destroy, and she managed to force enough food past her lips to stay alive.

The door swung open, and Mai stood rigidly awaiting her fate.

The handsomest man she had ever seen stepped into her room. "I am Li Han-lin," he said. "I have come to return you to your family."

With a cry, Mai threw herself at his feet. "Thank you," she repeated over and over, her voice choked with emotion and tears rolled down her eyes that the freedom she had prayed for every waking moment was finally hers.

"Come." He bent to lift her from the ground, and then held her arm as he led her out of her cell. Han-lin's Yuen-li tong lined the walls of the house. Posing as customers, they had entered the house one or two at a time, and at the allotted hour seized the women and their guards. The way was then free for Li Han-lin to enter and rescue Mai.

He took her down the hallway and out the front door to the astonished gasps of the other women of the house. His men quickly followed.

Outside the house Han-lin lifted the girl, who was weak from physical and mental abuse, into his carriage and then got in and sat beside her. The coach sped off. "Don't worry. You are safe now," he told her, patting her hand. "No one will harm you here."

"I know," she whispered, and smiled shyly yet somewhat boldly as she looked at him. "Will…will my parents still want me after…"

"Don't worry. They do." He took her to her parents' home and quickly left amid the profuse thanks of the parents for the safe return of their child.

"Li Han-lin," the girl cried after him as he left the house. He turned towards her. Running, she caught up to him and bowed low as she said, "My lord, I have not properly thanked you. I cannot tell you how grateful I am; you are truly wonderful. My life is yours; I am yours, for whatever you wish."

"Then I wish you to enjoy your life."

Surprise and disbelief filled her face as she straightened and looked at him. "That's all?" she asked.

Han-lin smiled. "That's more than enough." He gave a nod, then turned and left.

As his carriage rode out of sight Mai stood watching it with a look that was close to hero worship.

o0o

Ruth came to enjoy teach the Li children very much. They were opening up to her, and displaying charming, gentle, yet warm dispositions. She developed a real affection for them, especially Pao-yang.

The next weekend was as uninteresting for Ruth as the previous one had been. The Greers gave a party in their home on Saturday night. Realizing that Mike Harrison had no place in Ruth's affections, Greer used the party as an opportunity to parade another set of prospects in front of his daughter, while telling her all the time he realized that they didn't meet her standard (in other words, himself), but that he did find them passable. They were not to Ruth, however.

The evening bored her. Greer wondered about this change in his daughter. He noticed that she did not even bother to flirt with any of the young men, which was unheard of. She normally had at least one beau that she was stringing along.

Ruth was happy when Monday morning finally arrived and gave her a chance to go to Chinatown again. It surprised and rather frightened her, how strongly she came to feel about it. She felt it to be a place where real life happened, life more vital and intense than anything she had previously known. She knew she was just an observer and could never really be a part of it, but Chinatown teemed with energy, and she loved it.

Dupont Gai was shrouded in morning fog. As was becoming her habit, she went to the little restaurant she had discovered earlier. The waiter had come to know her and greeted her with a smile and bow of welcome. After tea and *bao,* she explored some side streets until it was time for her lesson. At the Li household, the old servant Ruth came to know as "Lao-she" (the old one), opened the door. Ruth was becoming quite fond of Lao-she who always seemed genuinely pleased to see her.

Pao-yang was boisterous and practically jumping with joy to see his teacher. He was a fast learner, and filled with questions about the world outside Chinatown. He planned to travel when he grew up, and visit every place he could. Ruth was surprised that she, who never much cared for children, was always happy to be with Pao-yang and his younger, and quieter, brother and sister.

Mrs. Li was stoic but friendly, and was a surprisingly dedicated student. Ruth was also surprised by how much she enjoyed teaching.

And so, another week of lessons began.

oOo

The busy street was filled with shoppers in the warm afternoon sun as a voice rang out.

"Mai-ching!"

The girl turned to see a beautiful woman coming towards her, followed by an older woman.

"I am Li Jun, wife of Li Han-lin," the woman said, head high and eyes cold as she spoke. "Stupid girl! I have heard what my husband did because of you. If he is hurt, I hold you responsible!"

Mai felt a fear creep over her at these words, "Whatever do you mean? Is Li Han-lin in danger?"

"Of course he is! He may be killed."

"No! What has happened?" the girl cried.

Li Jun looked at her with utter contempt, "Nothing has happened yet, but it will—because of you. You!"

Mai shrunk back as Li Jun continued. "T'ang Tsu-shao, leader of the Wang Shao, is my brother. For some outrageous reason, he took a fancy to you. You had been his. He owned you. Then Li interfered and stole you away from T'ang's home. T'ang is furious. He has challenged Li to a fight—tong against tong."

Mai could hardly believe what she was being told. "A fight? Over me? No, it must be stopped."

"That's not so easy. T'ang was wronged yet Li will not let him take you back."

"T'ang was wronged!? What about me?" Mai cried, shocked at the woman's words. "But the past doesn't matter. What matters is to stop the fight. They must not battle."

"My brother is an outstanding fighter," Li Jun said. "Were this fight to go on, Li could easily be killed."

Mai was silent. She folded her hands and slumped back against the wall, thinking of Li Jun's words. She could not let the fight happen if there was anything in her power to stop it. There seemed to be only one thing to do.

"This fight," Mai asked Li Jun, "are you sure it is because of me? There were so many other women there for your brother. I find it hard to believe."

"You were T'ang's woman," Li Jun eyed her coldly. "Li Han-lin stole you away from him. I'm his sister, and Li took me away from him, too. T'ang and I were close. Very close. But since my marriage I've been forbidden to see him. And now, he's lost you. Li Han-lin goes too far this time. T'ang cannot sit back."

"But..." Mai's head was swimming, just where was Li Jun's loyalty and concern? "There's no similarity between your situation with Li Han-lin, and this incident with me, I just ..."

"Nevertheless," Li Jun interrupted, "that is the way it is. Will you help, or do you not mind seeing Li dead?"

"Of course I will help!" she cried.

"Good. I would hate for one so insignificant as you to be the cause of the death of one so great." At that Li Jun walked off, leaving the girl scared and shaken. Tears blinded her eyes as she somehow managed to find her way home.

oOo

When Mai's father returned home that evening he found that Mai was not there. Her mother, with a worried expression, handed him the note she had held all afternoon. She lacked the knowledge to read it, but she knew that it was in Mai's childish hand:

Most honorable parents,

I am returning to the house of T'ang. He treated me well and life was fun there. I go of my own choice. Please tell Li Han-lin that I am happy and wish that no one try to find me or take me away from T'ang. Please forget about me, and forgive me.

Mai

CHAPTER 7

THE NEXT MORNING, the moment Ruth stepped into the doorway of the Li house she knew something out of the ordinary was happening. She heard men's voices coming from the first room on the right—the room she had been brought to when she first entered the Li house. Her heart skipped several beats. She had become so accustomed to Han-lin not being at home when she arrived that to find him there actually was startling to her. She hurried past the closed door and went on to the back classroom, longing yet anxious at the thought of seeing him again.

The class was learning sentences now. Ruth launched into her lesson with high intensity, needing to blot out thoughts of Han-lin. She and the students were concentrating hard, and were half-way into the lesson when the door to the classroom flew open. As the children scrambled to their feet, Han-lin stalked across the room straight towards his wife, looking nowhere but at her, his eyes black with rage.

oOo

Han-lin did his best to not look in Ruth's direction as he stormed into the classroom. He had managed to avoid her for three weeks now, hard though it was. But as he told her, the one day they had spent together was one of the happiest of his life, and he knew that if he spent any more time in her presence, it could lead to disaster. She didn't hide that she found him interesting, but he believed she felt that only because he was like no one she had ever known before. He seemed "exotic" to her, perhaps.

And she seemed like a goddess to him. Beautiful, intelligent, and completely unreachable. It was dangerous enough that she entered his house to teach English. The most he could hope for was to catch a glimpse of her now and then, from afar, until she grew tired of helping his family and found something or someone else to take up her free time.

So he marched into the little classroom because of anger at his wife, and did not look towards the one person who brought any light to his days.

Li Jun stood and bent her head towards the floor, unable to look at the hatred in her husband's eyes. He fairly spat his words at her, speaking in Chinese.

"I heard you spoke to Mai-ching yesterday. Her parents came to see me this morning and brought me a note, a terrible, pathetic little note she wrote to them. She has returned to T'ang's house. She said she wished to. We know that is a lie. What did you say to her?"

"I said nothing."

"I want the truth!" Han-lin roared, grabbing her shoulders as if he were ready to shake the life out of her.

He noticed that his children scurried to Ruth and hid behind her skirts, while she looked on wide-eyed and frightened. He dropped his hands, but didn't stop glaring at his wife.

"I mean that I said nothing that should make her go to my dear brother's house." Li Jun thought quickly. "I only said that T'ang confessed to me that he truly loved her. That he was terribly upset when she left; that he said he had wanted to give her a wonderful life. That's all I said. If she decided to return to him, perhaps it is because she feels the same way about him." Li Jun lifted her head defiantly, looking straight into her husband's eyes, her jaw clenched, and lips pursed into a sneer.

Han-lin shoved her from him in bitter and complete disgust. "How can you lie so boldly? You are as despicable as your brother, to use a mere child for your evil doings! Stay out of my sight. You make me sick."

So saying, he turned and started to storm from the classroom, but

Ruth stood still, gaping at him. Her presence flooded over him like a wave on the shore. She must be protected from this disgusting business, he thought. He wanted to rush past and not see her, ashamed that she had witnessed such an encounter between himself and his wife, and glad she could not understand the harsh words that were spoken.

He stopped near the door and looked at her standing there.

Her gaze met his and she seemed to pale. He wanted to go to her and place his arms around her and tell her not to be upset, that he was sorry, and so much more. Of course, he could do no such thing, and turned to leave.

But then, as he was almost out the door, something stopped him. He could not go away without even a word. He faced her again, his emotions raw and heavy with a sad, world-weariness. "I have missed you," he whispered.

The words were softly spoken, for her ears alone, and then he was gone.

o0o

Ruth stood immobile as Han-lin shut the door behind him, her heart heavy at the harsh scene she had witnessed but did not understand.

She wished she had said something, made some gesture, and wished she had at least told him she had missed him as well. If only she had offered some help, or at least some comfort, over whatever was causing him this trouble, she wouldn't be feeling like such a dunce. But her chance had passed, and she had stood mute. She could barely forgive herself.

"Please," Li Jun whispered. "Stop lesson today."

"Yes," Ruth said. "Of course." She quickly gathered up her things.

"Tomorrow, come back, please, teacher," Pao-yang said, his eyes wide with sadness and worry.

She didn't have the heart to deny the boy, much as she thought she should stay away. "I'll come back, but only for a short lesson, okay?"

Pao-yang smiled. "Okay!"

Ruth left the house and hurried through the streets to the cable car and home. The rest of the day she puzzled over what she saw that morning. It had appeared as if Han-lin hated his wife. The manner he had towards her seemed far more than a momentary anger, but something that came from a deep well of ill-feeling. Also, Ruth was troubled, yet warmed, by the words he said to her.

She couldn't understand how his simple statement about missing her could make up for many days of disappointment and dismay, but it did.

CHAPTER 8

THE NEXT DAY Ruth arose early. She could scarcely sleep wondering if she might see Han-lin again the coming day, and wondering what he might say. Somehow, she needed to find him and talk to him, for a moment at least, and to let him know that she missed him as well—and that he didn't need to stay away from her.

In her short time in Chinatown she came to understand that for Han-lin to have revealed any emotion towards her was extraordinary. She wondered if it might be a portent of change.

She left her house earlier than usual, planning a leisurely breakfast in Chinatown, and hoping to take the time to calm her wayward feelings.

The fog hung thick and close to the ground when she got off the cable car. Ruth loved the fog and found it cool and refreshing before the heat and grime of the day. The streets seemed unnaturally empty to her, and when she arrived at her favorite restaurant, it was closed.

A strange foreboding came over her.

Not far off, she saw a group of men running out of Sullivan's Alley.

She had never walked through that particular alley, and wondered what was going on. She hurried toward it. Strange though it seemed, she had learned she was actually safer in Chinatown than elsewhere in the city. The police left the Chinese alone as long as they did nothing to harm any whites. If they did, the police came down on them hard and fast with the full extent of the law. As a result, it was hands off people like her.

Curious about what was going on, she entered the narrow alley. The walls on both sides were solid brick. Only a couple of times did she see a doorway or window, and it had no shops of any kind. She went a little farther, and decided there was nothing here.

It seemed to be empty, with no reason for people to have fled from it. Nonetheless, a creeping uneasiness filled her. She told herself it was due to the quiet and the fog, nothing more. Such thoughts, she told herself, were quite silly.

Refusing to give in to such foolish squeamishness, she plunged forward. She would go to the end of the alley, and then turn around and march out. The only way to overcome fear was to meet it head on.

In the distance, a large object lay haphazardly against a wall. Could that be what caused the men's fear? She walked towards it, and although she was looking it the whole time, not until she was almost upon it did her mind allowed her to accept and understand what her eyes were seeing.

"Oh, my God!" she cried aloud.

The decapitated body of a man lay before her. He wore traditional Chinese clothing; the body and the sidewalk under it were saturated with blood.

It took another moment or two before, several feet away, she saw the head in a grotesquely tilted pose. The mouth was opened as if in a scream, the eyelids wide, and the eyes rolled back.

She gasped, and stumbled backwards towards the opposite wall. The freakishly screaming head seemed permanently etched in her mind. She wanted to run out of the alley, but she could barely manage to stay upright.

Reaching the far wall, she bent forward, unable to stop her stomach from spilling its contents. Her knees were close to buckling, and she wasn't sure she could stand without the wall supporting her.

This had to have been the site of one of the infamous "hatchet men" battles. Nothing else could have caused the ugly wounds and decapitation she saw on that body. She would need to go to the police. She used a handkerchief to wipe her brow and held it to her mouth as she tried to gather strength to run from the alley.

Then she froze. Her breathing stopped; even her heart seemed to stop beating.

She thought she heard her name. She stood absolutely still a moment, listening.

Nothing.

It's just the wind, she told herself, just the wind.

She took a deep breath, her hand pressed against the wall as if it were a lifeline. She told herself she had to leave, but it was almost as if something held her back. She did hear her name! She wasn't imagining it. The sound was barely a whisper.

She forced herself to go deeper into the alley. Up ahead was a doorway. She strained to see what was there in the fog. Another body; another death, but this man she recognized.

It was one of Han-lin's men. One of his bodyguards. And past him she saw another.

She felt faint.

They were dead; they hadn't called her name. Then, she knew the one person who might have. *God, no!*

"Han-lin?" she cried, going deeper into the alley. "Han-lin?"

She barely made out the shape of someone lying on the ground, his arm extended towards her.

She ran to him.

As she approached he whispered, "Ruth," and then let his arm fall back down as if the little strength he drew upon to raise it had evaporated.

She fell to her knees. He was deathly pale and blood flowed from his upper back and arm.

"I'll go to your home and get help," she cried. "Or tell me where and I'll go get a doctor."

"Get no one," he said. "Help me home. I can't stay here. The police will come ..."

"But you need a doctor! You could bleed to death! I'll get help."

"Please, home." As he tried to stand, a fresh gush of blood spewed out of the gaping wound on his shoulder.

"Wait, I've got to stop the blood!" She placed her hand on his chest and had him lay back down.

Using her teeth and fingernails that broke from the effort, she tore strips of cloth from her petticoats.

"The cuts are too deep, Han-lin. I need to get help for you!"

She placed some of the cloths on his deep shoulder wound. He held it there, pressing down hard, as she wrapped long strips under his arm and over his shoulder to hold the cloths in place.

"My friend, across the alley," he whispered. "See to him, please."

She hurried to the first man she had recognized, and then to the other. One look was enough to tell her they were beyond help, but she touched their necks trying to find a pulse. "It's too late," she said. She fought against tears, fearing he, too, would die.

He nodded, and looked at her in silence, then murmured, "Go."

"No. I won't let you die." She put his good arm over her shoulders and somehow they managed to get him to his feet. He was weak from loss of blood as well as the shock and pain of the deep gashes, but her strength gave him the will to try to reach help.

She held him by the waist, and in that way she slowly walked with him through the alley. He leaned heavily against her, causing her to stumble a couple of times, but somehow she managed to right herself and urged him forward, whispering the whole time that he would be all right, that she wasn't going to let anything happen to him.

They stepped out of Sullivan's Alley when she saw two men running towards her. She didn't recognize them, and feared whoever had tried to kill Han-lin had come back. She wanted to run, but he was too weak. She could only stand there, holding him, knowing she would do whatever was necessary to protect him.

Two men stopped and stared at them. Then they nodded at her, bowing quickly while saying words she couldn't understand, but she did understand the gentle way they took Han-lin from her, and hurried as best they could towards his home.

Ruth was aware of a few other people on the streets, but as they were some distance away the fog provided a protective cover for them.

She felt Han-lin's need for secrecy and to not let the police find him in this state. She was just as glad when they entered Ross, another alley, which seemed to be quite empty. She prayed that the fog would remain thick as they took side streets, not main ones.

They were near Waverly when one of the men gestured to her to take his place. She didn't understand why, but did as told. He turned and ran off. With the other fellow, she continued towards Han-lin's home.

Han-lin seemed to go in and out of consciousness, and when he would slump heavily, it was all Ruth could do to keep her own balance. She struggled to hold him upright while still moving forward, and she realized she never could have made it alone. She, who had never had to use a single muscle before, suddenly had to call up all her reserve strength, and found she had very little. When that reserve was gone, she still would not give up. Through will-power alone she took one step then another. Tears streamed down her eyes as they trudged along, step after step. "We'll make it, don't worry, just a little further," she said time and again to encourage Han-lin, as well as herself.

He slumped, no longer able to hold himself up, no longer taking steps. Fear that he was beyond help filled her. She knew how much blood he had lost. Tears rolled down her eyes. "Han-lin, don't die, please," she whispered. "Stay with me. We're almost at Waverly. Just a bit more."

Her brain could think of nothing but how exhausted she was, and that she couldn't let him slide from her arms onto the ground. He needed to stay upright, to keep moving, if he had any chance of surviving. The pounding of the blood rushing through her own body made her feel faint, but she would not cease. Onward and onward she went, until, strangely, her burden became lighter, and then it was no longer there.

"Han-lin!" she whispered. "No!" She opened her eyes, not having even realized they had been shut for the last few yards. They were near the Li house, and two of Han-lin's men had taken over from her.

She felt a strong hand take her arm, and a soothing voice trying to calm her. It was the elderly servant, Lao-she.

They stepped inside the front door and Ruth gripped the bannister to the upstairs. She stood there a moment, trying to catch her breath and to stop the quivering of her muscles. Her cloak was soaked with Han-lin's blood. She pulled it off, and tossed it aside.

The front door opened again, and the man who had run off came in, bringing a man who carrying a satchel. Ruth imagined he must be a doctor. She followed them upstairs.

Han-lin lay unconscious on a chaise lounge, pale as death.

Two worried men stood over him, talking quietly. His wife, Li Jun, huddled alone against the far wall, her face ashen.

Ruth saw with dismay that the doctor was a Chinese herbalist. She wondered if she should persuade her own doctor to come here. The herbalist mixed several powders together as Lao-she removed Ruth's make-shift bandages. He cleaned and sewed the wounds closed, then sprinkled powder on them and wrapped them with clean bandages. Ruth was thankful Han-lin was unconscious for that ordeal.

The doctor gave Lao-she a number of concoctions and lengthy instructions on their use, and then left.

Lao-she left the room with one of the vials, and after a while returned with a small glassful of the mixture. She and Ruth attempted to rouse Han-lin enough to give him the medicine, but could not. They tried to spoon some into his mouth, but were not very successful at that either. All they could do was sit and wait, Ruth, Lao-she and his four men. Li Jun had left the room.

EARLIER THAT MORNING, Mai received a summons to T'ang's room. She dressed and followed the guard.

"There you are!" T'ang beamed as she entered. "I have good news!"

She looked at him in horror. He was dressed in a white traditional uniform, with a black sash about his waist, but it was covered with blood. She cried out.

"Yes, whore, your observation is right." He gave a loud, boisterous laugh as she stared at him. "It is blood; and guess whose? Ha! Guess whose!?"

There was only one person whose spilt blood would have made T'ang so happy. Mai felt her insides crumble, and it was all she could do to stare at him. "I have no idea," she lied. "I don't know what you're talking about."

T'ang spoke his words slowly and excitedly, relishing in the grief they caused. "This is the blood of Li Han-lin. Your precious Li is dead. I killed him. Yes, I did! After all these years I killed Li Han-lin!" He laughed, all but dancing around the room like the wild maniac he was.

"We had a battle of our tongs," he continued, "just like in the old days. He fell under the blow of my hatchet, a long, deep, gashing blow across his neck! It was wonderful!"

The world seemed to spin as Mai heard these words. Softly, she whispered, "You're mad," and shook her head in denial.

"You can't deny it. You know it's true. If Li were still alive, I would not be."

Mai felt hysteria rising in her at his every word, knowing the truth of what was said. She wanted to kill him.

"Why would you and Li fight?" she cried, unable to control her tears any longer. "Why? I am here, of my own free choice. You have no cause!"

"Fool!" T'ang laughed again, grabbing her long braid and pulling her head back until she could not bear the pain. "You think one so insignificant as you would be worth either of us risking ourselves or our tongs over? Of course not! This fight was about the past, and the future. It determined who will rule Chinatown one day. Me! All tongs will bow before the might of the Wang Shao!"

Mai felt as though she too had died with those words. She shut her eyes and did not move, beyond even tears in her sorrow. Suddenly she felt T'ang's arms around her.

"Come, we must celebrate!" he whispered, unbuttoning her jacket as Mai wished for the release of her own death.

CHAPTER 10

As THE DAY WORE on, Han-lin showed no sign of improvement. Ruth and Lao-she were afraid to change the bandages in case the bleeding should start again, but they kept a careful watch for any signs of infection.

As night fell, Lao-she made some soup and rice for the family and brought some to Ruth and the men. The four men left when the hour became late. Ruth gave one of them a note to have sent to her parents telling them she was caring for a sick child and wouldn't be home that night.

About midnight, Lao-she got up from her chair to see how Han-lin was doing. Urgently, she cried out to Ruth. He was burning with fever. Lao-she made up another brew from the herb doctor's medicines while Ruth sponged his face and neck with cold water.

This time they managed to get him to take the medicine, but it didn't break the fever. Throughout the night, Lao-she and Ruth took turns giving him medicine and keeping cool packs on his head and neck, watching and waiting for whatever the morning might bring.

The next day, a number of men came to the Li house to pay their respects. The doctor visited several times, usually just to stand over Han-lin and wring his hands. He changed the bandages, put new powder on the wounds, and gave a new mixture of herbs to Lao-she. The children peeked in the doorway two or three times, and Li Jun did once.

Lao-she and Ruth simply waited.

Ruth wondered about the situation at her home with her having been gone for so long, but she would not leave Han-lin. Twice his fever spiked, and twice she and Lao-she pulled him through. So she sat and waited and prayed harder than she ever had in her life for him to recover. Lao-she would pat Ruth on the shoulder or squeeze her hand by way of encouragement and gratitude.

Evening came. Lao-she made a light supper for the household. After dinner, they settled down for another long night when Han-lin's eyelids fluttered. Ruth and Lao-she immediately jumped up and stood beside his bed. Slowly his eyes opened. He tried to say something but was unable to speak.

Lao-she quickly gave him an herb mixture.

He slept another hour, and then when he opened his eyes the fogginess that had clouded his mind seemed to have lifted. He looked at the two women standing over him, simultaneously worried, concerned, and yet happy just seeing him awake. Haltingly, he murmured a few words to Lao-she. She answered him at length, then smiled and quietly left the room.

He turned to Ruth. "Thank you," he whispered.

Ruth sat on the side of his bed, her eyes glistening with unshed tears of joy. "You're most welcome. I'm glad you've wakened. I was so worried!" Her voice carried all the emotion that had gripped her over these two days.

He lifted his hand and she quickly took it. "I can see how tired you are," he said, his voice barely a whisper. "I'm sorry you were involved in something so ugly ... so brutal." The look he gave her said everything about his feelings for her at that moment. Her fingers tightened on the hand she held to show him that she understood.

"I'm fine," she said, her heart soaring, "now that you will be."

"I remember that street," he continued. "I remember hearing your voice cry out. I know your voice as well as my own. I expected to die when I fell there, and I know that my men thought me dead. Another inch or two, and the blade would have done its duty. When I heard your voice, I thought I was dreaming. But you were real. How scared you must have been, but how brave. After I saw you running towards me, I can't seem to remember ..." He stopped and seemed to be lost in thought.

"It doesn't matter. Don't talk; you need to rest." Ruth pressed her cheek against his hand.

His fingers tightened on hers. "I do remember that you kept calling me, bringing me back, giving encouragement. I owe you my life."

"Just get better."

She asked him more about how he was feeling—if his head was hurting or if he had pain anywhere aside from the wounds. Her fear was that he had sustained some unknown internal injuries, but it seemed there were none.

Lao-she came back in the room carrying a bowl of chicken broth for Han-lin, which she helped him eat. She had much to relay to him as he ate a small amount.

After the broth, Ruth suggested that he try to sleep a bit. He wasn't sleepy at all, however, so Ruth decided to read to him from one of the small collections of English books he had in the room used as her classroom. She went to select a book and was amused to find *The Legend of Sleepy Hollow* among them. She took the book back to the parlor where Han-lin told her he never did have time to read it, although he had wanted to.

With Ruth giving as animated a reading as she could, the tale of the headless horseman and malcontent Ichabod Crane did much to entertain him. She continued to read through the night, and Lao-she brought more broth and medicine. They all talked quite a bit, with Han-lin interpreting, and even managed to laugh a little.

The next morning, Ruth awoke on a thick mat on the floor in Han-lin's room. A symptom of how exhausted she must have been, she didn't even remember lying down on.

"Good morning, sleepy-head," Han-lin said with a smile. Li Jun stood beside his bed and it was clear they had been conversing. Ruth quickly sat up without speaking.

The bright morning sun cast a harsh light over the room, making everything suddenly seem cold and forbidding where last night in the yellow glow of the lamplight, it had seemed warm and friendly.

The previous day, Li Jun had not entered the room at all.

"Forgive my wife for waking you," Han-lin said. "It was thought-less, of her. I'm ashamed."

"It's all right," she said with an abrupt shake of her head. "Your wife certainly has the right to speak to you anytime. Anyway, it's good I've awakened, I must go home. I'm sure everyone there must think I'm down with the plague or something." She spoke coolly, and quickly got up and began bustling about getting her things together. She suddenly felt irritated at everyone and everything, and especially at herself for feeling so.

"Ruth—"

"Yes?" Her tone was brusque.

Han-lin said nothing as he studied her in silence, and then said only, "Chang will take you home." Lao-she was just coming into the room and he gave her instructions for his coachman.

In a moment, Ruth was ready to leave.

"When will you return?" Han-lin asked.

She stared at the floor, not wanting to meet his gaze. "You will be better soon," she said. "I don't believe I'll be needed." She forced her voice to sound nonchalant, as if none of this was important to her.

He seemed to study her, to look into her heart. "You are needed here." His voice was gentle. "I would like you to come back, if you wish to. But if you don't, I understand."

Ruth shut her eyes; she both wanted and hated hearing those words from him. She simply didn't know what to do or say, but seeing his wife standing by his side told her everything that was wrong with her constantly running back to his house like a love-sick puppy. Yet, she knew there was no love between the two of them, and also knew, from the way he looked at her ...

She shook off the thought. Everything about this situation was wrong. Han-lin was so pale, and looked so weak and vulnerable she could hardly bear it. "I'm very tired. After I rest, I'll see what will be."

Li Jun's English was not good enough to understand the words, but she clearly understood the undercurrent in the room.

"Eat and sleep," Ruth said with a small smile. "You'll be fine soon." She glanced at Li Jun before adding, "Good day to you both."

As Ruth hurried out of the room, a lump of emotion in her throat made it hard for her to breathe. Behind her, the two of them said "Good-day" to her, their voices in unison, combined as one, as they themselves were.

And she, the outsider who had pretended to be a part of that world and that life for these few days, now needed to return to her own reality, to climb alone into the coach that would take her back to the life she belong in, to the people she belonged with, and who gave her no pleasure and brought her existence no meaning. Deep inside, she had never felt so empty.

CHAPTER 11

WHEN RUTH ARRIVED home, she ran up the stairs to her room, not wanting her mother to see the state of her dress with dried blood splattered on it. She had discarded the cloak she had been wearing.

Blanche didn't move from the living room sofa, and only called out that she hoped Ruth carried no fatal Asian germs into the house, and that she would call some fumigators the next day.

Ruth went to her room without a word to bathe and change the clothes she had worn the past two nights.

Newspapers had been saved for her as she was an avid reader of current events. As she spread the papers out to find the one with the earliest date, a headline caught her eye and made her blood run cold.

TONG BATTLE BLOODIES CHINATOWN

The hacked-to-death bodies of three Orientals were discovered in a Chinatown alley early yesterday morning. One man had been decapitated and the other two apparently died from multiple blows from a hatchet.

Residents expressed shock over the incident. It is believed the men were members of opposing gangs, which the Chinese call Tongs. No one could say if this marks the beginning of another Tong war in Chinatown.

The street was bloody in areas other than where the bodies were found, indicating that many men must have been injured in the fight along with the three that died.

The Mayor has called for an immediate police investigation. Chief of Police Hanson said that although the police haven't gotten to the bottom of this incident yet, white San Franciscans need have no fear, as Tong wars in the past have always involved only the Orientals.

The rest of the article was filled with speculation about what might have happened that night, followed by a brief history of tongs and their battles. Although the word "tong" simply meant "association" and some were no more dangerous than a rotary club, a few were involved in illegal activities—"highbinder" tongs was the name given them by the local press. Those activities and the turf battles that resulted from them gave tongs, per se, a bad name. The larger and more powerful a tong became, the more it tried to expand, causing turf battles, or tong "wars" as they came to be called.

Ruth read the newspaper's description of a tong battle with horror. The battles were formally arranged ordeals. In an alley, members of opposing tongs would line up along opposite walls and face each other, each man holding a hatchet. Suddenly, one of them would move, signaling the others into action. Like two massive snakes, they hurled themselves at each other. A blinding clash of steel would sound as blades hacked the air. Then, just as quickly as they came together, the two sides fell apart and all who could, made their escape, leaving the victims bloody, helpless and dying on the street. The actual battle lasted but a few seconds.

The latest battle had the police completely baffled, as was the usual situation in their dealings with the city's Chinese population. No one in Chinatown would talk to them to say who was involved or why, although it was held on good authority that most people did know.

Ruth put down the newspaper. She felt as though she had been struck by a thunderbolt. It all fit together now, why Han-lin had been left in that way, why he feared being found, and why so many men were always around him. Perhaps even the gambling parlor they went to was part of his tong.

No, it's not so! Ruth told herself. How could she think Han-lin was some sort of tong hatchet man? Possibly a murderer? It was crazy. Impossible!

He was the gentlest man she had ever met. His words were soft and gracious. He had an appreciation of the beauty of life, and was not unwilling to show it and share it with her. She had thought of him as perfect as a sonnet, and now this. She could not reconcile it.

But she also realized that Han-lin was a complex, many-faceted person, that she knew little about him, and had seen but one side of his nature. She never imagined, however, that the other side could be cruel, bloody or vile.

Ruth looked for follow-up articles on the tong battle. One battle was always good for several days' copy. One such article speculated that one of the tong's involved was the "Yew-en-lee," one of the largest of those that ran Chinatown's gambling parlors. The opposing side, however, was not known, nor was the reason for the battle discovered.

The Chief of Police decided to make a few pronouncements and offered the opinion that he "would be happy if all the tongs would get together in one massive battle which would continue until every one of their heathen kind were dead." He went on to assure San Franciscans that the police fully intended to "keep the lid on this thing" and contain the battles solely within the confines of Chinatown so that the rest of the city would be safe—apparently forgetting that on the previous day he assured everyone that tong battles never occur outside Chinatown.

oOo

The next day Ruth was still very tired but knew that despite the troubling newspaper stories about illegal tongs, she had to see Han-lin and find out his condition. She had no confidence in the ability of the herb doctor to heal the wounds, and had heard of far less severe cuts festering and becoming gangrenous.

Han-lin's eyes lit up when Lao-she led her into his room. He had been surrounded by several men when she arrived, but he abruptly dismissed them from the room.

For the next week, Ruth visited him daily, watching as he slowly regained his strength. She never stayed too long because he refused to rest while she was there. Ruth asked about Li Jun, but was told she was ailing and did not wish any English lessons at that time. Ruth decided not to mention the newspaper articles on the tong battle, nor did Han-lin offer any explanation as to what had occurred.

CHAPTER 12

WINSTON GREER DIDN'T understand his daughter. He never had, and probably never would. But he was growing increasingly agitated over her fascination with the Li family and everything Chinese. She had been buying books on China, its history and people, and her room looked like a Chinatown junk shop.

For her to have become an "English teacher" and to leave the house early each morning for the sake of the students was simply not Ruth. His suspicions grew as the days went on.

There's a catch, he thought. There's something she's not telling me that is causing her to be fascinated with this Li bunch—or someone, or some place, in Chinatown. The more he thought about it, the more convinced he became that he needed to find out the true story. Finally, he told two of his men to follow Ruth and give him a full report.

The men followed her nine times. Since Han-lin was recuperating, she went straight to the Li house and joined him in tea and Chinese rolls for breakfast, so the men didn't even have the novelty of following her to a Chinese restaurant or through back alleys.

They had to report to Greer that she did in fact go straight to a house, stay all morning and leave about noon. The only people the men saw were the Li children and the servants, Lao-she and Chang, who they assumed were the Li's.

Han-lin had heard about the "white devils" watching his house the first day they set foot in Chinatown. He knew why they were there, and had been expecting for weeks that Winston Greer would send spies out to watch Ruth. If he had been Greer with such a lovely but headstrong daughter, he didn't think he'd ever let her out of his sight. He didn't tell Ruth about the spies, knowing she would be furious and only make matters worse.

Instead, he put out word that while the men were there, no one was to come to his home unless it were an extreme emergency, and if spoken to by the men, everyone was to pretend they didn't understand English.

As Greer listened to his men report what Ruth was doing, he was very puzzled. He did his best to go about his own work with an easy mind, but he knew his daughter too well for that. His spies were missing something, and he wanted to find out what it was.

CHAPTER 13

THE LARGE, BALDING AMERICAN surveyed the scene before him with pleasure. "Very nice salon you have here, T'ang; all the comforts of home, and then some," Winston Greer said as he eased himself onto the divan and drooled over the food and women, feeling stirrings of equal desire.

"'My house is your house,' Mr. Greer. I understand that is an American saying," T'ang added.

"Actually, it's *mi casa*...well, forget it. Means a lot more when you say it, boy!" Greer guffawed along with the burly men beside him— business associates he called them.

T'ang nodded at two of the women who proceeded to sit on each side of Winston Greer and hand feed him delicacies from the sumptuous table. The other Americans with Greer soon enjoyed similar favors. Chinese rice wine flowed freely.

When the meal ended, T'ang turned from its idle chatter to business. "The problem I wish to speak to you about, Mr. Greer, is that there are not enough women here in Chinatown to meet our needs. Men came to this area, Gold Mountain, we call it in China, to make their fortune and then return home. Unfortunately, many of those men spend the money as quickly as they earn it, and are not able to return home, and your country has passed laws that have made it nearly impossible for my people to legally enter the country, or to return to it once we leave. But our men need women for pleasure, and also to marry, to settle down and make our community strong."

"Oh, ho, so that's it!" Greer and the others laughed, which T'ang ignored.

"I have a simple, yet profitable solution," T'ang continued. "I propose we import women as we do any other desirable commodity." He paused to be sure his words were understood before he continued. "We import them from China, on your ships. Once here, we sell them to the highest bidder."

"They'd be stopped by customs agents," Greer said. "The only way to get them in the country would be to smuggle them."

T'ang smiled and nodded.

"These women," Greer asked, concern on his face, "will they want to come here, to this kind of life?"

"Of course! We will buy them in China. Their parents will not object to getting money for them. Daughters are plentiful, and of no importance to anyone. They will be happy to do whatever we ask of them."

Before Greer could respond, the man to his right said in disgust, "What you're proposing is a slave trade, man! That kind of thing ended forty years ago in this country! We fought a bloody Civil War to stop it."

"Not at all!" T'ang sounded indignant. "I know slavery is illegal in this country. This is quite different. Poor, lonely women will be brought here to be married, to find happiness. And think of the profit involved! There is a fantastic profit in this, as you can well imagine. Everyone profits, even the girls, uh, women involved. At least they won't be starving to death in this country." T'ang turned his back on Greer's underling, and said with a smile. "My plan has great potential. We would have them immigrate if it were possible, but it since the Chinese Exclusion Act was passed, immigration has been effectively cut off for us. Surely, you see that!"

"I don't know," Greer began, but already thoughts of those profits began to swell in his brain.

"There is no danger to you or your business, as you have already discovered in our opium dealings. All we need are your ships. My men will pick up the women. We will have all the necessary papers for each so that they will look like legitimate passengers. Your crew will have the ready excuse of not knowing Chinese and not understanding our ways if anyone were to question them. But no one will; who in their right mind would question Winston Greer's cargo?"

Mai looked with interest at this man called Greer. His name sounded so familiar, but she could not think of why. She couldn't think of anything these days it seemed. The opium T'ang routinely gave her took away much memory, and much pain. She lived each day as if in a perpetual dream.

She should have been horrified by the conversation, but even that was too much of an effort any more. She reached for more wine. As T'ang's woman she did not have to feed the Americans, but sat apart from them in a black silk dress that emphasized the childlike delicacy of her body. Her simple braid was gone and in its place her hair was piled high and lavishly arranged with combs and ornaments, adding some years to her youthful demeanor, now garishly colored with nearly white pancake makeup, blackened and lengthened eyebrows, and cherry red coloring on her lips.

"He does have a point," Greer said loudly to his associates. "And, what the hell, what do we care what one group of Chinamen do to another? We have a business to run, damn it."

"It could be risky," Greer's goon cautioned.

"It isn't," T'ang said. "But to allay your fears, why don't we try it once? Why not just a little run, only fifteen to twenty women? You will see how easy it is to transport them here."

"The price must include a premium for the risk—a hefty premium," another American interjected.

"That is understood," T'ang said with a smile.

"Let's try it," Greer decided. "The details can be agreed upon later."

Toasts were raised to celebrate.

"Now," Greer spoke eyeing the women about him, "maybe we should become a little better acquainted with our new cargo. What do you say?"

"Sounds good!" his friends agreed, while T'ang just grinned at the suggestion.

"Personally, I like that one," Greer pointed at Mai.

"She is my very own," T'ang said proudly. Then, looking at the girl and remembering how displeased he had been with her ever since the night he told her of Li's death, he decided a lesson was in order. "However, in the spirit of our newest, and hopefully, good and profitable partnership, I would be most proud if you would give my poor mistress the honor of spending time with her this evening. She is very beautiful and skillful; I'm sure you will find her pleasing."

"Very big of you, old boy, very big," Greer said, trying to stand on wobbly legs after the wine.

"My men will show you and your friends to most comfortable quarters. The women will await your pleasure."

Mai took one last, long swallow of wine before leaving the room with the other women.

"Maybe this will teach you to be friendlier to me next time!" T'ang laughed in her ear as she passed by, but his smile turned to a scowl when she was out of sight.

She continued to believe Li Han-lin was dead, when she was able to remember enough to think anything.

T'ang did not tell her of Li's recovery and threatened death to anyone who did. The mere thought of how Li survived threw him into a black rage. He was a laughing stock because of it. Li would pay.

o0o

Much later that evening, Mai returned to her room feeling more alive than she had for ages. Not because of Greer. Happily for her, he was too old, too fat and too drunk to perform. Surprisingly quickly, he gave up and spoke with her, probably wanting to pass a little more time to look better in his friends' eyes.

Mai couldn't understand much of what he said, although her English was becoming much better since living with T'ang because many of the customers were Americans. She strained to understand, however, when he asked if she knew a family called Li. He said his daughter taught English there and one of the Li's took sick and his daughter stayed until the person was out of danger. He wanted to know what the Li's were like, but Mai disclaimed any knowledge of them.

She racked her clouded brain trying to remember the past. Greer...wasn't that the name of Li Jun's English teacher? American names all sounded so funny to Mai she scarcely remembered any of them.

But it must have been that name. Why else would it sound famil- iar? The Li family had a serious illness and the Greer's daughter had stayed until there was a recovery. Hope began to grow within Mai at the news.

The timing was right, she thought. If Li Han-lin had died, the American woman wouldn't have stayed. She would have told her father the person had died, not that he had recovered.

Dare she hope Li Han-lin still lived? She must find out. She knew no one here would tell her. There was only one way to do that. She must cause T'ang to trust her again and let her out from under his guards' thumbs.

Her body ached for more opium, to dull the pain she was in, even to dull the hope she had in case such hope proved false. Somewhere her mind told her she had to stop smoking it if she were to ever be truly free, but for the moment, she could not stop.

CHAPTER 14

WINSTON GREER'S PLANS to profit from a cargo of women for Chinatown's sing-song houses proceeded nicely. Every exigency had been planned for; all that was left was the execution. Nevertheless, Greer felt an anxiety about this deal that he hadn't felt since the old days when he was no more than a two-bit wharf rat, breaking heads and swindling sailors to man his boss' tramp steamers.

It wasn't until he picked up a few grams of opium for a cheap price and then sold them for a higher price in the U.S. that he learned how easy it was to become rich. That was the start of a business that eventually led to a legitimate shipping enterprise. It was lucrative, but never as much fun as those early days on trampers.

The fun was over now. Greer had a reputation to uphold and decided, all in all, the best course of action was to be out of the city when the first boat full of women arrived.

A business trip provided a good excuse to leave.

He decided to take Ruth with him. The last thing he wanted was for her to nose about and discover anything suspicious about his latest cargo. Also, he had some hopes that once out of San Francisco she would realize that her Chinatown involvement was an aberration and should be forgotten about. He hoped to stay away for a month or two, but told Ruth they were only going to Los Angeles.

oOo

Ruth argued against accompanying her father on a business trip, but Greer said he needed her.

In fact, she was of two minds about the trip. She hated the thought of not seeing Han-lin, but she was at the point, too, of finding it difficult to stay here and be with him. The more she was with him and the better she got to know him, the more she wanted to be with him. Finally, she had to admit that she had fallen in love with him.

She felt foolish. He was married with three children. He was alien to her. She recognized that he held back so much, she didn't really know or understand him, and she wondered if she ever fully could.

If he knew how she felt, he would probably feel pity for her. She doubted he could be in love with her, and she knew she was making a spectacle of herself going to see him every day, pretending to take the role of comforter when she knew that was something his wife should be doing. But his wife was never with him. Li Jun seemed to feel nothing for Han-lin, and he seemed to look at her with distaste. Or, so Ruth thought. Sometimes she wondered if she was just fooling herself about the relationship between the two, seeing what she wanted to see, and not what was.

At times, she felt nothing but humiliation over her foolish heart. Yet, she, who had always been so proud, hadn't the strength of character to stay away.

And so she agreed to go with her father.

oOo

The next day Ruth told Han-lin about her trip.

He looked at her intently, studying her. "It is necessary for you to go?"

"Not really." She tried to make her reply sound light and carefree. "Perhaps it will be more like a vacation."

He nodded thoughtfully. "Yes, a vacation. I can see where a vacation is called for. A time away, that is always good."

"You're probably glad to be rid of me," she said with a joking tone to her voice, but her eyes sparkled with tears.

"Yes," he replied, lying back with a sigh.

The color drained from her face; she didn't want to believe what she had heard. *He wants to be rid of me.* Her mind raced, feeling very foolish at the way she had believed he welcomed her visits. She clamped her jaws firmly shut to still the quivering of her lip, and silently, rose to leave the house, never to return.

Han-lin reached up and grabbed her arm. She looked at him, unable any longer to hide the hurt she felt, hurt pride as well as emotions; she wanted to speak, but no words would come.

He pulled her down to his bedside, then put his arms around her, crushing her to him as he kissed her mouth and her teary eyes. Then his mouth was on hers again, holding her even closer, his kisses, strong and brutal, almost as if he hated her, hated having anything to do with her, yet wanting to possess her totally. Her head spun as she wanted to pull away out, but instead found herself kissing him back, returning each kiss with one of equal passion. His hands caressed her breasts, stole along the length of her back, her thighs. Fire flooded her body, leaving her unable to think, only to feel, and she felt completely lost in the glory of the feeling of his lips, his touch. She gave herself up to the pleasure of him, desiring more, much more from him than she had ever before wanted from a man.

Suddenly, he pushed her away. For but a fleeting moment she thought she saw a flicker, almost of pain, in his eyes, but before she could be sure, it was gone and the mask, the veil that he could pull over his features to hide any expression, fell once again. But he could not hide the anger in his eyes.

"Never again say I will be glad to be rid of you," he demanded, his voice harsh. "But you must leave here. Go with your father and forget this house. I don't want you to return. There is nothing here for you but pain."

She stood and looked at him in silence. She understood why he had stopped what had passed between them. And she knew he was right to stop it.

She must leave. She felt no bitterness at his words, only deep sorrow and emptiness. He was attempting to make the inevitable easier for her.

She shut her eyes a moment, to gather strength. "You're right," she said finally. "I understand." With that, she leaned forward and gave him one last quick kiss. Then she stood and looked at him until she could bear it no long, and turned away. Keeping her back straight and her head erect, she walked out of the house, saying nothing and not looking back.

It was the hardest thing she had ever done in her life.

oOo

After two weeks in Los Angeles, Greer decided he and Ruth needed to a real vacation and the two set sail for Acapulco.

After another couple of weeks, even Greer tired of the enforced quietude, and decided they should journey across the country to Mexico City.

They weren't in Mexico City long before he became involved in an affair with a married Mexican woman. Because of her marriage, the affair had to be carried on in secret. It was filled with intrigue and clandestine meetings, which Greer thoroughly enjoyed. The affair was not secret enough to keep Ruth from finding out about it, however.

She knew it would run its course in time, but until that happened, she couldn't get her father to leave Mexico, and he refused to give her the consent, or the means, to return home alone.

In Mexico City, Ruth did not lack for attention. Her father's reputation for wealth preceded him wherever he went and Ruth found herself being wined and dined by the cream of Mexican society. A number of young men called upon her, and she went out with them simply because the activity made the time pass more quickly than inactivity did.

She also hoped that seeing so many prospective suitors would allow her to meet someone she could care about. Instead, the suitors caused her to realize she didn't want to meet more men; that she had met the one man who could ever mean anything to her.

And he was the one man that could never be hers.

Instead of helping her forget Han-lin, meeting others only made him all the more precious to her.

The path she took was a wrong-headed, and she knew it. She threw herself into her father's business as she had done in the past. But this time, he kept a good deal of it away from her, and she didn't understand why. All the paper work that he normally had with him, the telegraph messages and other missives about the shipping company, had been left at home. It was as if he had abdicated his responsibilities to his office manager. Whenever she demanded an explanation, he said that he, too, needed a vacation from work.

At times, she couldn't face any more parties or the phony gaiety on display at them, and refused to leave the house Greer had rented for them. She would sit brooding in her room for three or four days at a time, refusing to see anyone, including Greer. Greer ignored her during those times, and pursued his own pleasures.

CHAPTER 15

TWO MONTHS HAD PASSED when Soo Chen-gai, Li Han-lin's best friend and right arm in the Yuen-li tong, heard a timid knock on the door to his tiny, two-room apartment above a sweetmeats store on Dupont Gai. Opening it, he was amazed to find Mai-ching. She bowed, then quickly entered the room and shut the door behind her.

"Soo Chen-gai, I am so relieved to find you at home! I had to come, to find out the truth about the night T'ang's Wang Shao tong fought the Yuen-li."

Chen-gai was stunned at her words. He pulled a chair up for the daughter of his cousin. "Certainly, Mai-ching. Please, sit here." His heavily jowled face rumpled with compassion at the young girl. Chen-gai was about ten years older than Han-lin, heavy-set, with rough, weather-beaten features. He was coarse and uneducated, but had a warmth about him that made him well-loved by all who knew him.

"I have only a moment," she said. "I must go before it is suspected I am anywhere but shopping. I was told Li Han-lin had been killed, but I believe that is false."

Chen-gai smiled at her words. "I am happy to be able to report he lives. It was truly miraculous. T'ang and three of his men all attacked Li at once. We saw him go down under T'ang's blade, and when T'ang did not give another blow, we all thought the one that struck Li was fatal. The cry went out that the Wang Shao were victorious and the rest of us ran, I am ashamed to say. The blow we thought killed Li took the life from us, too. We no longer had any will to fight.

"When the Wang Shao left, we went back for Li Han-lin's body, but the American woman who is Li's friend had already found him alive. Some swear he had died, and she brought him back to life with her love—it is clear to everyone how much she loves him. But others believe they only say that because they are filled with shame that they abandoned him. Whatever the truth may be, she had somehow managed to get him to his feet and out of the alley. We helped her carry him home. The American and that old servant of his who loves him like a son pulled him through."

Mai's eyes shone with joy hearing this news, "My prayers have been answered," she whispered.

"All of ours have," added Chen-gai.

"But tell me, is the American named Greer?"

"Yes."

"Then you must warn Li Han-lin to be wary of her. No matter her feelings, her father works with T'ang. He is an evil, disgusting man, but is very powerful. He is using one of his ships to bring women from the homeland to fill T'ang's brothels. Her father places money and profit over all human decency. Li must be careful that the man's claws do not reach to him through his daughter."

"That is an outrageous story, Mai-ching. Are you sure of it?"

"Absolutely."

"I will give him the warning. Thank you, child."

"I must go now."

"Must you go back? Your parents grieve constantly for you."

"I must return, and my parents must learn to accept it."

"Why, Mai-ching?" Chen-gai softly touched her arm, remembering her when she was just a small child, how happy and playful she was, and how he could make her laugh just by making funny faces. Why had fate been so cruel as to make that child the unhappy woman he saw before him?

"Surely you understand," Mai looked up at him, her eyes searching his. "I have learned to use the opium pipe to make it through my days, and now I find I must have it or I cannot bear the pain. T'ang is most generous in that regard, and it is a costly burden and shame I could not inflict on my parents. But more than that, if I were to leave T'ang that might give him an excuse to battle Li Han-lin again. I would never do anything that might allow that to happen, never. Li must beware. It isn't over yet, not until the final battle. T'ang's hatred of him has quite unhinged his mind, he is dangerous and capable of anything. We are all in less danger if I am with him; I can at least watch him."

Chen-gai nodded, "Go with an easy heart, Mai-ching. I, too, fear for Li. He was lucky once. At least the tong is there to protect him. Maybe something can be done to stop this war before any more people are killed, but I doubt it. I will speak to your parents. We will keep your secret."

Mai bowed deeply and turned towards the door.

"Mai," Chen-gai called to her, and held out his arms. She ran to him and buried her face in his big barrel of a chest, as he gave her a bear-like hug just as he had when she was young. "Come anytime it is safe for you."

She nodded unable to speak for the affection she felt for this dear man, and quietly slipped through the door and into the crowds enveloping Dupont Gai.

GREER AND RUTH STAYED in Mexico City five weeks until Greer's romance cooled. Ruth wasn't sure what had happened, perhaps the lady's husband found out, but whatever it was she was ecstatic to be returning home. She had felt like a prisoner, but at the same time, she was glad for the time away, to collect her bearings, and to put Li Han-lin and everything about the strange world he lived in out of her mind.

She wondered what strange spell had been cast over her that she ever thought she could love a man like him. Tongs … hatchets … wives. She must have been temporarily insane.

The return journey seemed endless. Greer was in a bad humor most of the way. When they finally arrived back in San Francisco, nearly four months had passed from the time they had left.

Blanche Greer brought a number of Ruth's and her father's friends to the pier to meet them as Blanche had decided to hold a "coming home" party. Neither Ruth nor Greer was in the mood for a party, but they were friendly, realizing they shouldn't hold Blanche's thoughtlessness against those who agreed to come to meet them.

As soon as she could get away, Ruth ran up to her room and shut and locked the door behind her.

It felt good to be in her own room again.

She went over to her desk and looked at four months accumulation of mail. There was one bit of mail that was different from all the rest. It was wrapped in a tube with no return address. Intrigued, she quickly opened the package, to discover inside a clever and humorous picture drawn in black ink of the headless horseman and Ichabod Crane!

There was no note with the sketch, but Ruth knew who it was from.

He hadn't forgotten her.

And he was a skilled artist.

Tears sprang to her eyes, her emotions roiling. Unable to stay alone with her thoughts, she ran downstairs to rejoin the party.

The next morning, she didn't allow herself to do what her heart wanted, to go back to Chinatown.

Later in the day, she walked to the cable car line and watched one car after the other pass her by. Finally, she returned home. She would not go, no matter how much it hurt to stay away.

Instead, she went to her father's office, and threw herself into the family's shipping business. As night fell, she returned home with armfuls of reading material, her refuge once again from the world.

The next day she went downtown with Blanche to do some shopping, an activity that Ruth never found of particular interest. Once home, Ruth retired to her room to read the memos, papers, and budget reports she had picked up at the office. She felt the need, more than anything, to occupy her mind so that she would not be tempted to think about the Li family, Chinatown, or anything that might be happening there.

She stayed up late reading reports and going over the accounting books. She hadn't been asleep very long when something woke her. She opened her eyes and looked about in the darkness. She saw and heard nothing, but felt sure some sound had caused her to wake. Then she heard it again, a slight tapping at the French doors that lead to the balcony off her bedroom.

She sat up with a start. It must be the branch of a tree or some such thing blowing against the window panes, she told herself. She got out of bed, walked to the French doors and drew aside the curtain.

For a moment she thought she must still be dreaming. Han-lin stood on the balcony. He was dressed all in black, and seemed to blend with the night.

With hands shaking so badly she could scarcely work the latch, she unlocked the doors as quickly and quietly as she was able. Eventually, she flung the door open. She wanted to run to him, and hold him close, but she dared not move, and said nothing.

Han-lin stepped into her bedroom, shutting the door behind him. She stood in a white nightgown, her long red hair hanging loose to her waist. He, too, said nothing and seemed unable to move.

She didn't know which of them broke the spell, but suddenly she was in his arms, clinging to him, holding him and kissing him as if she never wanted to let him go.

His hands molded her body against his as he caressed her.

She pulled back her head to look at his proud, noble face. "Han-lin," she cried as their lips met again. Her arms tightened, as if she couldn't get close enough to him to know that she was really, finally, holding him again. She felt lost in the heady, sensuous feel of him and knew she wanted him completely, right then, right there, in her own bedroom.

She knew she had to break away, to somehow control these wayward feelings.

She pushed herself away from him, holding him from her with outstretched arms. She stared at him with wonder at the feelings he aroused in her, at the longing and desire she had never before experienced, with emotions that came from deep within her soul—and with wonder at the realization he desired her as well.

Han-lin placed his hands over hers as they lay against his chest, and holding her gaze, tried to explain. "I spent many hours, Ruth, wondering what to do when you returned, if you would return. Your trip lasted so long I was beginning to doubt it. I thought about you with other men, men who would make you forget that you had ever known me. Then I heard you were back.

"I waited, to see if you would come to Chinatown, despite my words to you when we last met. But you did as I asked, and you did not come." He shook his head. "I couldn't bear it. I could not pass another day knowing you were in the city and yet not seeing you, not knowing how you were, or how you felt. Can you forgive me for coming here?"

"Forgive? Of course! You being here ... it's what I've dreamed of. But let me look at you! You seem to be completely recovered. Are you, my darling?" She carefully placed her hand on his shoulder and arm.

"I'm fine." He laughed and pulled her closer to him, capturing her against him once more.

It felt so good to be in his arms, she didn't know what to do. It was as if she had only been half a person and now she was complete, as if she was finally where she belonged.

His eyes locked with hers, growing smoky with intensity, and suddenly the smile left his face. His searching look found her lips, full and sensuous, and he slowly lowered his head towards them.

Ruth felt the warmth from his hands and arms on her body through her thin nightdress, and smelled the clean, masculine scent of him. Her breath caught in her throat as she saw the desire in his eyes, a desire that was matched by her own and frightened her in its intensity.

"I don't think…" she whispered, just before their lips met.

"Yes," Han-lin said, his voice deep in his throat as fingers intertwined in her hair and held her still while his mouth descended on hers. She felt his whole body tremble as their lips met and he pulled her closer, his arms like steel bands about her, his kiss like a heady wine, totally enveloping her, making her lose her senses, all her reason.

Her arms reached upward for him as well, caressing him, reveling in him as he did in her.

His lips took full possession of hers, parting them as he roused her even further. His hand slipped under the thin strap of her gown and slipped deeper, caressing, loving, feeling her warm beauty in a way no man had before.

It was not until he laid her on her bed and stopped kissing her for the moment it took him to lay beside her that the full impact of what was happening hit her with force and shock. Before he was able to take her in his arms again, she stood and walked across the room, clutching the window sill, trying to still her pounding heart.

"Ruth, come here, don't be afraid," he said softly, his hand outstretched towards her.

She shook her head, and shut her eyes, biting her lower lip to keep from returning to him. But all the reasons not to came flooding over her, like waves of nausea—he was married, and to even think of making love to him went against all her years of rigid upbringing. She could not toss so much aside, no matter how strong her feelings were.

Loving him, wanting him, she had nothing left of who she was but her honor.

She reached for her robe and put it on, then faced him, her eyes shimmering and her cheeks aglow with emotion. She could have cried with relief and love as she saw understanding in Han-lin's eyes.

He sat up, still on the bed. "You're right," he said.

She nodded, knowing that if he held her, kissed her, again, she might not have the strength left to deny him anything. And that made her love him even more.

"Tell me, how did you get past my father's bodyguards?" she asked, deciding that conversation at this time was the safest course. "Someone usually patrols the perimeter of this house."

"To make one's way past some watchmen is hardly a difficult task. As for your room, Chang noticed by watching the lights a few times after he brought you home which room should be yours. He showed me which it was, and he awaits me outside, hidden, now."

Ruth crossed the room to him and sat, somewhat stiffly, on the stool by her vanity.

"I've missed you terribly," she said. "I've been worried."

"Worried? Why is that?"

"Because of what happened the night you were hurt, I was afraid it would happen again."

"Don't even think about it."

"How can I help it? Please tell me, was it a tong battle as the newspapers said? The papers frightened me. They said once these wars start they don't stop until everyone is dead!"

"It's not that bad!" Han-lin tried to jest, but he saw how seriously Ruth looked at him. He faced her squarely. "It's only right I give you an explanation, but I'm not sure you'll understand. The papers were correct, a tong battle was involved. My business, if you can call it that, is the Yuen-li tong."

"A tong," Ruth cried, her heart sinking. "But how? Why? You're so gentle, so good. I don't believe it!"

"I'm not those things, Ruth. However, tongs are also not necessarily what you read in the newspapers."

"But the wars, the battles; so many deaths. Surely those bodies are not just journalistic fancies. You nearly died! Why, Han-lin?"

"Sometimes there is no choice but to fight. The Yuen-li tong tries to find other ways, but they are not always available. Tongs exist to protect their members. If a man does harm to another man, what recourse does the victim have? The police won't help him—or can't. They don't understand our ways. We are aliens, not citizens. We have few rights. It is necessary to provide our own laws."

She was determined to learn, and to try to understand. "Tell me about the Yuen-li tong."

"It started in China," he began. "And when I came to this country I was able to use certain ties from China along with newly formed ones to get the group organized in such a way that it quickly became powerful. The gambling parlors we went to were mine. My technique was simple enough: to make gambling accessible to whites. I have several places in Chinatown that white people know are safe. The police are both paid off by me not to raid, and warned not to do so by the establishment because of the big shots they might unwittingly arrest.

"In all, it became very lucrative, yet caused little displeasure among established tongs because I did not take away their business, but expanded to a new one. Only a few fights were necessary."

"But the battle you nearly died in," she said, "wasn't that connected with your tong?"

"Yes, in a way. It is a shameful thing for me to speak of, because it involves my family. My marriage, as traditional in China, was arranged by my parents. My wife comes from a wealthy family. My family had little money, but we were all well-educated by our standards. So the marriage was seen as a good mix.

"I was twenty-one and my wife seventeen when we married. She is extremely pretty, so for a while I was pleased. However, I soon discovered her shallowness. I came to realize our marriage had no bond, we shared a house and bed, but ..." He stopped and shook his head. "These are things I should not speak of. In any case, I am ashamed to confess that, for a while, I sought the company of other women, but it was not a good situation. We had children, but even they did not help. Finally, I decided to come to America.

"I brought my wife back to her father's home. He had been providing her with money all this time to keep her in lovely clothes and surroundings. I fully intended never to see her again. Although I was sorry to leave the children, I knew they would be well provided for.

"I came to San Francisco with some close friends from my village.

Since I spoke passable English and not the 'pidgin' jargon heard so often, I was able to find out how things run in this city. I made connections, set up a small gambling parlor in the back of a friend's pottery shop, and got the word out that it was there for non-Chinese as well.

"After I had been here a short while my brother-in-law, whose name is T'ang, turned up. He wanted to join Yuen-li and get his share of the action. He has always been, for whatever reason, very jealous of me, my knowledge, my tong—even that I was given his half-sister to be my wife. I told him I wanted nothing to do with him. Two years ago, he returned to China, got my family and delivered them on my doorstep.

"I took them all in. We moved into the house on Waverly; eventually T'ang found other quarters. T'ang constantly caused trouble. Because he came from a wealthy family in China, some men listened to him and agreed with his ideas, thinking, I suppose, that his money could help and protect them.

"As he found more people to follow him he began his own tong, which he calls Wang Shao, roughly translating into 'Association of Harmonious Prosperity.' He tried to move into Yuen-li territory and has proclaimed that Wang Shao would take over Yuen-li. It was necessary to protect Yuen-li's interests from this assault, and the only route left was to confront T'ang.

"My wife, I know, would gladly take T'ang's side in the conflict and go with him, but she knew she could never get the children out of the house and she would not leave them behind.

"Our tongs have had several small skirmishes, but our one traditional battle—the one in which I was nearly killed—was not fought because of any of that. It was waged, in theory at least, over a sing-song girl, a relative of my best friend, Soo Chen-gai, who was stolen from her family and made to work in T'ang's brothel."

"That's horrible!" Ruth cried.

"It happens to many women from my country. Too many of them, I'm sorry to say. In any case, on the night of the battle, I was actually surprised that T'ang showed up. We each knew one of us was supposed to die, and our men were there to try to both save us and help kill the other. But the battle did not settle anything; our fight goes on.

"My recovery was marveled at by all of Chinatown. It made quite a laughing-stock out of T'ang. He has lost face, and we will always be deadly enemies."

At that point, Han-lin stopped speaking and looked at Ruth with a question in his eyes as to her reaction to his story of blood and greed.

"Maybe he will leave here," she said.

"No, that won't happen." He paused a moment. "Look at how light it is becoming outside. I have talked most of the night away. I must leave. I wish it weren't necessary." He stood and walked towards the French doors.

"As do I," she whispered, following him. "It seems wrong not to be with you. Should I come to your house?"

Han-lin hesitated, but then said, "If you have no objection, I know a place where we can meet in private. At my house many are watching us, how we act, and the tone of what is said, even if the words are not understood. I don't like that."

"I…don't…" She, too, hesitated.

"You need not worry about meeting me alone. You should know I respect you. I promise that I will never touch you, despite how I feel, unless you wish me to."

"I know," she said simply, and then, her voice firm, asked, "where is this place?"

"It is a little cottage on a very small street, more of a walkway than a street. It's called Macondray Lane. I bought the cottage shortly after my family was brought to this country, as a place to be alone. It's not in Chinatown, but near the top of Russian Hill. The cottage has a view of San Francisco Bay. I often sit by the hour watching boats come and go through the straits of the Golden Gate. No one, except Lao-she, Chang and Soo Chen-gai know of its existence."

"It sounds lovely, Han-lin. I would like to meet you there."

"Tomorrow night, at seven o'clock? Chang will wait for you at the corner east of your house."

"That would be fine."

"Until then," Han-lin said. As he looked at Ruth, his body seemed to lean towards her. She longed more than anything to have him kiss her again, to feel his strong arms, his lean, hard body next to hers. But instead he abruptly turned, quietly opened the doors and disappeared into the night.

CHAPTER 17

THE NEXT DAY, RUTH convinced herself not to go to meet Han-lin. Whatever had she been thinking? Was she mad?

She would send Chang away when he arrived for her. It was a belittling, demeaning situation, and she cursed the day she met Li Han-lin!

That evening at seven o'clock she stepped outside her house, walked one block and there spied Chang waiting beside the carriage. She started to speak to him, when her earlier resolve vanished. Almost against her will, she got into the coach.

She rode from Pacific Heights down through Polk Street gulch and then to the top of Russian Hill. The going was slow because the steepness of the hill made it difficult for the horses. Eventually, they reached Macondray Lane and stopped before a brown cottage.

Ruth hesitated, her hand paused on the door handle. She looked at the small house and thought of Han-lin waiting for her inside. She knew she should tell Chang to take her back home. She was crossing a boundary that was impossible to ignore. But she could not leave.

Raising her head high, she descended the carriage and went up the walk, across the veranda to the front door and knocked.

Han-lin opened the door and at the same moment Ruth heard Chang's carriage pull away. They were alone.

Saying, "Won't you come in?" Han-lin stepped aside and let Ruth get a full view of the interior of the cottage.

Her surprise at what she saw almost wiped away her anxiety at being there, and, a broad smile flashed across her face. "I don't believe this!" she exclaimed as she walked into the living room. It was furnished casually and comfortably in a purely American style. No exotic teak and hard chairs here. The wood was pine and the furniture upholstered. Even an old wooden rocking chair had a seat cushion in a patchwork quilt. She had to laugh at the contrast between this cozy house and the one on Waverly Place.

"I do think you're a Yankee at heart," she told him.

"Have a seat, please," Han-lin said as he went out to the kitchen.

Ruth soon heard the banging and clanging of dishes. She was tempted to go see what was happening, but remained where she sat, and ended up glad she hadn't spoiled her surprise at seeing Han-lin enter the living room carrying a tray with two large mugs of coffee and powdered jelly doughnuts.

"I want you to feel at home here," said Han-lin obviously pleased at pulling off his "Western" treat.

The treat broke her reservations about being with him. Han-lin lit a fire in the fireplace, and they turned the lights out and sat on the floor in front of the fire to talk. Only to talk. It was a wonderful evening.

Shortly after eleven Chang returned. Han-lin was going to his gambling parlors, but first he escorted Ruth home. She allowed herself only a brief kiss as she left him, and they made arrangements to meet again in two days.

Han-lin and Ruth's next meeting at the little house was very much like the first. He told her about his childhood in China. She was fascinated by his stories, and asked many questions about the villages and the people, what the houses were like, what people wore, and so on. Ruth discussed her own childhood, and they found that even growing up on opposite sides of the world they had much in common in feelings, emotions, and in their hopes for the future.

She felt spiritually closer to Han-lin than she imagined could be possible with another human being, and was almost absolutely happy in her relationship. Only one thing marred it, and she felt as if she were on a tightrope, struggling to balance, and knowing the precarious position she was in could not last. Being close to him, getting to know him, caused her desire for him to grow until it had become a physical ache, nearly impossible to deny. But deny it she must.

So she held her rendezvous, the sweetest time and the bitterest time for her, but a time she would never willingly give up.

The third meeting took place one week after the first. When Ruth arrived at the cottage she was surprised to find no fire in the fireplace, and nothing on the stove in the kitchen. "How would you like to go out with me this evening?" Han-lin asked.

"Of course," she said, looking at him quizzically. "But why?"

"I thought you might become bored here," he said.

Something told her there was more to it than that, and she couldn't help but suspect he was finding it as difficult as she did to face another romantic, fire-lit evening being proper.

"I would never be bored with you," she admitted. "But I'm happy to go."

Han-lin stepped into the bedroom to change. He put on a beautiful jacket. It was silk, a deep maroon color, almost black, and had delicate embroidery work on it in lighter shades of maroon silk thread. Ruth felt her breath catch in her throat as she saw how handsome he looked. The rich, warm color of the jacket cast red highlights against Han-lin's shiny, black hair.

He stood so tall and straight, it was all Ruth could do to stop herself from reaching out for him. But she did not.

Chang was waiting by the coach for the short ride down Russian Hill to Chinatown.

They went to a theater with a traveling troupe. The theater was filled with both Chinese and whites. The troupe sang many of the popular songs of the day, some so beautiful they brought tears to Ruth's eyes, which she tried to hide from Han-lin, although it seemed he might have watched her more than he did the performance.

After the theater, Han-lin took Ruth to a gambling parlor. It was different from the one they went to previously. This one was smaller, more intimate and less crowded. This time, also, Ruth understood the deference being paid to Han-lin as she took his arm and walked proudly beside him. A number of people bowed and smiled at her, knowing of her rescue of Han-lin, and made her feel welcome among them.

It was well after midnight before they left the parlor; the evening had been far too nice to bring to an end. Chang was waiting with the carriage, and with a sigh Ruth got in, knowing the ride to her home would be all too short. She sat in the coach and looked at Han-lin, studying his dark, exotic profile and feeling overwhelmed with pride and love at being with him.

He turned to Ruth, feeling her intense look, his face carefully controlled to show no emotion, but his eyes were like smoldering coals as they watched her in the darkness. In what seemed to be mere seconds, the carriage stopped. They were at Ruth's house, too soon, as usual.

"Tomorrow?" Han-lin asked, with a searching, penetrating look. Ruth's green eyes gave him the response he sought, but before she could say a word she heard Chang cry out. Han-lin's body became tense, like a cat ready to spring, as the door to the carriage suddenly was hurled open with a crash.

There, in the darkness, his face livid with rage, stood Winston Greer. The blood vessels in his temples bulged. Ruth never saw him so furious.

"So this is how you spend your nights!" he bellowed, "running around with God-damned Chinks! You've had it. You'll never be so sorry for anything in your life."

Ruth's immediate reaction was fear for Han-lin's safety.

She turned to him and said "Just leave, please!"

She stood to step down from the coach, but at the same time, Greer reached into the carriage and grabbed her wrist. With one furious yank he pulled her out the door. It felt to Ruth as though her arm were torn from her shoulder. She tumbled from the carriage. Greer slapped her face so hard she fell onto the gritty pavement.

The taste of blood rushed into her mouth and made her want to gag. She was on her hands and knees, stunned. No one had ever hit her before. She shut her eyes tight, expecting another blow when she heard Greer gasp, and then, nothing.

She opened her eyes. Han-lin stood in front of Greer with a six-inch knife lodged against his throat. Greer was the color of ash. Slowly, cautiously and with clear intention, he raised his hands, palms open, over his head.

Greer's men, who came running as soon as they saw Han-lin leap from the coach, had stopped dead in their tracks. Chang stood behind Han-lin, a revolver in his hand.

"Ruth, are you all right?" Han-lin asked, not taking his eyes off Greer. He knew that only by endangering Greer's life did he have a chance of getting past Greer's henchmen alive.

"Yes, I ... I will be" Ruth rose to her feet, slightly dizzy, and held the carriage for support.

"Get inside the carriage, Ruth," Han-lin almost whispered, his voice choked with emotion.

She stood still, not yet able to accept what had happened.

"Don't you listen to this bastard," Greer snarled. "Get in the house where you belong."

She looked at Greer. Where she belonged—yes, it was so. Her home, the business—the business she had been groomed for from the time she could talk. She loved that business, and the power it gave her. She could rule men's lives, and watch them live for better or worse according to her whim. From the outside, she watched others live, as she had done for years, always watching but not really living herself.

"Come with me, Ruth!" Han-lin called, his voice desperate.

"I'm sorry I hit you, Ruthie." Greer lowered his voice. "Don't throw everything away on this ... on him. Ruthie, use your head!"

Han-lin's voice seemed come from some great distance, "Ruth, if you go in there you know he will send you away somewhere with no money, no way to return. I love you. I can protect you."

"Don't you listen to his filthy talk!" Greer raged. "What do heathens know of love? Let him put this knife away and we'll see who can really protect you!"

"Come with me!"

"Go in the house! Now!"

"Stop!" she shrieked, alarming them both by the vehemence and hysteria of the tone.

"Please stop," she whispered. Her face was white except for the livid red blotch where her father's hand struck her. She looked on the verge of passing out. She turned towards her father, fighting back tears. "I've used my head too much! I'll use my heart this time. I've always loved you, father, but I've finally met your equal." She turned and stepped into the coach. Chang got into position as driver.

"No!" Greer cried, but he couldn't move as long as Han-lin's cold blade pressed against his flesh. He glared at Han-lin, "I'll kill you for this! You'll live just long enough to regret the day you thought you could cross Winston Greer! You're a dead man."

Han-lin smirked and dropped his voice low so that Ruth could not hear, "Yes, I know another killing would mean nothing to you, not after fifteen of the forty women on your boat died. What's a little murder to you after that mass slaughter?"

Greer didn't want Ruth to hear any of that, and in an equally hushed but deadly voice said only, "Shut your filthy mouth!"

"You know what your daughter will think of you if she learns what you're involved in. Call your men off, and let us pass."

Greer felt an overwhelming desire to lunge past the knife and break Han-lin with his bare hands; but as he stood, he realized the futility of going up against that blade. He was beside himself with rage. "You'll pay," he whispered between clenched teeth.

"Let us pass!" repeated Han-lin.

Greer looked at him with deadly fury, and waved his men back.

With lightning speed Han-lin leapt to the carriage. The instant he did so Chang drove off.

Han-lin watched the street until he saw that Greer did not sent anyone after them. He turned towards Ruth. She was sitting huddled and trembling in a corner of the coach with her hands clasped. Her hands and arms were bloody and scratched from the pavement and one side of her face bruised and swollen.

Han-lin put his arms around her, gently at first, but then clutched her tight as if to persuade himself that she had chosen him, and he would not give her up for anyone. He wanted to envelope her, to take her body and her being and make them his, so that no one could ever hurt her again.

They reached the cottage. Han-lin picked her up in his arms and carried her into the living room to lie down on the sofa. He went into the kitchen where he warmed some water for her to cleanse her cuts, and made some tea to soothe the inner body just as the outer needed care.

She carefully washed the dirt and grime of the street off her face and hands. The two did not speak as they sipped the strong tea Han-lin made. The trembling Ruth experienced subsided, and she gradually began to feel somewhat better. She sighed deeply as she rose from the sofa and walked to the windows facing the bay. The lights of a large ship leaving the city were playing on the water.

"I'm so sorry for all this trouble, Han-lin," she said at last. "He'll come after you. And me. He's a powerful man with even more powerful friends. I should have known better! I'm so sorry."

Han-lin rose from his seat and stood at her side. He, too, faced the bay, not daring to look at her as he said "You are no trouble for me. I want you here. I always have."

"You are good to me, good *for* me," she said. After a moment, she added, "You surprised me, saying what you did on the street by my house .... I never dreamed ..."

"That I love you?" Han-lin turned her so that she faced him. "How can that be a surprise when from the day I met you, you've been everything to me? I thought I would go crazy while you were away. I've felt as awkward as a schoolboy around you. I guess I usually acted like one, too."

She looked into his eyes as she whispered, "No, not at all."

He put his arms around her and slowly drew her towards him as her arms circled his waist. He placed a hand by her face and studied the bruises until he was sure that they needed no further doctoring. He then proceeded to softly place his lips over each in a gentle kiss. Ruth shut her eyes and raised her lips to his. He took the kisses she offered, tentatively at first, cautiously, being careful of her as he had so long in their relationship.

Slowly, the two grew into their kiss, realizing that the need for hesitancy was behind them.

The hunger and emotion she had felt for so long and had tried to contain was finally freed. His desire matched her own and carried her along to a fevered pitch.

They went to his bed, and he lay beside her, holding her against him even as he shedded unnecessary garments, kissing her, touching her, until she gasped in surprise and ecstasy that her senses could be made to feel so exquisite.

She clung to him, her fingers exploring his sleek body, wanting to know him just as he was learning about her, shyly at first, then more boldly as she became aware of the pleasure that her touch gave him. A pulsating heat spread through her; the essence of her being throbbing with desire for him.

"Love me," she whispered, "please love me." And with that invitation he caressed her until every particle of her cried out with desire. Every sensation tingled and was so rapturous she had no idea how it would end, how it could stop, until he showed her that as well, the grand climax to their passion, more sublime yet more furious than she had ever imagined it could be.

When it was over, she lay unable to move, holding Han-lin inside her and not wanting to ever let him go.

Slowly, he moved from above her to lie at her side on the bed. Putting his arms around her, he held her close through the night. As he slept, she rested her head on his shoulder in such a way that she could see his profile in the darkness, that profile she had come to love.

She lay awake watching him until the early hours of the morning.

CHAPTER 18

*L*AO-SHE CAME TO THE house the next morning. She didn't knock, but instead just shouted her arrival and rattled the doorknob a few times. Han-lin rushed to open it and Lao-she began an outpouring of words to him. It sounded as if she were scolding him, but Ruth had discovered already that Lao-she often sounded as if she were scolding someone. As she spoke, Lao-she walked into the kitchen and deposited two large sacks she had brought with her, one full of food and the other Chinese clothes for Ruth. After putting the sacks down Lao-she came back into the living room and marched to Ruth, who sat in an easy chair. She took Ruth's face in her hands and looked carefully at the bruises. She then stood back, patted Ruth's shoulder as if to pronounce everything all right, and with a few more words to Han-lin, went back to the kitchen.

"Lao-she was quite concerned about you," Han-lin said, finally able to get a word in. "Chang told her what happened at your father's home and that we were here. She berated me at great length for treating you, how should I say it, too much like a man and not enough like a doctor. I'm sorry—"

"It's all right, Han-lin. I'm fine." Ruth could see his worry about her embarrassment over the position she was in, "I love you; I don't care who knows it."

They had expressed many words of love to each other the previous night, but to see her state her feelings so openly, in the light of day, seemed to trouble him. He sat on the sofa, studying the soft carpet of woven Chinese silk. "If, at least, I did not have a wife..."

"It's not important," she said.

He held her eyes. "It is because ... because I would do all I could to convince you to become my wife."

"I know," she murmured, her heart breaking. "But even if you and I were free, we couldn't be legally married in this state." She drew in her breath. "California has anti-miscegenation laws."

He looked confused. "Anti-mis—what is it? Do you mean we could not marry because I am not American?"

"No." She was embarrassed. "It's because you aren't white."

He reared back slightly, then shook his head. "It's very strange to see some people's prejudices written into the law. Your country's Chinese Exclusion Act is wrong—but this law you mention is even worse. In China we could marry. In fact, many men who can afford them have more than one wife. Usually it's an old one, then a young one; a rich, ugly one, then a beautiful one. But, I will admit, many in China also have strong prejudices against non-Chinese. The most common word for foreigner translates into 'barbarian'."

She had studied enough about China to know its name meant "Middle Kingdom" and not only did the Chinese consider their country the center of the world, but were quite proud of their history and traditions. That boorish Americans would discriminate or look down on them in any way, was met with fury. "Poor Han-lin," she said with a gentle smile, "stuck with a barbarian. Whatever will your friends say?"

"We could go to China to marry. Would you marry me, Ruth?"

Ruth left her chair to sit beside him on the sofa, putting her arms around his shoulders. She knew that under the Chinese Exclusion Act he had mentioned, if he left the country, it would be difficult if not impossible for him to legally return. "Hush, dearest. Don't worry about it, I'm not. I love you, I'm here. That's all that matters." Her thoughts turned to Greer, what he might be doing or planning at that moment; she shuddered, holding Han-lin closer, wanting to protect him at any cost.

Lao-she must have been aware of the sadness pervading the living room, because she suddenly entered, chattering cheerfully as she opened the sack of clothes she brought to Ruth, and began to pull garments out, one by one.

Ruth was overwhelmed by Lao-she's thoughtfulness, as well as intrigued by the clothes, especially the trousers. Ruth had never worn slacks, not even as a little girl. Han-lin had to explain, with Lao-she's assistance, what some of the underthings were. In all, Ruth was amazed at how little clothing Chinese women wore in comparison to the reams of material, petticoats, camisoles, corsets, stockings, etc., that American women had to put on each day.

Ruth grabbed an outfit, gave Lao-she a hug, and rushed off to change.

CHAPTER 19

ALTHOUGH LAO-SHE COULDN'T understand Ruth's words, her expression and tone of voice told Lao-she every-thing she needed to know. She enjoyed Ruth's happiness tremen-dously, but more than anything, she was thrilled to see the warmth in her sorrowful boss's eyes. She had perceived the changed relationship between the two lovers immediately upon entering the cottage that morning, and since then she was having great fun teasing Han-lin about it.

She enjoyed seeing affection and she enjoyed life. Even though she was old and alone now except for the Li family, she had known love in her time and had even borne several children while in China. To her sorrow, they had all died in infancy or had to be given away because she didn't have enough food or money to keep them and raise them. Scarcely a day passed without her thinking about the chil-dren she had found homes for, wondering if they had survived and if they were happy.

It was probably because of the children lost to her that she had such affection for Han-lin. She knew that in her heart she thought of him as a son, and for that reason she felt good about his happiness with Ruth. She had seen him spending years growing more bitter over his marriage, and often was frightened by his increasing reck-lessness with his tong, almost as if he did not care if he lived or died.

She had worried as well about Han-lin's growing fondness for

Ruth. She alone knew how important Ruth had become to him, but she also knew that Ruth was rich and spoiled. She feared Han-lin was nothing more than an interesting diversion for the white woman, a diversion who would be cast aside if someone or something more interesting came along.

Thus, Lao-she could hardly believe it when she heard from Chang how Ruth had defied her own father to be with Han-lin. She hoped Ruth had learned what it meant to truly love someone. In any event, Lao-she knew she would do everything in her power to see to it that Ruth was happy in her new life.

"Look at me!" Ruth shouted as she threw open the bedroom door. She stepped into the living room wearing her new Chinese outfit—loose trousers and a tunic top with a Mandarin collar, in a plain, dark blue material. "I will never give these clothes up. Never!" She hugged herself and twirled around the room. "I feel so free! For the first time in my life no corsets, no stays, no laces, no tight waists, full skirts or binding sleeves! These are the most comfortable clothes in the world and I love them!"

Han-lin caught her and pulled her towards him. "Poor little rich girl." Then he murmured in Chinese how he would enjoy helping her out of them. She didn't understand, but Lao-she did, and decided this would be a good time to leave the two of them alone. She said good-bye until the next day.

She was accustomed to walking, and she traveled down Russian Hill towards Chinatown on foot.

oOo

As she entered the edges of the Chinese community she heard her name being called. An old lady friend, Lao-mah, was running towards her up the hill.

"Lao-she, it is very dangerous," the old woman cried, breathless. "Do not go home."

"Whatever do you mean, Lao-mah?" she asked.

"The police have come. They arrested Chang. Everyone is talking about it. It seems the American woman who saved Li is missing. The police say she was kidnapped and they are holding Chang responsible."

Lao-she could hardly believe what she was hearing. Somehow

they must save Chang. She could not return to the Li house on Waverly Place. The police might pick her up for questioning, or even as an accomplice. Worse, they might follow her back to Macondray Lane where Ruth and Han-lin could be found. She would have to warn Han-lin not to return to his house on Waverly, but first she had to find out Chang's condition. Just as she knew many white San Franciscans had fears for their safety when going into Chinatown, so too did she fear what could happen to a Chinese in the hands of white San Franciscans—especially the police.

Lao-she knew of a lawyer in the city, not too far from Chinatown, who was having a secret affair with a Chinese woman. The woman believed he would marry her except for the state's anti-miscegenation laws. Others felt the lawyer believed that if knowledge of the affair got out, that alone would destroy his career among white San Franciscans. As a result, the liaison remained a secret outside of the Chinese community.

The lawyer's house was easy to find and luckily both he and the woman, who translated for him, were home. The attorney, Devlin Wilcox, asked Lao-she to remain at his home while he went to see what Chang was being charged with.

Greer had decided to press charges against Chang as an accomplice to a kidnapping. Chang refused to say anything at all to anyone —including Wilcox.

Back at his home, Wilcox explained the charges to Lao-she, and also said that Ruth's father was a very rich, influential man who could have the city and surrounding counties turned upside-down looking for his daughter and the man she was with.

Fear filled Lao-she at those words. She thanked Wilcox and promised she would bring him his fee as soon as possible if he would help Chang. Wilcox agreed.

It was sunset by the time Lao-she got back to the little house on Macondray Lane. The lights were on, and it looked very friendly, warm and cheery—just as she expected its inhabitants to be. Her main fear was that Han-lin had returned to Waverly in her absence.

Han-lin opened the door in response to her knock, and relief rushed through her. He was surprised to see her again, and at her distraught and exhausted appearance.

Lao-she told Han-lin all that had happened. Ruth understood Chang's name in the conversation, but that was all. Han-lin became increasingly upset and paced the floor. To Ruth's inquiries he would only say, "I'll tell you later."

Han-lin sat quietly in deep thought while Lao-she hungrily ate some dinner. She was less than half-way through when he rose and told her he was going out for a while, and that she was to stay with Ruth. Lao-she grabbed his arm and pleaded with him not to go back to Waverly or near the jail, but he was adamant.

Lao-she covered her face with her hands, scared for Han-lin, and at what he might do.

oOo

Han-lin was about to walk out the door when Ruth grabbed his arm. "You can't walk out of here without telling me what's going on! What has happened?"

He was torn and his thoughts swirled. Soon after meeting Ruth, he could see she was a head-strong woman who would do what she thought best, and, once she decided something, she could be all but impossible to stop. He feared that if he told her what had happened to Chang she would march right into the police station and demand that Chang be released as she had not been kidnapped by anyone. But he also he feared such an action would not result in Chang's freedom.

"I cannot tell you yet," he said finally. "I must go out. I may not return for several hours. Lao-she will stay with you. Do not leave this house under any circumstances. Will you promise me that?"

She wasn't about to take no for an answer. "Where must you go? Tell me what's wrong! Is this about me? Or ... it's my father, isn't it? What has he done?"

"I will take care of your father."

Ruth's eyes widened in fear. "No, you won't! I demand to know what's going on!"

"Don't worry. He won't be harmed. But neither will he bother us any longer."

"He's not a man to be dealt with easily. I know him. Believe me. He may be my father, but—I'm sorry to say—I don't trust him to be honorable."

"Promise me you will stay here." He wavered, then added, "Or don't you trust me to do what's right?"

She studied him a long moment and he realized her next words would tell him everything he needed to know about how she felt about him. Trust and loyalty were the virtues he valued most, and he would accept nothing less from her.

He wondered if she could read his mind when she said, "All right. I trust you, and I will remain here. But when this is over, you will tell me what's going on!"

At that, Han-lin smiled, kissed her and quickly left the house.

CHAPTER 20

*H*AN-LIN KNEW THAT above all else Winston Greer wanted revenge. He owned the city, the mayor and the police. He would claim his daughter had been forced to say she was not kidnapped by threats, derangement or whatever. In any event, Chang's release depended on what Greer said, not Ruth.

If Ruth were to walk into that police station, or in any way make her whereabouts known, Han-lin knew he would never see her again. Greer would pick her up and have her spirited off to some far corner of the world. He could not imagine how Ruth could handle that sort of enforced imprisonment. And he could not imagine how he could face going back to a life without her. He would do anything in his power to keep her with him.

Han-lin went straight to his largest gambling parlor and called a tong meeting. He then sat, waited, and thought.

Slowly, the men started to arrive. Two hours later, twenty-three of the thirty active tong fighters were there. Just by their expressions Han-lin could tell that they had heard quite a bit about what was going on.

And he felt he had to tell them more.

"As you may have heard," he began, "the American woman that was teaching English to my children has left her home. She is the same woman you have seen me with on several occasions. Her father is, not unexpectedly, very angry about her departure, and has had my houseman, Chang, arrested as a kidnapper. He is also having me sought by the police.

"Now, I will not say where the woman is. I will only say that she is all right and staying where she is of her own free will. This is not a police matter. Nothing illegal has been done. You are all instructed to pass the word throughout Chinatown that no one is to speak to anyone about this situation. If asked questions, they know nothing. If word reaches me that anyone has said anything that could lead to the discovery of the woman, or to cause more harm to befall Chang or anyone else, I personally shall take revenge on that person—and if I am not able I expect this brotherhood to fulfill my revenge. I repeat that this is not a police matter. Nothing illegal has happened and only evil will come from those and to those who unwisely speak. Are there any questions?" he raised his eyes to steadfastly look at the group around him.

Most members of the tong simply shook their heads. Only Soo Chen-gai dared to speak, "Li, why do this? I know she is important to you, but only disaster can come from getting mixed up with the whites. You are head of the Yuen-li tong! Your men look up to you, and are willing to die for you. Only you can stop this, before it's too late. We all know she is Winston Greer's daughter, and that Greer works with T'ang running opium and prostitutes. But Greer also has the support of the white mayor and city council. Their reach is long. I fear for you, for all of us."

Han-lin looked at Chen-gai and was not surprised that he, of all the tong members, had spoken. Chen-gai loved Han-lin and was devoted to him, watching over him in an almost avuncular way. He had a stable, accepting personality while Han-lin tended to be more fiery and emotional. He recognized the dread that had spread over Chen-gai at the thought of his young friend's involvement with a white woman, and knew that Chen-gai feared greatly for his safety.

Han-lin looked at him steadily. "You have spoken, Soo Chen-gai. Perhaps others agree with you and so do not wish to help me. I will not stop what has started. I will not turn back. This is the path I have chosen and must follow to whatever end. Will anyone here help me? Can I count on you, or shall I try this alone?"

One by one, each man said he would help, Chen-gai included.

"I thank you," was all Han-lin could manage to say after the poll was completed and he realized his men's concern for him. He paused a moment before going on. "You are correct, Soo Chen-gai, that it would be wrong for me to endanger the lives of the men of the tong. We must think of another way to save Chang, to free him from the hands of the barbarians."

As Han-lin continued to speak, he paced across the room, and back. "The man who put him in jail, Winston Greer, can get the police to do whatever he wants, whenever he wants. I saw Greer only once. I have always heard that he is a fierce man. Our one meeting showed him to be so.

"I do not trust him. I do not trust that there will be any justice for Chang, nor any safety for anyone associated with this whole matter. Greer could easily have Chang or anyone else tried, convicted and hung on flimsy evidence without the least protest from any official."

Finally, he stopped pacing. "This is how I see it. I think the only way to save Chang is by our own means—perhaps extra-legal, but at least just. What do you think?"

When Han-lin finished speaking the tong members didn't know what to say. They were not prepared for this.

It was Wang Pon-chin who spoke first, "What do you mean by 'our own means'? This is the San Francisco police you are talking about. What can our steel and few guns do against their arsenal?"

"Of course, friends, I do not suggest we go up against city jail in a frontal attack. That would be suicide. But perhaps there is another way that can be explored? Does anyone know of any access to the jail?"

"Well," said Wong Lon-po, "my cousin runs a laundry service for the prison, a good 'Chinee-laundee.' What else, right? Anyway, he does have access of a sort, through a back door to a room full of dirty sheets and towels that the prisoners have used."

"Can you contact him tonight?" asked Han-lin.

"Sure."

"All right. Meet with him and explain about Chang being held and that he must be freed. Have him find out tomorrow which cell Chang is in, and get all the information you can from your cousin about the lay-out of the prison, the number of guards and so on. Report back to me."

"My cousin might fear for his job," said Lon-po.

"And I," said Han-lin sternly, "fear for Chang's life. Gentlemen, let us meet tomorrow night at Soo Chen-gai's home. My wife will be questioned, if she hasn't been already, and this place may not be safe for us."

The meeting broke up soon thereafter and Han-lin returned to his cottage.

He entered the house to see Ruth standing in the bedroom doorway wearing a make-shift nightgown. He stepped into the bedroom, quietly shutting the door so as not to disturb Lao-she, who slept in the small second bedroom.

"Still awake at this hour?" he whispered as he took Ruth in his arms.

"I couldn't sleep with you gone. I was so worried about you."

"Everything's all right now. Don't worry any more. I'll explain another time. Now is not the time for so much talking."

As their bodies intertwined, Han-lin last rational thought before being swept away in a blaze of passion, was that whatever the future might bring, to be here with Ruth, now, made it all worthwhile.

CHAPTER 21

AS LAO-SHE HEADED towards Wilcox's home early the next morning, Han-lin's money to pay him carefully tucked in her pocket, she decided to go by way of the Li house. The street was strangely quiet as Lao-she approached, and the plainclothes policemen were all too obvious as they tried to nonchalantly lurk about doorways within a block of the Li house.

Lao-she could not get very close to the house, and her heart was heavy as she walked away without being able to see the children. She could only hope that they were being well-cared for.

The attorney and his friend were again at home when Lao-she arrived. She gave Wilcox the money and asked for him to find out how Chang was doing.

Wilcox looked at the money, carefully counted out a very minimal amount to cover the prior day's expenses, and returned the rest to Lao-she. He explained that there was no way he could find out any more about Chang. If he went into the police station asking anything he himself would be stopped and questioned, made to tell why he was interested and who was paying him for the information. They might detain him until he talked, or they might simply follow him and any Chinese person who spoke to or visited him. Greer had the case clamped shut. It would do Chang no good for Wilcox to go to the jail, and might cause Chang and others even more harm.

Though Wilcox did not say it, Lao-she understood that he had made inquiries after seeing her the day before, and had learned that he needed to stay far away from this case. She could see that he was aware of how this case could harm his career. She could also see why he would not be more open in his relationship with the Chinese woman. Suddenly, she felt very sorry for the woman.

Lao-she hurried back to tell Han-lin what had transpired.

"It is as bad as I feared for Chang," he said.

That night, Han-lin went to Soo Chen-gai's house to meet once more with his tong. The group arrived at a plan which would go into effect the very next day.

That night all members of the tong who would take part in the next day's activities stayed at Soo Chen-gai's house. They decided to consult the *I Ching*, a book of ancient Chinese oracles, regarding the next day's events. Han-lin used yarrow sticks and tossed them in the manner dictated since antiquity. The sticks told him which of the numerous oracles in the *I Ching* he should read.

The selected oracle told them that everything was in motion, and by perseverance, there was the possibility of success. The tong was pleased by that, and went off to sleep.

As they slept, however, Han-lin reflected on the *I Ching*.

His relationship with Ruth was foremost in his mind and he decided to seek guidance on it. Alone, he asked the *I Ching* what his relationship meant. He tossed the yarrow sticks, and then turned in hope to the oracle:

The Judgment
  After completion, success in small matters.
  Perseverance furthers.
  At the beginning good fortune.
  At the end disorder.

The Image
  Water over fire: the image of the condition
  After completion.
  Thus the superior man takes thought of misfortune

And arms himself against it in advance.

Han-lin threw the book on the floor and laid down on the cot that had been set for him. He tried to sleep, but found he could not. The book was warning him: disorder and then misfortune. The image of fire danced in his mind; he must prepare, but how?

CHAPTER 22

THE SMALL LAUNDRYMAN walked up to the guard who watched over Chang's cell-block. The guard was sitting on a chair eating an apple as Shao diffidently approached.

"Oh mastah," he said in his thickest pidgin, "Look like linen door way down hall him still locked. Poor Shao no can do work. Please come unlock door for me." Shao bobbed and bowed during this little speech.

The guard looked disgusted. "Can't you do anything right? Here's the key. Open it yourself. I'm not your flunky!"

So saying he gave Shao the key ring and indicated which key opened the linen closet.

As Shao walked down the hall he silently and quickly looked through the keys until he found the one to Chang's cell. He held a small piece of wax in his hand while talking to the guard. The heat from his hand had sufficiently softened the wax so that he was able to make a perfect imprint of the cell key on it. He then pretended to unlocked the linen closet door, put the wax in his pocket, and returned the key ring to the guard.

Later that morning, he left the jail long enough to give the wax to a member of the tong who then rushed it over to a Chinese locksmith to have a key made.

By early afternoon the key was ready. Three carriages, each with four men hidden inside and a fifth sitting in the driver's seat looking like hired coachmen, pulled one by one into prescribed places near the jail.

The first trick was to get Shao's accomplices inside the jail. One was Pu-yin, chosen simply because of his great resemblance to Shao. The other was Han-lin, who insisted on taking part because he refused to endanger any more of his men then absolutely necessary.

The two men each carried a large bundle of soap, cleaning fluid and scrub brushes as they walked up to the guard at the back door of the jail. He hardly looked at them and they realized that to the guard they were scarcely human, not worthy of his attention. He nodded in the direction of Shao's laundry room, and let them pass without a word.

They walked into the room and saw Shao standing alone. "Everything is set," Han-lin said.

"In a little while it should be over," added Pu-yin.

"Good luck to you," said Shao.

The three men bowed to each other. "I'm sorry," said Han-lin, bowing again. He then made his hand into a fist, reared his arm back and struck Shao on the jaw with all he was worth. Shao stumbled backwards onto the floor. The two then struck him several more times to make more bruises on his face, tied him up and lifted him into his laundry cart. Han-lin jumped in also, while Pu-yin covered them with sheets.

Pu-yin then put on one of Shao's workmen's outfits and began pushing the cart towards Chang's cell-block.

Pu-yin breathed a sigh of relief at the guard's absence as he continued wheeling the cart down the long hallway. Just a little farther …

Pu-yin heard a noise, looked up and there, at the other end of the cell block the guard was opening the iron gate and entering. What was he doing there? He should have been far from this area making his rounds at this hour. Pu-yin slowed his pace greatly and lowered his head.

The guard also walked slowly from the other end of the hallway, checking prisoners as he neared Pu-yin.

He glanced up. "You back again! Can't you ever do your work right!" He glared at Pu-yin who was doing all he could to divert his face from the guard, but a little flicker that something was wrong crossed the guard's face. He realized what it was. That wasn't the launderer!

In a split second Pu-yin was upon him. He lunged forward and with what appeared to others to be almost effortless, he gave the guard one blow to the front of the neck and another to the back. The guard slumped to the floor as if dead.

Pu-yin quickly turned to the other prisoners who were watching the strange scene with a morbid, yet quiet, fascination.

"If you are all quiet, you will all have a chance to escape." So saying Pu-yin lifted the keys from the guard's pocket and dangled them in the air.

Han-lin jumped out of the cart and unlocked Chang's door with the key Shao had made. Chang could hardly believe the daring of his friends as he recognized them. They lifted Shao, who was now pretending to be unconscious, out of the cart and placed him in Chang's cell. They dragged the guard in with him and locked the door.

Chang and Han-lin climbed back into the cart as Pu-yin placed sheets over them. He gave the guard's keys to one of the prisoners.

"Since there is safety in numbers," he said to them, "I suggest you unlock all of your cell doors first, and then try to escape together as a large body. Be quiet. Good luck to you."

The prisoners silently waved their thanks to him.

Pu-yin quickly pushed the cart out of the cell block and through the halls to the laundry room. He knew he had little time before the prisoners' escape would raise a ruckus. Depending on their luck, the escape would either cause a diversion or cause the police to mobilize in such a way that they, too, would be trapped.

Once in the laundry room, Chang quickly removed his prison uniform and put on the extra clothes Han-lin had brought for him.

The three men picked up enormous bundles of dirty laundry to try to get past the one last guard again. They had just stepped out the door past him when they heard gunfire start.

Almost immediately, the sirens sounded to signify a jailbreak.

"Stop there," the guard shouted at them at which point they threw down the laundry and began to run. "Halt!" the guard fired a shot at them and began shouting for others to follow him.

Soo Chen-gai was holding the reins of the coach horses and as soon as he saw the three he started it in motion towards the jail house. They saw him and began running as fast as they could. As they reached the sides of the coach the horses too began to run. "Jump—hurry," Chen-gai shouted as the horses picked up speed. The men hurled themselves to the running board and those inside helped them hold on as the coach turned to head away from the jail.

The city police opened fire on the carriage, but it was far enough away that no harm was done by the bullets. As the carriages with the other tong members saw Chen-gai's coach pick up the men and escape the police, they too quickly left the scene, all going in different directions. The tong members were soon out of reach, free and clear.

Back in the jailhouse, the guard and Shao were coming to. The guard helped remove Shao's ties, and Shao gave his greatest performance as he explained to this guard and later, others, how he was brutally assaulted by members of his own race while he was just trying work. By the grace of his good acting, Shao kept his job.

The carriages brought the tong members back to Chen-gai's home. Han-lin leapt off the coach, and opened the door to let Chang out. Compassion, and then anger, flashed across his face the longer he looked at Chang.

"How could they have done such a thing!" he roared.

Chang slowly stepped down from the coach as the other tong members stood about him, hardly believing what they saw. "It is nothing, master, I am accustomed to it already."

"Those barbarians! I thought they hadn't done that for twenty years!" Han-lin slowly walked around Chang, his fury mounting.

"Bastards!" Soo Chen-gai added, "those police are worse than filth."

"Do not distress yourself, master," Chang could not help but run his hand through his newly cropped hair. "In this country, it doesn't matter. In China I wore my braid with pride, as did all Chinese, ever since the Manchu rulers decreed that true Chinese must wear their hair in queues as a sign of slavery, and we turned it into a sign of honor. Throughout all these years I wore it proudly. The police called it a pig's tail and hacked it off with one quick cut. At first I was furious, I would have like to kill them all, I saw it as my sign of being a Chinese. But then I realized that in this country, I need no such sign. You, master, do not wear the queue. It is not necessary for us. I don't care anymore."

"But I do!" Han-lin said. "What they have done brings dishonor to all Chinese. They will pay for it."

"The loss of their prisoner will be a payment enough, I think," laughed Chen-gai, "especially when they have to explain what happened to Winston Greer. "

A few others murmured the same thing.

"And the continuing inability to find one woman right under their noses may also help even up the score a bit," Lon-po declared.

"And I don't care," Chang said. "My hair will grow back if I wish, but right now, I may like this easy-to-take-care of hair cut!" He ran his hands through his hair, and laughed.

"I may cut off mine as well," Soo Chen-gai said. "I'm sick of it!"

At that, everyone, including Han-lin, began to settle down. When Pu-yin finished telling his story of what happened within the cell-block for the third time, Han-lin decided it was time to return to Macondray Lane.

"Chang, come with me," Han-lin said. "Waverly is home to us no more. Lao-she and the American woman are at Macondray Lane. You will join us there."

"No, master. I do not wish to be disobedient, but I cannot go with you," Chang announced. "Photographs were taken of me in the prison, and they will soon be distributed throughout the city and the surrounding areas. I think I must travel fast and far. I have a cousin in Los Angeles, where there are many Chinese. I believe I can live in safe anonymity there."

Han-lin thought about this. "You may be right, Chang," he said sadly. "To remain in San Francisco would mean spending years in hiding. That would be no life for you."

Pu-yin spoke, "I know a merchant who will be traveling to Bakersfield tomorrow. I am sure the man will be willing to give Chang a ride that far in the back of his wagon. I will speak to him."

"If he is not available," Chen-gai added, "there are others. It is best for Chang to go south. We will see that he does."

"It is settled," Han-lin said looking at his old servant and his friend. "We part here. Soo Chen-gai, be sure that Chang gets suffi-cient money to help him start his new life."

Chen-gai nodded his assent.

"Good-bye then, dear friends." Han-lin grasped the older man about the shoulders and hugged him. "I will always be indebted to you. If you are ever in need, get word to me and I will do everything I can for you."

"I am grateful this poor servant could help my tong leader." Chang bowed to Han-lin.

Han-lin realized all that Chang was giving up: his home and his friends of many years, because of Han-lin's folly. If only what had happened did not impose upon others, he thought. But it did. So many others. He saw a room full of them right now. Quickly, he rose, and said good-bye to his men. He felt his heart in his throat as he tried to say a last good-bye to Chang, and quietly hurried from the house.

With Chang gone the police lost their main hope for finding out anything about Ruth's whereabouts. They brought Han-lin's wife to the police station for questioning. However, it soon became apparent to the police that Mrs. Li, too, was a victim in a sense and that she had no idea where her husband was either.

When asked what her husband's business was, she said he was involved in imports and exports and worked out of their home. She stated that she had no idea who any of his clients were.

The police searched the Li house and found nothing, nor could they get any more information out of Mrs. Li. She knew enough not to mention to the police a single word about the Yuen-li tong. When she heard of Chang's escape, she knew Han-lin and the tong were still at work. She became fearful of her safety and would say nothing.

The police, too, felt sure a tong was involved because of the absolute wall of silence that confronted them wherever they went. Even their usual informers were being close-mouthed on this one.

Eventually they did learn that Li Han-lin was head of the Yuen-li tong. They knew that tong mainly by reputation as it hardly gave them trouble because it was only involved in gambling, a minor offense for Chinatown. Still, they knew that any man who tried to cross the Yuen-li in the past had ended up dead, so they had no more love for the Yuen-li than for any other of the highbinder tongs.

When the man who had named Li Han-lin as head of the Yuen-li also disappeared, the police were completely stymied.

During this time, Winston Greer spent money like it was water trying to turn up leads on where Ruth had gone, but he, too, ran into the same blank wall of silence. Even his so-called partner, T'ang, would not tell Greer anything.

T'ang had his own reasons, reasons he would never admit to Greer, for not helping the white barbarian.

T'ang believed if anyone were to kill Han-lin it should be him. Whites and Chinese did not kill each other; to start that would only wreak havoc on Chinatown and bring the police descending on it in droves. T'ang had far too many ideas for his own future success and wealth to permit such a thing to happen.

This way, too, Li was essentially out of his way. T'ang felt that the man was so besotted by his new love, he scarcely had time for any other interest and that gave T'ang the chance to make inroads.

Also, he got to see his sister as much as he wished now that Han-lin had moved out of their house. She was his dearest treasure, the only woman who ever truly understood him, his needs or his desires. She often visited him for several days at a time, leaving the children at home with servants. If only Li were dead, T'ang thought, life would be perfect.

CHAPTER 23

*A*S TIME PASSED, with the lack of success of the police and Greer to find out anything about Ruth's whereabouts, she and Han-lin grew bolder in leaving the cottage on Macondray Lane. Han-lin quickly realized that a woman who was influential in running a multi-million dollar shipping concern needed to do more with her life than housework, dinners, and visits to his establishments to keep her happy.

Ruth's thoughts had gone along the same lines, and the two made plans for starting their own shipping company. She knew how to run such an enterprise, and Han-lin had a surprising quantity of money. He also had connections with Chinese dock workers throughout Asia. The more they talked, the more they realized such a plan was not only doable, but it had potential to succeed beyond their wildest dreams. Han-lin was especially thankful of the possibility, over time, for the Yuen-li tong to move away from its illegal gambling parlors and into a legitimate business in the China market.

On the evening of April 17, 1906, their plans came together. They retired early that night, after deciding to begin serious negotiations to create such a business the very next day, and their love-making was joyful, fun and teasing.

Han-lin felt he had hardly gotten to sleep when something jarred him awake.

"What is it?" Ruth cried, reaching for Han-lin as a loud, rumbling sound, from the depths of the earth, thundered ever more loudly about them. The little house began to shake so violently they feared it would come down. Ruth felt paralyzed. She sat up and watched the ceiling visibly move up and down. She waited for it to crack and fall, crushing her to death.

"Earthquake!" Han-lin jumped out of bed, and immediately discovered he could barely keep his balance. "Get under the doorway!" He started to make his way, stumbling about, towards Lao-she's room when he realized that Ruth remained on the bed, too petrified to do as he said.

"Move!" he ordered, then reached for her hand and dragged her off the bed. She snapped to attention and ran after him, stumbling and knocked about by an earthquake that refused to stop shaking. Lao-she appeared, terror-struck, in the doorway.

"Why doesn't it stop?" Ruth cried to Han-lin. "It's so strong. I've never felt a quake like this one." She could barely be heard above the roar of the earth.

"Let's get outside, the whole house may come down," Han-lin said. The three ran out into the backyard.

Then, as suddenly as it began, everything became quiet. The movement of the earth stopped. The trio looked at each other in amazement. "I've been in many earthquakes before, ," Han-lin said, "but that was the worst one I've ever felt."

"I could not believe how it didn't want to stop! It seemed to go on for ten minutes!" Ruth exclaimed, her heart still pounding with fear.

"Hardly a minute is more like it," Han-lin murmured, "but at least we are all safe." They looked at the house: windows and glass shattered; dishes, cups and groceries had fallen from their shelves; yet the structure of the house remained sound. And most importantly, they had survived unscathed. They smiled with relief. "We were lucky," Ruth said.

The quiet when the earthquake stopped was but a lull in the storm, for soon, the sounds of a city waking up in astonishment, awe, and terror reached the house on Macondray Lane. The whole populace seemed to have risen as one to go outside their homes and wail in fear. Sirens whirred interminably, and the horrible sounds of structures shaken loose from their foundations and slowly rending, cracking and shattering to the ground were heard.

Until that, Ruth thought that the most frightening noise she had heard was the terrible scream the land made in the midst of the quake as it slipped and shifted. It had sounded as if the earth was going to tear itself apart and swallow up those infinitesimal creatures on its surface that so arrogantly saw their petty trials as of near-cosmic significance. The immensity and strength of nature made Ruth recognize her smallness and mortality, and it frightened her.

But the sounds she heard now were far worse. They were cries of human suffering—the roars and rages, whimpers and murmurings of man and his structures, his city, mortally wounded. She could hardly bear to hear it.

"What can be happening to the city? How much destruction must there be?" Ruth wondered aloud. Han-lin gazed at her in silence. As one mind, their thoughts turned to Chinatown—to those flimsy wooden structures, and to the mass of humanity tightly crowded within them. What must it be like in Chinatown? A cold terror clutched at Ruth's heart. Han-lin's children. Could their house have withstood this quake?

Ruth read those questions in the eyes of the man she loved. She knew it was foremost in his thoughts as he stood. "Go to them," she whispered. "Lao-she and I will be fine here."

He nodded, fear of what he might find etched on his face. "Stay in the garden," he said. "There will be aftershocks. You'll be safe here in the open. I'll walk a little way, to see what's happening in the street, and then bring some blankets out for all of us."

When Han-lin returned with the blankets, his expression was grim.

"What did you see?" Ruth asked, stopping him.

He shook his head. "It's still too dark to tell much. The sun is just starting to rise, a strangely beautiful sunrise." He took a deep breath. "But what I saw was bad. People are wandering about, looking hurt, stunned, by what has happened. Many homes have crumbled. It is frightening to see. I must go." He took her hands. "Pray that my children are safe. I'm worried about those old buildings. They are weak, not well built."

"If there are aftershocks, and you're in Chinatown ..." she said, not able to speak her fears.

"I must go. I have delayed too long already. They are my children."

Ruth knew he was right. She knew he could not sit here safely on Macondray Lane and not know what was happening to his family.

The thought of him going filled her with a new fear, a foreboding. Deep within her she felt something was terribly wrong, and that this earthquake that shattered a city may have shattered a way of life as well.

She could not tell this to Han-lin. "Hurry back to us," she murmured as she held him as long as she dared, tears coming to her eyes although she didn't know why.

Han-lin said a quick word to Lao-she, kissed Ruth and was gone.

The two women sat in the garden, waiting. The minutes seemed like hours and the hours like days as they sat. The sun rose slowly, and soon brilliantly lit up the whole sky. Two more aftershocks were felt shortly after the big quake, but eventually the earth stilled.

Ruth went indoors for day clothes and fruit for breakfast. The day wore on, but still Han-lin did not return. The sense of foreboding that had been with her since the quake first hit grew stronger with each passing moment.

She kept looking up at the sky, but she couldn't really discern where this uneasiness came from. Finally, she decided it was time to go back indoors to start to clean up the mess of broken glass. She walked up the steps to the back door and turned to look down at the garden. As she did so, she caught a view of the eastern sky. "Oh, my God!"

Billows of dark, sooty, gray smoke filled the sky in the direction of Chinatown, while over the bay the horizon was light and clear blue.

Fire.

Lao-she saw Ruth's reaction and joined her on the steps. Without saying a word the two women walked straight through the house to the street and began climbing up the hill. They were heading for the top of Russian Hill, where Broadway Street crosses Jones, a spot they called "boat place" because of the spectacular view it offered of the eastern skyline and the bay.

As they walked, the sky darkened. Ruth could smell the fire in the air, but she couldn't yet tell where it was, or how many structures might be burning. Walking south along Jones Street the buildings blocked her view of the east, but she was astonished to see streams of people walking up ahead, all heading westward.

She ran towards them. It wasn't until she turned the corner at Broadway that she saw what was happening. She stopped walking, appalled and horrified at the sight. She and Lao-she pushed their way through the crowd to the overlook to see if it was really as bad as it had at first seemed. They discovered it was worse. The entire eastern edge of the city burned, from Telegraph Hill to Market Street, an area that included Chinatown.

Ruth felt physically ill at the destruction before her, and clutched the rail of the overlook.

Lao-she stood beside her. "Dupont Gai," she murmured, her voice tearful as she stared in the direction of the fire. She placed her hand over her mouth and stood as if transfixed.

Ruth faced the people slowly walking up Broadway to the top of Russian Hill, wearily moving away from the fire, many carrying small parcels of clothes or food, as if they had grabbed what little they could before fleeing their homes.

She hurried to a family with two young children.

"Is it as bad as it looks from here?" Ruth inquired.

"It's worse, ma'am," the man replied, breathing heavily due to the steep hill. "Don't go down there. Fire all over, and moving fast. Really fast. Lots of people dead—buildings crushed 'em or the fire got 'em. We got to get away. This here's all we could save from our old house." He motioned at the bundles they carried.

"Where are you going? Where is everyone going?" Ruth asked.

"Don't know. All we can think is to get away from the fire. It's outta control. The water mains broke in the quake, so the fire department's worse than useless. Most folks are heading west, like us. Maybe we'll all end up in the Pacific 'fore this is over." He took several more deep breaths, as he looked at his children who were happy to pause for a moment. "Some folks were headin' towards Market Street where it's a little flat. I wouldn't chance it, though. I'm afraid of the tall buildings there. Lots already came down in the quake, I hear. And more will come down 'fore this is over. Also, the fire is headed that way. You two had best move along. This whole area is doomed."

The family then continued on their way. Ruth stood speechless, unbelieving. Yesterday, she was happy; she and Han-lin talked about a new start, a new business, and now this.

The number of people walking up Broadway Street increased rapidly, most with nothing more than the clothes on their backs. Only the sound, now and then, of someone unable to control their tears disturbed the grim-faced, stony procession.

"Let's go," Ruth said to Lao-she. "We'll go home. Han-lin will be there soon."

As she started to walk back, Lao-she grabbed her arm, "No," she cried, shaking her head.

Ruth tried to make her understand, "We must wait for Han-lin. Han-lin will come home soon. We must be there to meet him."

Lao-she looked at the fire. "No. No Han-lin."

"What do you mean? He'll come back for us!" Ruth turned and hurried towards home with Lao-she reluctantly following. She had to struggle to get past the people and not get swept up in what had rapidly become a human wave pouring westward towards the ocean. The stories of death and destruction they shared with each other were horrible. No one knew what to do or where to go, and all were frightened.

Evening came.

Ruth sat at the window of her home, watching for Han-lin. The night should have been dark, but the sky was lit up by the fire casting its ominous glow. The streets had quieted. Lao-she was frantic to leave, but Ruth would not go without Han-lin. She had taken their most prized possessions, some food and clothing, and made them into three bundles—one each for Han-lin, Lao-she, and her to carry as they fled for safety. But she would not leave without him.

She settled down to wait.

The streets had grown ominously silent after the day-long constant drone of people hurrying by. The fire crept closer, and the area was no longer safe.

oOo

Lao-she stepped outside. The smell of the smoke was stronger now, fearfully stronger.

She didn't know what to do.

A clip-clop noise sounded in the distance. A horse—someone on horseback. Han-lin? Could it be? She ran down the street in the direction of the noise. She saw the horse, the man. Disappointment slowed her step for only a moment. It was not Han-lin, but it was help—a policeman. She shouted at him, surprised at her own boldness.

The policeman was every bit as surprised as Lao-she to see the elderly Chinese woman calling him. She gestured wildly for him to follow her, and he did so, right into the living room where Ruth sat waiting.

"Ma'am, you must leave here. It isn't safe," he said.

"I'm sure it's safe. The fire won't reach all the way up here. I'm waiting for my ... my husband to return."

"The fire's half way up Russian Hill. It's gobbling up a whole city block every thirty minutes or so, and once it reaches to top of the hill it'll start down so fast you won't believe it. There'll be no escaping then."

Despair filled her. "But my husband," she cried, "he's still in Chinatown."

"I'm sorry, ma'am, no one's in Chinatown. It's gone, completely burned down. Everyone's gotten out—if they could. Refugee camps are being set up to the west. You're husband's probably up in the Pacific Heights area or somewhere like that looking for you among the refugees right now."

"No! It can't be!" The words she had been so afraid to hear, yet fully expected, had finally been spoken. Tears threatened. "China-town can't be gone," she whispered, unwilling to believe it, yet knowing it was true. "It can't be!"

"Completely, and good riddance if you ask me," the policeman said with a snort.

Lao-she had picked up two of the bundles, and stood at the door, waiting for Ruth's decision.

Her heart empty, Ruth knew she must not let the old woman die. Perhaps the policeman was correct, and Han-lin and the others had fled westward. She picked up the last bundle. "In that case, we will leave." Ruth crossed the room, and when she reached the door she stopped and turned for one last look. Her eye caught the tiny, intri-cately painted dragon she had bought one day in Chinatown, and she went back into the room, picked it up, and put it in her pocket. She never explained to Han-lin why she collected fine representations of dragons; it was her secret. She gazed a long moment at the big over-stuffed chair that Han-lin loved so much. Then, before leaving, she gently placed her hand on the wall and gave it a loving pat. Quietly, she pulled the front door shut, and shuddered at the final click of the latch.

Some of the flames were already visible over the crest of Russian

Hill, giving the skyline an eerie glow. Ruth and the policeman fairly ran along the streets, with the horse trotting along carrying Lao-she and the bundles, the glow of the firelight silhouetting the strange procession.

When they reached the bottom of Russian Hill, the policeman stopped. "I must go back to see if anyone else is still in their home. Keep going west and you'll be safe. Ask anyone where the tents with food and such are. They'll help you. Good luck."

Lao-she dismounted and the policeman climbed back on his horse and headed back up the hill looking for more folks that he considered fools too sentimental to leave their homes for a mere reason like an entire city in flames around them.

Before long, a stranger directed Ruth and Lao-she to a camp set up by the Red Cross for people made homeless, like themselves. Hot food and blankets were available.

Ruth walked about the campsite. Yesterday, it had been a pretty neighborhood park; today, it was filled with hundreds of scared, lost people. White, yellow, or black, it didn't matter, they mixed together, helping each other face their mutual fears of more quakes and fire, comforting each other in their sorrow over family members who were missing or known to be dead. No one cared about the old prejudices that had separated them in the city, prejudices that had forced Ruth to choose between Han-lin and her family.

She realized the section of the city where her parents' home was located had been spared so far, although the fire was headed that way. If it couldn't be stopped, the entire city was in danger.

She couldn't think of that now. Tomorrow, Han-lin would find them. He would know what to do about getting food and shelter. Perhaps the fire would be out by then. By some miracle, perhaps the house on Macondray Lane would be spared.

All she had left that night was hope.

oOo

The next morning, devastating news of the fire and the destruction it caused spread through the camp. Men and equipment from all over the bay area joined in fighting it, but the fire raged on, consuming block after city block in the blink of an eye.

Each hour, the refugees heard new death tolls. Hundreds of lives were known lost, and thousands of people unaccounted for. When news reached the camp that the chief of the fire department had become, himself, a victim, even grown men cried. Despair hung heavy in the air.

Ruth spent most of the day wandering about the crowds hoping to spot Han-lin or one of his tong members. But she did not succeed. Another day passed; the fire continued.

The next day, news hit that the fire had burned down the west sides of both Russian Hill and Nob Hill and was heading towards the camp. Ruth, Lao-she, and the others picked up their belongings and moved further west to the Pacific Ocean.

The authorities decided there was only one thing left to do to stop the fire's relentless push towards the ocean. They needed to contain it by destroying and leveling a portion of the city that the fire had not yet reached. Van Ness Avenue was chosen as the fire line—the street that would be demolished, not by the fire or the earthquake, but by the city itself.

The Army dynamited Van Ness, and then cleared away as much of the burnable material as possible in hopes of stopping the fire from jumping the line. Everything to the east of Van Ness Avenue and north of Market Street—the heart of San Francisco—was lost to the inferno.

All day long the city was wracked with blasts of dynamite as Van Ness Avenue was brought to its knees. The plan had to work, everything depended on it.

Again, the Army came to break up the camp where Ruth and Lao-she were, and to move it to a safer area. By the fifth day after the earthquake, news reached the camp that the fire was finally under control. The dynamiting had worked. Soon, the fire would simply burn itself out, and the monumental task of cleaning up and rebuilding would begin.

Ruth spent the week in the camp. It was high on a hill where she could get a good view of the city. There were so many homeless people drifting about, that Ruth had little hope of Han-lin finding her, if he were still alive.

The city set up a make-shift morgue, and Ruth spent hours looking among the decaying bodies for Han-lin's. Not too many Chinese were there, however, which lead her to suspect that if he had died his body had probably been left in Chinatown to burn, and she would never know for sure what had happened to him.

About a week after the fire ended, the population of San Francisco awoke to the fact that the Chinese, who had always been more or less contained in Chinatown, were roaming freely about the city and living with everyone else in refugee camps. White San Franciscans had grown up with stories of treacherous hatchet men, tong wars, and innocent folks being shanghaied off the streets and never heard from again. An outcry began and soon grew so loud it couldn't be ignored.

The city's mayor called on the U.S. Army for help in rounding up the Chinese and placing them in a segregated temporary camp in the northern part of the city, so that they could be transported by boat to some permanent spot far from the city.

Ruth saw a group of soldiers enter her camp and immediately take hold of Lao-she.

"What is this?" Ruth demanded.

"All Chinese are being rounded up," the sergeant replied.

"That's the stupidest thing I've ever heard!" Ruth said to him. "This lady wouldn't hurt anyone. Leave her alone!"

"Sorry. All Chinese must go," he said.

"But she lives with me. I want her here!"

"You can come along too, then," he snarled. "You sleep with 'em, you can live like 'em."

Ruth was completely taken aback by the crudity of this reply, and felt her face flush hot with anger. "You despicable creature." The words spat from her mouth. She picked up her belongings and marched to the area where Lao-she and others stood awaiting their orders. If this round-up was going on throughout the city, Han-lin or some of his friends might be there, Ruth reasoned.

In a short while another soldier came by to help move the Chinese. He immediately noticed Ruth in the group.

"I don't think you want to go with these folks, ma'am," he said.

"I understand all Chinese in the city are being sent there," Ruth said.

"That's correct."

"Then I'm going."

The lieutenant looked at Ruth's determination and realized he didn't want to try to argue with her, and just walked away.

The little group was set up in a camp, but had scarcely settled in when they were told to pack up everything because they needed to be moved again. Ruth went to find out why, and learned that a delegation of property owners had descended on Army headquarters to protest the dangerous Chinese being placed near their homes.

They no sooner arrived at a second location when the same thing happened. And then a third, with similar results. Finally, in desperation, the Army put them on a cold, barren piece of U.S. government land near Fort Point overlooking the Golden Gate.

Ruth knew Han-lin would never join such a motley group, which, by the time of the final move had dwindled to about sixty Chinese and her. The others resolved that, destitute or not, they were better off fending for themselves outside San Francisco than being shunted about at the Army's whim. She had to decide her next move; but before she could think about the future, there was one thing she had to do.

CHAPTER 24

THE FOLLOWING MORNING, Ruth left the camp early and walked eastward from Fort Point to the Marina district. Most of the houses were still standing in the area, and the work of cleaning up from the earthquake had already begun. She reached a point where she could see Van Ness Avenue, or what had once been Van Ness Avenue, in the distance. The destruction was unbelievable. What had once been city streets filled with houses and people looked like a scene after a forest fire. Nothing remained but charred, blackened ruins where tall buildings and proud homes had magnificently stood. She was sickened by the devastation before her. Only by gathering all her will power could she continue into the ruins.

Ruth knew what to expect before she reached her home site.

The top of Russian Hill had not been spared. Macondray Lane had been unique because it had so much greenery for a San Francisco street, with trees and bushes and wild flowering shrubbery. Compared to the very concrete look of most of the city, it was like living in a park. Now, the beautiful trees were blackened and the shrubbery was no more.

She reached the location of the little house that had known such happiness. The walls and roof were gone, their remains so much rubble atop the foundation. All that still stood was the fireplace.

For the first time in days since the earthquake, she sat down and cried, not only for herself and those she loved, but for her city. The place she had grown up, the city she loved, was gone, and she had no idea if it could ever be rebuilt.

She sat on the hearth for a long while, the acrid smell of the fire stinging her nostrils and giving her an excuse for the tears that seemed unable to stop.

Finally, she rose. Without looking back, she walked down the hill to what was once Chinatown.

The shops, the written characters, the Cantonese opera, the restaurants, the foods, the smells—all those things that gave Chinatown its special and unique character, were no more. When Ruth arrived she saw that ground crews had already begun a massive clean-up. The little wooden hovels that housed so many people were gone and had taken a shocking number of lives with them.

Ruth's steps turned automatically towards Waverly Place.

The whole street had been leveled. It was as if Han-lin's house had never existed except in her mind. A number of people were there digging among the ruins, obviously trying to find valuables—whether their own or someone else's was anyone's guess.

Ruth was sick at heart. Nothing in her life had prepared her for this sort of devastation and human suffering. She wished it were a nightmare; that she would wake to find Han-lin with her, and all as it had been. But she could not awaken from this dream, she must live it.

How must Han-lin have felt when he reached Waverly Place? Let him be safe, she prayed.

As she looked at what had been the Li house, a small group of Chinese took notice of her. She saw that they were talking about her, but she did not recognize any of them as Han-lin's friends. She simply greeted to them in Chinese, having learned a number of basic words in her need to communicate with Lao-she over the days they had been together in the camp, and turned away.

One of the men stepped forward, "You Li Han-lin's friend?"

Ruth's heart seemed to stop. "Yes," she said, hardly able to speak.

"Very bad here," he continued.

"I see," said Ruth, straining to understand the words he spoke, and fearing she would not be able to comprehend his half-English, half-Chinese speech.

"We think—I very sorry—they all dead."

She looked at the small, scraggly man. He was toothless, and full of soot from digging in the ashes. He bowed and smiled as he spoke—smiled, not because of pleasure at what he was saying, but because it was simply a Chinese way, an expression, and a way to mask the expression of pain. How incongruous she thought, that at such a time she should think about his smile—perhaps because she could not bear to think about his words.

"The family," he continued, as others in his group moved closer to Ruth, alarmed at her frozen silence, "children, wife, inside. House come down."

She felt as if the earthquake struck again. The children…Han-lin's children. She thought she had no more tears, but they filled her eyes.

Only slowly did she realize he did not mention Han-lin.

She looked at him, her breathing so harsh and heavy she could scarcely speak. "Li Han-lin…is he, is he also dead?" she whispered.

"Li? No. You go find Li's friend, Wong Lon-po. He tell you."

"He's not dead?" She could scarcely believe him.

"You go find Wong Lon-po."

"Wong Lon-po? I don't know him. Where is he?"

"Dupont Gai. You ask. Many people know Wong Lon-po."

"Thank you," Ruth bowed. "Thank you so much!" The man bowed in return and broke into a huge, toothless grin.

Ruth turned and walked towards Dupont Gai. She could not think about what she had heard—Pao-yang, the two little ones, even the beautiful Mrs. Li. Maybe they were wrong, and all of them had managed to escape. She could not think about their deaths, it was too much, simply too much.

She concentrated on Han-lin, holding the man's words that he was alive like a talisman. She needed to know where he was, and what had happened to him.

She rushed up to the first group of Chinese men she saw standing there. "Wong Lon-po? Do you know him, where is he?" she cried.

They looked at her as if she were a mad woman and backed away, saying nothing.

She turned and ran from them. "Wong Lon-po?" she said to the next group. "I must find Wong Lon-po."

They just shook their heads. Ruth was beside herself.

"He was down there earlier," said a man who had been sitting on the street selling rice and had overheard her question.

"Oh, thank you! Thank you!" she cried, and hurried in the direction he pointed.

She rushed along the street asking even more people. Often, she was just met with blank stares, but many people did know Wong Lon-po and tried to guide her. For three hours she searched, growing ever more frantic and weary with each passing minute.

"Friend of Li Han-lin?" she heard someone ask and turned towards the man who spoke. He looked about Han-lin's age and build, but she did not recognize him. "I hear you are looking for me," he said.

"Oh!" Ruth cried, and almost felt faint in her relief that her search had ended. She caught her breath, her voice a mere whisper as she said, "I was told you might have some knowledge of Li Han-lin. I have not seen him since the morning of the earthquake."

"Come, sit down over here," he said, motioning towards some rubble that had been stacked up to resemble a bench. "You look very tired."

Ruth followed him to the place to sit. "I am tired, yes," she said. "But more than that I am worried! Where is he? Please, what do you know?"

"I don't know how to explain this," Lon-po began. "I can tell you what I heard and saw and perhaps you will understand."

She nodded.

"In Chinatown, during the earthquake many houses collapsed—among them Li Han-lin's house. Ah—you know that? Well, that makes it somewhat easier.

"I went with Li Han-lin to help him, but Li arrived at the place his house had been, he found his brother-in-law, T'ang Tsu-shao already there. T'ang was holding his dead sister's body and weeping very terribly. He had dragged her from the ruins.

"Li looked from his wife's body to T'ang, and asked, 'Where are my children?' T'ang pointed at the rubble and said, 'They are there, your children! Your responsibility! Look at how you failed them! You are their murderer, Li, not this earthquake. You could have saved them! Where were you?'

"Li began to push aside the fallen lumber and bricks with his bare hands, trying to find them. He found his wife's servant, but that was all." Wong Lon-Po stopped talking, rubbing a hand over his face as if overwhelmed by the memory. Finally, sad black eyes met Ruth's.

"There was so much destruction," he said grimly. "Li stayed there for hours and hours, pushing the wood and stone, furiously trying to find the children. No one could stop him, he would not listen to me, to anyone. The fire, which had started who knows where, was growing larger. We heard there was no water to fight it and knew we had to evacuate.

"I and others tried to tell this to Li, but he would not hear us. We were afraid, I will admit, to touch him or try to drag him away. He is the leader of the Yuen-li, our lord and protector.

"But also, we wanted nothing more than to help Li and protect him—for his is a dangerous position. The tongs are scattered, his enemies are all over. In a way, to help another helped us to bear our own losses.

"Li's grief was terrible. The fire was close. We could feel its heat, as together we joined Li in his awful search. For Li Han-lin, it was as if a mortal blow struck him. He had no thought of saving himself, and it seemed he would willingly have died there that day.

"Fortunately, Soo Chen-gai arrived. He is like a father to Li. He clutched Li by the shoulder, and finally, our leader stopped. The men clasped each other, their eyes wet with sorrow, and Chen-gai led him away from those awful ruins.

"We traveled southward most of the afternoon, until we found a camp where some volunteers set up hot coffee and blankets. There were many people there who were hurt, some who died before our eyes. There were many who lost loved ones in the catastrophe. I will never forget what I saw that day.

"We could not get Li to eat or drink or talk. He simply sat.

"Chen-gai had relatives in Oakland and the next day word came to us that little damage had been done to the Chinese quarters there. Li was like one dead, with no care as to where he was taken, and so, for safety reasons, we took him to Oakland.

"We found Chen-gai's cousins. They gave their bed to Li, and finally we were able to give him some proper care. But he believed the cruel words T'ang had spoken, and took the guilt upon himself for his wife and children's deaths. There was nothing we could say to console him."

Ruth had listened to the whole tale in silence, unable to speak for the pain his words caused as she learned of Han-lin's tragedy, and when Lon-po finished speaking, she simply nodded her head in understanding, her face devoid of expression, an immovable mask in the Chinese way. Over the short while she had known Han-lin, she had come to understand very well the sense of duty and familial honor that kept him bound to his first wife and children. She looked up at Wong Lon-po, determined to be strong in his eyes, and asked, "Is he still in Oakland with Soo Chen-gai?"

Lon-po shook his head, "One week after the earthquake, when I awoke in the morning I went to see how Li was doing. His bed was empty. I went about the house, inquiring after him, but no one had seen him leave.

"I believe the only person who may know where he has gone, is Soo Chen-gai. That afternoon, I returned to San Francisco to try to rebuild what I had here."

"I see. Tell me, did Li Han-lin ... did he say anything about me?" she asked.

"No, I'm sorry," Lon-po replied quietly, his eyes filled with understanding over the torment the woman before him must be facing.

Ruth stood slowly, feeling both numb and cold at the same time. "Thank you for the information," she said softly. "You have been very kind."

Lon-po rose and bowed low to Ruth, showing deep respect for her. He had liked the woman. Although he had seen her in the past, this was the first time he had spoken with her. Yes, he thought, he could see why Han-lin had been so captivated. He watched her walk down Dupont Gai for a time, and then turned and began again his task of cleaning debris from the foundation of his shop. He could start to rebuilt any day now.

It was night before Ruth arrived back at the camp, having walked there as one in a daze, scarcely aware of how she had gotten there.

She didn't know how she could face Lao-she and give her the terrible news. She knew that Lao-she loved those children, and had left them only because of her even greater devotion to Han-lin. Ruth found an old gentleman who had been kind to them who could break the news to Lao-she in a gentler way than Ruth could manage with her limited knowledge of the language.

It was heartbreaking for Ruth to watch as the man explained to Lao-she all that Ruth had learned that day, to watch Lao-she's old, careworn face go from surprise, to disbelief, to desolation. As the man finished, he stood and took Ruth's arm, to lead her from the tent.

Ruth stopped, wanting to stay with Lao-she, but the man shook his head. As Ruth followed she glanced back, and realized that Lao-she was doing all she could to control her grief until she was alone. Only then would she allow herself to crumble with heartache.

Alone, Ruth walked to the bay and sat by its edge for many hours that night, staring at the black waters and listening to the waves pounding on the shore as she tried to reconcile and accept what had happened. She tried to keep her mind blank as her a defense against the tragedies that had befallen so many, but she could not help but think of Han-lin. If she felt this way, how much more horrible this must be for him, especially with T'ang's accusations ringing in his ears? How was he coping? What was he doing now? Had he learned, yet, to accept?

When the chill in the air became too cold to endure, Ruth returned to the tent. No words passed with Lao-she as the two women saw the grief-ravaged expression of the other and silently prepared for bed.

The next morning, two more families left the camp. Ruth knew that if they did not leave soon, they would become wards of the city. She had to take care of Lao-she, and she had to find Han-lin. With no money, extra clothes, or food, she could only think of one place to go.

The two women packed their few belongings as they had done so many times the past weeks and set off for Pacific Heights, which had been spared from the fire by the dynamiting, and miraculously, had withstood being badly damaged by the earthquake.

Ruth walked up to the door of the mansion as Lao-she huddled close behind her. Facing Winston Greer would not be easy, and Ruth breathed so heavily with anxiety she felt faint. She gave her hair a final pat, smoothed the tired, dirty dress as best she could, and then knocked on the door.

A woman Ruth did not know opened it. Ruth was taken aback as she had expected their old butler, but then she realized that more people than herself and her Chinese friends must have been badly displaced by the fire. Somewhat apprehensive, she spoke, "Is Mr. or Mrs. Greer at home?"

The woman looked at her quite haughtily, obviously disgusted by Ruth's appearance and apparent poverty.

"The business entrance is in the back. The servants will attend to you there."

"I wish to see Mr. or Mrs. Greer," Ruth repeated.

The woman scowled at her. "I will see if Mrs. Greer is available. Whom shall I say is calling?"

"Tell her it's her daughter."

The woman's jaw fell open. "Oh, oh my," she said. "One moment, please." She rushed off, leaving Ruth in the doorway.

In less than a minute Blanche rushed to the door. She stopped when she saw Ruth, her eyes filled with tears, and she held her arms out. Ruth rushed to her.

"Don't cry, mother," Ruth said, holding her.

"I thought you were dead! We both thought you were dead! My God, my prayers have been answered. My baby has come home," she laughed and cried at the same time. She brushed the hair back off Ruth's face. "How you've changed. Just look at you."

Ruth knew what her mother saw, a once elegant young lady, now a woman in ragged clothing, half-starved, her hair pulled into a single braid down her back, and with skin on her hands and face coarse and darkened from the sun and work.

"We were in refugee camps since the earthquake," she explained. "Our home was burned. I had nowhere else to turn."

"Don't speak of that now. You're home again and we'll take care of you."

"Mother, I'd like you to meet Lao-she. She is my friend." To Lao-she she explained that Blanche was her mother.

Mrs. Greer brought them inside and ordered her servant, Smitty, to prepare them a hot meal, then asked Ruth to sit with her to talk over all that had happened since Ruth was last home. Ruth agreed, but first she found Lao-she a bed where she could rest, and made sure her mother and the servants treated the old woman well and with respect.

When lunch was ready, Ruth had Lao-she sit with her to make sure she ate. Lao-she had little appetite, little life in her, since learning about the Li children and Han-lin's despair.

After lunch, Blanche suggested a nice bath and change of clothes for each of them.

After the weeks of camp living, Ruth found the bath to be an indescribable pleasure, and luxuriated in it for a long while.

After the bath, she went to her room to lie down, hardly realizing yet how completely exhausted she was from the constant worry and tension of the preceding days.

Smitty had been instructed to awaken Ruth about two hours before her father's expected return, as she wanted time to dress before seeing him.

Ruth slept soundly for four hours when her mother came to waken her. "Your father is home, dear," she said, "I couldn't bring myself to awaken you, you looked so tired."

Ruth opened her eyes and for a moment couldn't remember anything. Then, suddenly, everything came back to her like a crushing, horrible weight.

She quickly got out of bed. All her plans to dress beautifully and style her hair, to show her father she was just fine, had flown by the wayside.

"It'll be fine, dear," Blanche encouraged her.

She put on one of her favorite dresses from her closet, and was horrified at the way it hung on her thin body. She pulled her hair back and held it in place with a ribbon.

Head high, she quietly descended the stairs and crossed the hall to the library. The door was open, and she stepped inside. Greer stood, looking out the window.

"Hello, Daddy," she said.

He spun around. Had he aged so much in just a few weeks, or had she never noticed the lines of age on his face before?

He seemed at a loss for words, and stared at her for the longest time. "Ruthie, you've come home."

"Yes," she wanted to explain further, but the words would not come. She saw tears in his eyes, and walked towards him.

"Come to your old Dad." Greer held out his arms and enveloped her in them. She couldn't help but remember the good times of the past, and how safe and secure she had always felt as a child when her big bear of a father held her close. "We thought ..." He was unable to speak for a long while, then he stepped back and held her at arm's length to looked at her. She had never before him cry before, but his cheeks were wet as he looked at her. "You will always be Daddy's little girl. No matter what happened in the past, all that is over and forgotten. It's good to have you in this house again."

"It's not quite as you think, Daddy," Ruth said, not wanting to hurt him, but knowing she didn't dare let him misunderstand her actions.

She walked to a chair and sat. He took a seat nearby. "There have been problems—many deaths, much destruction. We had no place to go."

"We?" Greer scowled.

"I brought my housekeeper who has become my friend, a fine, older Chinese woman."

"And the man?"

"I don't know where he is."

"He's run out on you?"

"No. You see, some people who were very close to him died in the earthquake. He has gone away to learn to accept their deaths."

"Sounds fishy to me." Greer raised an eyebrow as he looked at her.

Finally, Ruth could hold back no longer and tears began to stream down her face as in a voice broken with sorrow she said, "They were his children, father. His children."

Greer looked taken aback. "Oh, I see. Is he coming back?"

"I don't know. Excuse me, I'm ..." At that she rose to leave the room, hot tears stinging her eyes.

"Ruth! Don't leave. Please!"

She turned to look at him.

"I don't often say these words you know, but ... I'm sorry, Ruth. I'm even sorry about your friend's children, and how it has affected you. Stay here with us, please. This is your home. It's always been, and always will be."

"Oh, father." She couldn't seem to stop her tears. It seemed she was doing nothing but crying these days, and Ruth Greer was a woman who never cried. "I need time to think. I don't know. I'll stay for a while, at least."

Greer breathed a deep sigh of thanks.

CHAPTER 25

AO-YANG, YOU MUST study! You will grow up to be an ignorant beggar if you don't. Your father will be so ashamed he will disown you." Mai-ching looked at the boy with some dismay.

"I don't like these lessons. They're no fun!" he answered.

"Just because your school building burnt down, it doesn't mean you can spend all your time playing. Now study!" Mai's rage did its trick and Pao-yang put down the toy soldiers and went to the table, sat down and opened a book with a huge sigh of frustration. Mai frowned at him. The boy was getting to be a bit much for her to handle, far more difficult than his younger brother and sister.

She had been surprised that Li Han-lin's wife hadn't come yet to pick up her children. But Mai had no idea what was happening because T'ang kept her and the children isolated from everyone else. She wasn't even sure how long they had been in Oakland. Three weeks? A month? Time had run together and she could no longer sort it out.

The younger children played quietly as Mai sat and watched Pao-yang go over his arithmetic book. They were bored and unhappy by this enforced confinement.

Mai could take no more of this, and left them to search for T'ang. "There you are," she cried, coming upon him sitting in the parlor. "I must speak to you!" she ran and knelt before him.

"Hmmm?" he mumbled, barely looking up from his newspaper.

"The children are miserable. They need be allowed outside, to play, or at least to walk around the block."

"No."

"Please. You know I wouldn't try to run away with them."

"I have told you many times, I do not want them or you outside."

"But why? This is not healthy for them."

"No! For the last time, no!" he bellowed.

Mai would not back down. "We are all going mad here. I can't stand these walls any longer. I want to see something new."

T'ang did a slow burn at these continued questions. "How many times must I tell you the same thing! Don't ask me again!"

"But the children will get sick. Children must move about. What will your sister say if she finds them sickly when she comes to get them?"

"Comes to get them? Huh!" T'ang snorted.

"That's right! That's just what I said," Mai cried. "They must stay well cared for. You don't want your sister or Li Han-lin to be angry, do you?"

Mai had finally gone too far. The look T'ang gave her was withering.

"My sister is dead," he roared. "If she was alive, she'd be here with me. Are you really so stupid or so addled by opium you don't know that?"

Mai gasped in horror. "I don't believe you."

"She died in the earthquake while her loving husband slept in the arms of his whore. She was crushed to death when her home collapsed on her!"

Mai was shocked. "Why didn't you tell me this earlier? Why did you let me think they were both alive?"

"It was better for the children not to know, and you would have given it away. Let them learn later, so they will not suffer as I have at my beautiful one's loss."

"And Li Han-lin, how is he?"

"How is he! How is he! Your concern overwhelms me!"

"But he was not with her. Why doesn't he send for the children? Where is he?" Mai would not give up her questions.

T'ang turned to her in fury. "'Why?' you ask! 'Where is he?' you ask! He's run off, that's why! Like a child. He thinks they are all dead, his children as well as his wife. How do you like that? He thinks they are all dead and that it's his fault. He abandoned them. They could be dead, you know. And him too. He should be! Dead like my sister!" He began to sob. "My beautiful Jun. How can I go on without her? I loved her so much; she's the only woman I ever loved."

Mai looked at him in horror. Li Jun was dead and someone, T'ang perhaps, had told Han-lin that his children were dead as well. She must find him and tell him the truth. Without a second's hesitation she ran from the room to the guard at the door.

"T'ang said you are to get the children and bring them to him at once. They are in the study. I must go back to him now."

The guard looked puzzled. "Me? Why should I?"

"I don't know. Do you wish to ask him? I must go back to him immediately; he is in a terrible rage."

The guard was horror-struck at the thought of questioning T'ang.

"No, I'll go get them." The guard started up the stairs as Mai made as if to go back to T'ang's room. As soon as the guard was out of site, however, she quietly opened the door and slipped out.

On the street she ran for all she was worth to put as much distance as possible between herself and T'ang's home. After two blocks she saw a fire-escape hanging near the street. She jumped up onto it, climbed, and then pulled it up behind her. She quickly scrambled to the roof and from there hid until she saw T'ang's men circling about looking for her. She had known they would be close behind her.

Her heart pounded as they drew nearer. They didn't pause, but continued down the street. Mai descended the fire escape and ran off in the opposite direction from the searchers. She didn't know Oakland's Chinatown area at all and, in the need to keep out of sight, made slow progress. She saw no one she knew, and couldn't risk making the wrong encounter.

As night fell. Mai saw wagons with food being dished out to the few remaining refugees who hadn't yet managed to find a way to care for their needs, but she still dared not show herself. Even the restaurants had people lined up at their back doors waiting for scraps and leftovers, closing that source of food for her as well. Finally, she found a doorway to an old warehouse that seemed to offer some sanctuary from the cold night air, and curled up in it to rest.

At the first light of sunrise she went to the Chinese area's main street and surveyed until she found a spot where she could be well hidden but yet observe all the passers-by. The idea worked well, for not two hours later did she recognize a member of the Yuen-li tong.

He quickly led her to the home where Soo Chen-gai was staying. They knocked on the door, awakening Chen-gai who had spent most of the night drinking and gambling. He opened the door and one eye at the same time.

Mai burst in upon him. "Oh, Soo Chen-gai, I have heard terrible news. Is it true that Li Jun is dead and that Li Han-lin thinks his children as dead as well?"

"Mai-ching," Chen-gai mumbled, trying to get his faculties together. "Uh, yes; yes, they are all dead, I'm afraid."

"But they're not! At least, the children are safe. They are with T'ang; I myself have been taking care of them."

Soo Chen-gai looked at her in amazement then smiled and let out a cheer. "What wonderful news! The best news possible! We must tell Li as soon as possible. He will kill T'ang for this deception, and that one's death would be well deserved! Their unholy truce will be over."

"Let me tell him," Mai asked.

"He's not here," Chen-gai said. "He's gone a long way. He had to get away from so many memories."

"Let me go to him, Soo Chen-gai. Where can I find him?" Mai placed both her hands on Chen-gai's arm and looked at him imploringly. Chen-gai was silent for a long while as he carefully pondered the situation.

"Well, Li said absolutely no one was to follow him, but your news may be just what is needed. I will arrange it."

Mai ate a hearty breakfast, lunch and dinner that day, and slept warmly that night. Before dawn the next morning she started out in a buckboard driven by tong member, Bao-yi. They traveled all day, stopping to eat and drink only when the horses needed rest. Bao-yi seemed to know exactly where to go, for by late afternoon they arrived at a small farm just outside Sacramento. An older woman came out to meet him and, after quick greetings, explained that most of the men were out working the land, but Li Han-lin had returned a short while ago and was in the bunkhouse. Mai asked Bao-yi if she could be alone with him, and Bao-yi consented.

Mai walked with some trepidation to the small building where Li was. He must have heard her approach for, before she arrived there, he opened the door and stepped out into the daylight. She was surprised at how wan and pallid he had become.

"Mai-ching! How is it that you are here?" he demanded.

"My lord, I have come to bring you wonderful news," she cried, bowing low as she spoke.

He stepped back and looked at her with skepticism. "What is this news?" he asked quietly, with no emotion or interest apparent in his voice.

She kept her eyes on the ground. "T'ang lied to you. Your children are well. They were at his home when the earthquake struck. I have been taking care of them. When you left her, Li Jun was in a rage and took the children to T'ang. She moved there herself. Occasionally, she would go back to your old house just to have some time alone. That's what happened the night of the earthquake."

Han-lin reeled from the shock of her words. He grabbed Mai by the shoulders, his hold so strong she winced. "You are telling me the truth?" he demanded.

This time, she did look into his eyes, and the pain she saw there startled her. "Of course. I would not lie to you about such a thing! I didn't know until two days ago that you had been told they were dead. T'ang brought us to Oakland, to a cousin's house. There, he kept us as prisoners, never allowing us to leave the house, never allowing anyone to see us. I thought you were preparing a home for them, and that was why you didn't come to get them. Only yesterday did T'ang tell me how horribly he had lied to you."

He looked at her but did not really see her, then sat on the door step and held his head in his hands. "Thank God," he whispered over and over. "Thank God."

Mai sat beside him and put her arms around him. She held him thus and rocked him, until the emotions that overwhelmed him were once again under control.

He sat up and took her hands and kissed them. "Thank you for bringing me this news."

Her eyes filled with tears at his joy. "I came as fast as I could. My heart breaks to think how you have suffered under that man's cruelty."

A dark cloud passed across Han-lin's face. "Does he treat them well? Do they like it there?"

"He provides for their wants, but, as I said, he does not let them leave the house at all. They don't know yet about their mother's death. They seem to think the two of you are busy rebuilding the house for them."

"And in time they will forget us. Is that what T'ang hopes?" Han-lin's eyes had a far off look to them.

"I suppose he may think that. I'm sure he knows he can't keep them a secret forever."

"Is his house roomy for them?"

"It is a good house. I don't know if he will stay there in Oakland or return to San Francisco."

"I hope he stays in Oakland, for their sake. It is safer. There may be another earthquake and fire in San Francisco," Han-lin said quietly.

Mai's eyes widened his words, "What do you mean, 'for their sake'?"

"I mean," Han-lin murmured as if in a dream, "it is because of him they are alive. Because of me they could have died like their mother."

"No! What happened was not your fault. You are their father!"

"Enough! I will not discuss it," he stood. "How did you get here?"

She nodded in the direction of the farmhouse and began to say, "Bao-yi—"

Han-lin strode off in the direction she indicated. He found Bao-yi with the wife of the owner and spoke with them.

oOo

Mai spent the next day helping with the farm chores while the men went off to work in the fields. She did not get to see Han-lin again until evening.

"I guess I should be returning soon," she said to him when they were finally alone. "Will you come back to Oakland with us?"

"There is nothing there for me," he replied.

"Soo Chen-gai would like to see you, as would others."

"He is a true friend," he replied. "Did he speak to you about others in our tong and what has happened to them since the fire?"

"A little."

Han-lin's voice turned soft and quiet as he asked, "Did he mention Ruth?"

Mai knew it took great effort for him to ask the question of her.

Mai loved him, and knew the relationship with the white devil was no good for him. She remembered with disgust the Greer woman's father and his willingness to work with T'ang. She was much better for Han-lin, and in time, he would realize it. She took a deep breath. "People say Ruth has gone back to her parents' home. It is over for her. The fire made her realize all she had almost lost. She left a message to tell you good-bye. She doesn't want to see you again."

"I see," Han-lin said quietly. He remained silent a long while, then gave a small nod. "She's right. It is best this way. I had once thought ... many foolish things. But now, all that is past. She is a very practical woman. Americans are that way, aren't they? Very practical. And Chinese ... as much as Americans think we are cold because they don't understand us, I think we follow our hearts too much. It causes us to do senseless, imprudent things." He shut his eyes as he took a deep breath. "She has made the correct choice. I am glad for her."

Mai breathed a sigh of relief at his words, but her brow knitted in consternation to see him get up and walk away without a word. Mai wanted to say something, declare her love, and that she would never leave him, but decided she should wait.

Han-lin did not join them for the rest of the evening.

That night, Mai did not get into her bed. She waited until the house became quiet, until everyone else was asleep.

Han-lin was feeling alone and rejected. More than ever before he needed a woman to love him and for him to love in return. What better time was there for her? She felt she must act or would go mad with longing and anguish.

Quietly, she crept out into the clear, country night. She felt a sense of freedom and oneness with nature that was totally non-existent in the close city atmosphere in which she dwelt.

In the bunkhouse, she silently crept to the corner where Han-lin slept. Her night dress fell to the floor as she stole under the covers beside him. He immediately awakened. Mai's arms went about him as she pressed her body against his, letting him know her nakedness.

"I love you," she whispered, as she showered his face, neck and shoulders with kisses, her hands roaming freely over his body, feeling his hard, sinewy muscles and the ultimate maleness about him. "I have always loved you."

"Mai, stop this madness." He shoved her away from him and sat up.

"But I love you," she insisted. "Love me, Han-lin, please." She tossed aside the covers and let him see her. She had been told often that her body was beautiful, and knew that in the moonlight enhanced the ivory creaminess of her skin.

"Get dressed," he ordered. "Leave me!"

She wanted him so much she could hardly bear it. "I can help you forget the pain of the past," she pleaded. "I've learned much; I know how to make you happy." She took his hand and placed it on her breast, "Am I not soft, and warm? Let tonight be ours."

He quickly removed his hand and his eyes looked at her with pity. "You're little more than a child. I don't want you to feel this way about me. I don't mean to hurt you, but you being here is wrong."

She felt suddenly ashamed, and seemed to shrivel before his eyes as she used his blanket to cover herself. "Is it because of T'ang? Because he has known this body you feel I am defiled, a thing beneath even your contempt."

"No, Mai, of course not. You are a kind and good person. It's just that I...," he hesitated, never having spoken so openly to any woman other than Ruth about his feelings, but he felt she deserved an explanation after all she had done for him, "I love someone else. Even though she's gone from my life. I will never forget her."

"You must forget her, my lord! I can help you forget. You should not be alone at such a time!"

"She's gone back to the world she came from. I'm glad she's done that. And it doesn't make me love her less. Maybe you can't understand me, but I want no other woman. Not you, not anyone."

Mai looked at him and knew he spoke the truth.

She turned her back to him as she replaced her chemise and walked out into the night as softly as she had come.

oOo

The next morning Bao-yi entered her room with the news that Han-lin had gone, had left during the night without a word to anyone. Mai looked at him in shock, and then turned away so that he could not see her bitter tears.

CHAPTER 26

RUTH WAS AT HER wits' end regarding Han-lin's whereabouts. The head of the Yuen-li tong simply did not disappear into thin air. She knew someone must have some idea where he was, and she had to find a way to get that person to tell her or Lao-she. She had been to visit Soo Chen-gai many times, but he told her he didn't know where Han-lin had gone.

The clean-up of Chinatown, in the meantime, hit a snag.

The destruction of the sector had been a priceless loss for the Chinese. The temples, theaters, and tong and family association headquarters had housed numerous antique, elaborate, and irreplaceable pieces brought from China. All were now gone.

For the white population, however, Chinatown's destruction was seen as the one blessing of the fire. They saw it as an end to unsanitary conditions, crime, murders, opium dens, tong wars, sing-song girls, and a general corrupt and corrupting element in the very center of the city. As soon as the flames began to die suggestions were offered as to what to do with the old Chinatown site. No one considered allowing the Chinese to move back again, nor, apparently, did they foresee any strong opposition to relocation from the Chinese.

The city fathers looked forward to putting beautiful, elegant, and sophisticated buildings on the prime real estate. They even renamed the main street from Dupont Gai to "Grant Avenue" to go along with its new, modern image.

The Chinese protested all of this quite vehemently. They refused to settle elsewhere in the city, and called the Chinese ambassador from Washington D.C. to negotiate on their behalf. The city refused to listen until the Chinese announced, with the backing of the Empress of China, that if they were not allowed to resettle on the old Chinatown site, they would move to Portland, Seattle or Los Angeles and then, because of this terrible treatment of them by San Francisco, every Chinese merchant throughout Asia would boycott the city.

Winston Greer and other shippers were up in arms at this pronouncement. Most of the city's trade and income came from the Orient. Such a boycott, on top of the losses already suffered from the earthquake and fire, could send San Francisco into a financial downward spiral from which it might never recover.

Almost like magic, word of relocating the Chinese disappeared from public discussion.

The Chinese had won.

After this battle, the pace of rebuilding in Chinatown picked up speed.

oOo

Ruth heard a timid knock on the door of the Greer mansion. Shortly after, Smitty came to her, "There is a young China-woman at the door. I don't know if she wants to see you or the old gal. I can't understand her and she can't understand me."

"All right," Ruth said, wondering who it could be. "I'll take care of it."

She quickly walked to the front door, "Whom do you wish to see?" she asked slowly and meticulously in Chinese.

"I wish to see you," replied Mai in her heavily accented English.

Ruth looked puzzled.

"I come about Li Han-lin," Mai added.

Ruth's eyes grew wide with surprise and apprehension over what the news might be. She led the girl to the parlor.

Ruth had no patience left and got right to the point. "Who are you and what do you know?" she asked coldly.

Mai breathed heavily from nervousness over what she was to say, over being in the presence of the wealth and splendor of the Greer mansion, and particularly over the cold, forceful demeanor of the

Greer woman. Finally, she mustered up the courage to speak. In a strange mixture of Chinese and English, the two women managed to understand each other. "I am called Mai-Ching. Li Han-lin, my lord, has been kind to me. But now, he needs help and I … I am not the one who can give it to him."

Ruth saw the heartache in the girl's eyes, and heard the catch in her voice as she spoke.

"Have you seen him recently?" she asked.

"Two weeks ago."

Ruth sat on the edge of her chair at this news. "Is he all right?"

"He is strong," the girl said.

"Where is he?"

At that the girl shook her head and sobbed. "I don't know anymore."

"You don't know? What do you mean you don't know?"

The girl cried harder.

"What is it?" Ruth was beside herself, wanting to grab the girl and shake the news out of her. She forced herself to wait.

Mai stopped her tears, but continued to look at the floor. "I brought him news. Good news," she said. "He believed his children were dead, but they are not. It was a trick, an evil, vicious trick by a man named T'ang Tsu-shao, who owns me."

"T'ang? Han-lin's brother-in-law?"

She glanced at Ruth only a moment before dropping her gaze once more. "Yes. The children were with me at his house on the night of the earthquake. We got out before the fire. We went to Oakland where I cared for them. They are fine."

"They are fine?" Ruth stared at her in amazement. "Thank God! It's a miracle!"

Mai just nodded, then continued, "I thought that just hearing the news would make everything better for Li, that he would want nothing but to come home. I'm sorry to say it didn't happen that way."

At that, Mai looked Ruth in the eye, hesitating about what to say next, wondering just how far she should go. Ruth met her gaze and saw the questions there, the uncertainty, but above all the loneliness and sadness. Instinct told her that Mai loved Han-lin. She waited to hear what more the girl had to say.

Mai shut her eyes and spoke softly, almost to herself. "I tried to help him. I tried everything I knew—everything. But he does not love me, not even a little." The tears rolled silently down her face.

Ruth nodded, understanding, and sat in silence.

The next words spewed from Mai in a torrent. "I then told him that you had returned to your father's house, and no longer wanted to see him, or to have anything more to do with him."

"What?" Ruth jumped to her feet, hurt and puzzled that a stranger would speak about her in such a way. "That's not true! Did he believe you? Why would you tell him such a thing?"

"He believed me, I think. I know why I said it, and I am ashamed, but, it didn't work. And now, I don't know where he has gone. The people at the farm suspect he moved on to the mines along the Sierra Nevada foothills, probably to a place called Chinese Camp. There is work there, difficult work, and life is very rough. Li is strong, but he is not a laborer. His life would be shortened in that environment—and it's my fault! It's all my fault!"

The girl cried hard, her head turned away from Ruth in shame. "He must not be alone. If T'ang finds him without the tong to protect him ... T'ang is not an honorable man."

"I see." Ruth clasped her hands so tightly they ached.

Mai stood. "I pray you will be successful in finding him."

"Lao-she is here," Ruth said quickly, realizing the girl was about to leave. "Perhaps you know her? You must tell her everything."

They went to the back of the house where Ruth found Lao-she in her room. Mai and Lao-she greeted each other like old friends. They sat, and Mai told her all that had happened. Through tears of joy Lao-she asked many questions.

Ruth found it maddening that Lao-she was probably learning a lot more than she ever could with the language barrier she faced. Finally, the two women stopped talking.

Mai stood. "I must leave now."

"Where are you going? What will you do?"

Mai shook her head, "I don't know. I'm tired of the fighting, and the cruelty."

"You can stay here," Ruth said. "Lao-she and I can help you."

Mai lifted sad eyes. "Thank you, but no. I cannot do that."

Ruth understood and led Mai to the front door. "Good luck to you, Mai-ching. And thank you for telling me everything. I know it must have been difficult."

Mai bowed, "Good fortune to you as well, Ruth Greer."

As she left the house, Ruth folded her arms tightly against the shudder that overtook her body.

CHAPTER 27

RUTH DECIDED TO leave as soon as possible to search for Han-lin, even though the thought of traveling to the Sierras filled her with misgivings. It was lawless area. Few women went there; life was hard and held cheaply.

Winston and Blanche were horrified at Ruth and Lao-she going to such an area alone, and gave all the reasons they could think of against it, but Greer didn't push the issue. He saw Ruth was adamant, and he had a healthy respect for staying on her good side. He carefully gave no ultimatums.

Ruth's apprehensiveness increased geometrically as she packed her bags the night before she was to leave—especially as she placed the new snub-nosed revolver bought especially for the trip into her handbag.

The morning after Mai-ching's visit, the two travelers were ready.

They took a train Stockton. Once there, the women were surprised to learn that the old stagecoach company only went through the Sierra foothills twice a week. The gold country had far less activity than in years past. They had missed the early Wednesday coach by a few hours. The next wouldn't leave until Saturday.

They took a room in a small hotel, and Ruth immediately sent Lao-she out to the local Chinatown to ask if anyone knew of or had seen Han-lin.

In the meantime, Ruth decided to explore on her own. She returned to the coach station.

"Is there any other way I can get to Chinese Camp before Saturday?" she asked the ticket salesman.

"I'm sorry, ma'am." He looked irritated to see Ruth again. "Not many people go up that way. If we ran a coach up there more often we'd be broke in no time."

"But surely there must be other means of transportation."

"I'm not in the business of finding other rides for people!" he bellowed.

Ruth spun on her heel and left in a huff. Just outside the door she heard a voice say, "Old Sam is a grouch with everyone. Don't take it personally."

She turned and saw a man leaning against the building. He had a serious expression on his face, but his clear, blue eyes were laughing mischievously.

Ruth attempted a look of hauteur, raising her eyebrows and sweeping her eyes from the top of his curly brown hair down his long, lanky frame to the floor. With a toss of the head, she turned and walked away.

"I heard you want to go to up to the Chinese Camp," he said, falling in step beside Ruth as she headed down the street.

"That's none of your business."

"I can get you there."

"I'm not in the habit of going places with strange men." Although she said those words, she gave him a sidelong glance, curious about his proposal.

"I've been told I've got an unusual personality, some say a charming personality, but I've never been called 'strange' before."

Ruth grimaced. He was wasting her time. "You know what I meant. Go away and stop bothering me." She reached her hotel.

He stepped between her and the hotel's door. "Bother you? Me? Here I offer to help you, a damsel in distress. What if Guinevere had turned away Lancelot and told him he was 'bothering' her?"

"Perhaps Camelot would not have been destroyed." She tried to get past him, but he kept blocking her way. "You, sir, are no Lancelot!"

"Okay, maybe that wasn't such a good metaphor. But wait. Listen to me. You want to get to Chinese Camp, I need money and I'm going that way, anyway. For $10 I'll escort you there on my buckboard—right now, if you want."

"Oh?" She gave him a hard look, as if trying to figure him out.

"That's right. No problem. You can trust me, ask anyone."

"What's your name?"

"Brett Starr," he said, standing a little straighter as he said it.

"Hah! You've seen too many Wild West Shows!" She pushed him aside and reached for the door.

"Well, the Brett's mine—Brett O'Higgins," he said, following her into the lobby. "Who'd trust someone named O'Higgins? Starr, on the other hand, that has class. I guess I just haven't learned to say my new name with enough conviction yet to stop people from laughing at me."

"You're crazy."

"Now that *is* something I've been called before."

"Mr. O'Higgins or Starr or whoever you are, please leave me alone."

"Okay, but you'll find three days a mighty long wait. No joke, ma'am. I will help you, sure as I'm standing here."

Her lips pursed. Three days was very long, indeed. She eyed O'Higgins a moment, and then said, "I'm traveling with a friend. An elderly Chinese lady."

He studied her a moment. "Chinese women are usually pretty tiny, but I'd still have to charge another $5 for her."

Ruth's eyebrows lifted at that, but then she said, "Sold."

They left the next morning before dawn. The ride to Chinese Camp was a long one, over eight hours because of the need to often stop and rest the horses. The road was rough, and the ground rose quickly in altitude from the central valley to the Sierras.

With every step the horses took Ruth found herself farther from the civilized world she knew, and farther into a land almost pagan in its anarchy. It was wild and beautiful, treacherous yet serene, divine but cruel.

Brett talked almost nonstop, telling numerous, outrageous tales about the Old West even though Ruth wasn't able to clear her mind of other things enough to listen and Lao-she couldn't understand.

Finally, however, both women heard when Brett said, "You can just see the town out there. That's Chinese Camp."

Ruth's heart did a two-step.

"When we get there do you want me to help you find whoever it is you're going to meet? I know you've got a China-woman here, but sometimes those coolies are dangerous, even to their own kind, you know," Brett said.

"I can take care of myself." Ruth's immediate reply was indignant. "But, on second thought, I'm not sure he's here. Maybe it would be best if you waited a little while until we find out if he's in this camp. If not, we'll need to go on to another mining town."

"That sounds okay by me, but it'll cost you more money."

"Of course."

"Who is it you're looking for anyway? Some relative of the old lady's or something?"

"He's a friend."

"A friend of yours? You mean a white man? You'll find no white men hanging around Chinese Camp."

"He's Chinese."

He couldn't hide his surprise. "You know a China-man? And you're bothering to go look for him?"

"Stranger things have happened."

His mouth scrunched. "Not many."

As they neared the town, a few people were seen walking along the road. Ruth and Lao-she leaned forward in their seats, hoping to find Han-lin among them. They didn't.

The town itself was appalling. Most of the buildings were no more than hovels made out of what looked more like twigs than lumber. It seemed a strong wind could completely level it. The men—she saw no women—seemed to blend into the woodwork. All had similar dusty, lost, and forlorn expressions.

As the buckboard neared, the townspeople stood silently as if transfixed and stared at them.

Brett stopped in front of the Wells Fargo office. "I guess this is as good a place as any to start looking."

Lao-she and Ruth got out of the buckboard and Lao-she immediately went off on her own to talk to people about Han-lin. Ruth entered the express office.

She walked up to the clerk. "Excuse me, I'm looking for someone that I believe is living here."

"Who would that be?" The clerk was a mousy little man, with eyes that couldn't quite look at Ruth but kept darting from side to side.

"His family name is Li, given name is Han-lin."

"Han-lin Li. Li Han-lin. Nope, neither way it don't sound familiar. But you know, miss, a lot of men, women too, change their names when they come up to these camps. There's usually something, or someone, they either want to forget or are hiding from. Sometimes one person comes here and picks up packages for himself with two to four different names on them. I always ask why he wants all those and he says they're all his. It's common."

"That's true, he may have changed his name. He only would have arrived over the past three or four weeks. He's in his thirties, tall for a Chinese, and quite thin."

"There's about a dozen men I know of who could be him. Lots of people come and go through here. There's a lady down this street, Madam Leong she's called, that you should see. She'll rent you a nice room. Then you can look around yourself. I think looking is the only way you'll find him."

"I suppose you're right. Well, thank you for the information. Good-day."

"Good-day," he replied, unable to hide the curiosity from his face.

Ruth returned to the buckboard where Brett waited, and told him what she had learned. "It looks like Lao-she and I will have to stay here a day or two, at least, to look for Han-lin," she added. "If you come back this way soon, Brett, could you look us up? If we miss the stagecoach we might be forced to remain here a week before another comes by."

"Actually," Brett said, "I think I'll stick around here a while myself. Maybe I can help you look? Anyway, I always wanted to go to China. After a few days here, I'll believe I'm in Peking itself. How's that? Save myself plenty of boat fare too!" Brett laughed at the thought in such an infectious way, Ruth had to join him.

"It's good to hear you laugh, Miss Greer. That's the first time you laughed."

"Maybe it's because I have high hopes of finding my friend. Or because I'm finally doing something besides sitting around."

"That's some friend, I think." Brett looked at her intently.

"Yes, he is," Ruth replied proudly, meeting his look straight on.

Lao-she soon returned and told them she also had no luck. Everyone was quite close-mouthed in the town, which came as no surprise in this sort of a place. The three got into the buckboard and

Brett drove them around the town looking for Han-lin until it grew dark, when they rode to Madam Leong's.

Madam Leong was not in the least bit surprised when she opened the front door and saw the travelers standing there asking for a room. Their presence had been well-noticed and everyone knew where they would stay.

The three were quite surprised at what they saw, however. Madam Leong was obese and piled her hair high on her head with large curls fluttering about her face and neck. She wore a great deal of rouge and eye make-up, and was dressed in a flowery kimono that appeared Japanese rather than Chinese. As Ruth stood gaping, and Lao-she eyed the woman with not a small amount of disgust, Madam Leong smiled and asked them all to enter.

She had enough empty rooms for them each to be given a private one. Before going to her room, Ruth asked Madam Leong if she knew if anyone named Li Han-lin was in town. Madam Leong's response was only that Chinese Camp was the sort of place where no one used their real name.

Ruth sat on the bed in her room, glad to be able to rest awhile after the exhausting travel that day. She then freshened up and changed her clothes for dinner.

Brett was waiting for her as she entered the dining room. "You look beautiful tonight, Miss Greer. You make my staying here all the more worthwhile."

"I hope you are not inconveniencing yourself, remaining on my account."

"Not at all."

"I fear it might be a boring place for you."

"Quite the contrary. In fact, when Madam Leong showed me to my room she gave me a rundown on what to do in this town at night. It's not boring—and besides," he looked into her green eyes, "I like the scenery."

"Don't flirt, Brett, and don't flatter me. I'd like your friendship, but nothing more."

"Ouch!"

Lao-she came out of the kitchen carrying a tray for her room. She felt uncomfortable eating in the dining room. Madam Leong nodded with understanding.

A tasty Chinese meal was served for Ruth, Brett and the other guests, two Chinese gentlemen. Madam Leong was a good hostess and kept them entertained and comfortable throughout dinner with her many stories and jokes.

She told them tales of the mining camps and how lively and rough they were in the old days when Madam Leong was young and first came to Chinese Camp. She had started out as a "sing-song" girl in San Francisco, but money grew tight when the law attempted a crackdown on Chinatown and some over-zealous missionary women started going about rescuing sing-song girls from their tong leaders. Madam Leong was rescued three times herself. After each rescue, however, she found that she had no other means of support and went back to her old employer. One day she simply packed up and headed for the mining camps where she found "sing-songing" much more lucrative because of little competition. Soon she built a good-sized nest egg and bought the boarding house. She expected she would be moving on again soon, however, since the local mines had all but dried up. Chinese Camp most likely would soon turn into a ghost town. Madam Leong wasn't worried about it; she knew how to take care of herself.

After dinner, Ruth took Brett aside. "Are you going to the gambling house tonight?"

"It seems that's where most of the action is," he said.

"I'd like to join you."

He blanched. "That's not such a good idea, ma'am."

"Why not? I've been to gaming parlors before."

"You have?" He looked shocked. "I'm sorry. I don't know what kind you went to, or how you were kept safe, but I know these camps. It's not a place you should go to. Too much drinking, too many men, and not near enough women. Even the old lady might be in trouble."

"I see," Ruth said, understanding his meaning. "Well, all right. I won't go, but perhaps you could do me a favor? Han-lin, Li, that is, liked gambling. He might be there. He is tall, distinguished looking, actually quite handsome. His hair is Western style, parted on the side and a bit long. Sometimes, a wayward lock falls onto his forehead, and—"

"And I'll bet his hair is black and his eyes are so dark they seem black, too." Brent wore a smile as he spoke.

She stopped. "Yes. I see what you mean. Well, anyway, could you sort of look at the people there and see if anyone, at all—"

"I can do that."

"Thank you, Brett. You've become a good friend."

"You just stay in your room," he said. "And lock the door!"

"Good-night." With that, she went upstairs.

oOo

Ruth lay on top of the bed, trying to relax, but couldn't.

Anxiety over Han-lin grew. She got off the bed and paced around the room. The rooming house had grown quiet. Madam Leong's other guests had long since departed, Lao-she was sleeping peacefully, and Brett most likely was still out. She wanted to know if he had learned anything about Han-lin. After a while she knocked on his door in the off-chance that he had returned, but received no answer.

Back in her room, she felt more restless than ever. The room itself was stultifying. She continued to pace until she could stand it no longer. She put the snub-nosed revolver in her pocket, and then left the boarding house.

Outside, the air was fresh. She saw men in the distance and turned in the opposite direction, sliding her hand in the pocket to grip the gun. She needed to walk a bit, to help her become tired. She left the main street, having learned in Chinatown that it was not the main street that was the most interesting, but rather the side streets and alleyways. Also, Madam Leong had spoken of a gaming parlor behind the general store. She headed towards it.

Ruth heard the loud click-clack of mah-jongg tiles hitting together before she saw which building held the gamblers.

A door and window were open up ahead. She hurried to it, and saw a few men in the doorway, and others by the window. It sounded as if there was a good crowd inside.

Suddenly, a figure filled the doorway and started towards her. Ruth moved back into the shadows and crouched down. The man did not see her as he made his way along the path she had just traveled.

Two other men entered the house. Ruth felt a kind of fascination as she hid there watching the building as men came and went.

After all those faceless men appeared in the doorway, Ruth found it almost startling when she recognized Brett. She decided to make her presence known to him and have him walk back to Madam Leong's with her.

But rather than leaving immediately, Brett waited for another figure to join him. Ruth gasped, scarcely able to believe her eyes, as Han-lin stepped to his side.

The two men walked out of the casino and together turned down the road away from where Ruth stood. She remained frozen on the spot. In her mind, she had always thought that when she found Han-lin again she would immediately, happily and lightheartedly, run to him and everything would be all right. But now, actually seeing him, her feet felt like lead. She wanted to stop him, to call out, but couldn't. What was happening to him? What was his life now? Why was he talking with Brett?

She didn't know what to do—but doing nothing was equally unbearable. She would not watch him walk out of her life again.

She forced herself to move, first one small step, then another. She started walking towards them, slowly at first, but then she realized how rapidly they were progressing away from her. Soon they might be gone—disappearing into the night, and she might not be able to find them.

No, I won't let that happen.

She began to run.

The two men turned when they heard footsteps hurrying toward them. When they saw who it was a look of incredulity flashed across their faces.

Han-lin did not move from where he stood beside Brett. Ruth stopped as she neared him. He looked so much older she could hardly believe it. He had lost more weight, and lines of exhaustion marred his face. His clothes—Western clothes—were ragged and dirty, and there was an infinite sadness about his eyes. She could scarcely believe the change in him. Her heart went out.

Unable to bear being separated from him any longer, she threw her arms around him, burying her head against his shoulder and holding him tightly, not saying a word, not caring whether he wanted her or not. If he didn't want her, so be it, but she had to let him know that she still loved him. But also, she wanted to feel the strong grasp of his arms about her, the hard steel of his body against hers, and feel his love once more.

"Ruth," Han-lin gently tried to free himself from her grasp, his hands on her waist.

"No." She couldn't hold back her tears, and held him tighter.

He didn't have it in him to push her away a second time. He shut his eyes and his arms circled her as if from their own volition while his whole body melted towards her. He buried his face in her hair, breathed in the scent and warmth of her, and ruefully acknowledged the love and longing she awoke in him.

Finally, he lifted his head back to look at her, and she in turn did the same. In but a moment Han-lin's mouth was on hers, crushing, possessive, drawing her into him so that she felt weightless and dizzy from the passion of him, and all she could do was hold him and respond, respond with not just her body, but with her entire being.

Brett coughed. "Well, ahem," he said, "guess I'll head off. I, uh, guess our plan can be forgotten about."

Han-lin looked up at Brett, remembering what had just been said. Ruth, too, looked at him, but kept both arms around Han-lin's neck as she did so.

"Will you be here tomorrow?" Han-lin asked him.

"I think so, sure."

"We will talk again." Han-lin reached out his hand to shake Brett's, then Brett left.

"How do you know him?" Ruth asked.

"We just met tonight. He is a good person, and very fond of you," Han-lin replied, running his hand along her beautiful face, drinking in everything about her with his eyes.

"Oh, Han-lin, I couldn't bear being away from you."

"But to be away would be the best thing."

"No. Never."

"Let us go to my room. We can talk there."

Holding Ruth close to his side, they walked back to the main street and up to a small house. Han-lin opened the door and went down the hallway to a back room. He had a key to unlock the door and Ruth entered as he lit a lamp.

It was an extraordinarily miserable room. The walls were black with dirt. There was a mattress on the floor and a rickety dresser along the wall. That was all.

"It's cheap," said Han-lin as he noticed Ruth's look.

"Things will right themselves, in time," she said. "We'll start over. Life will be as it was."

"That's not possible, Ruth. Start over? I feel like all my life has been spent trying to start over. I don't think I can do it again."

"Yes, you can!" she urged.

"You don't understand. Everything is gone—everything. China-town itself. The gambling houses were all destroyed. Most of the cash money I had was in a safe. It was broken into by looters after the fire and the money is gone. My wife is dead because of me. The children are safe, but lost. It's too much, Ruth." He gazed at her. "I'm no longer the man you fell in love with. It would be best for you to return to your family, to forget about me."

"Mai came to my house and told me all that happened. You must get your children back, my love. You cannot leave them with T'ang."

"He's their uncle. He won't hurt them. Besides, they're better off without me. I deserted them, I am no father to them. I'm ashamed."

He walked away from her, turning his back on her.

Ruth sat on the mattress that passed as a bed. "Don't do this to yourself. T'ang is crazy; you've said that many times. Your children need you. And I need you. I need you so much I don't know what to do without you!"

"Ruth," Han-lin turned and knelt on the floor beside her feet, unable to bear seeing her tears, and took her hand in both of his. "You are everything to me. I have learned these weeks how much you mean to me. But it is because you mean so much to me that I must never see you again."

"This is madness."

"No, it is practical. Perhaps being practical is a kind of madness—who knows? I have little money, no means of livelihood. Even my children are better off without me. That is obvious."

"No!"

He stood and walked away from her, near the room's tiny, grease-covered window. "I thought you had already left me for good. And I was relieved when I heard it. I knew then that you were one person I could no longer hurt." He couldn't look at her as he continued. "I could hardly believe when I heard of the beautiful red-haired woman who arrived in camp this afternoon. It would have been better if you had not found me. There is no legal tie binding us, Ruth, and in this country, there never can be.

"Our ties are strictly emotional, and emotions are funny things," he continued. "They dull over time, and what once seems to be such a catastrophe that we could not live from the pain, becomes only a fond memory. It is the good we tend to remember, not the hurt. That is what will happen to us. Many men can love you. You will find—you deserve to find—someone who will bring you happiness."

"I could never love anyone but you." She went to him, and placed her hands on his arm. "It took me years to find you. I had given up, you know. I thought love was for others, not me. Then you came into my life and all that changed. No one will take your place, no one ever could."

"In time..."

"So much time does not exist. All I can hope is that there is enough time for the pain that you feel to ease. At least we're together. Together we can face anything."

"Ruth, I have seen...."

"No," she covered his mouth with her hand. "Don't speak." She ran her fingers over his cheek, along his ear, through his thick black hair. "Sometimes I can scarcely breathe I'm so filled with love for you."

Han-lin reached out for her and kissed her eyes as he murmured for her to stop her tears. She wrapped her arms about his neck and kissed him as he slowly lowered her onto the mattress. She felt as if she were on fire from the feel of the man, and a deep moan escaped from her throat. The muscles in his body quivered in response to her cry, as his hands ran over her as if to convince himself that she were really with him. She began to unbutton his shirt.

His flesh burned where she touched him, as hers did at his touch. She clung to him, his hands and lips exploring her, raising her to heights of unimagined passion. She loved him wildly, passionately, compulsively, as if she feared she would lose him again.

They didn't sleep that night, unwilling to lose a moment of this time together, but instead talked and loved until the sun was high into the sky.

Han-lin got up from the bed and dressed in silence. Ruth did the same, not knowing what was coming.

Finally, he faced her. "You are correct in saying I cannot hide from all that has happened. I must face it."

"Yes! Together we—"

"No. I will return to San Francisco. I must see my men, see to the situation with my children, with my property. I must do this alone, Ruth. I will need time."

She didn't know what to do or say, but simply looked at him, then nodded. She knew his anger and hurt had made him not believe in anything in his life. Simply returning to San Francisco might be a way to begin his healing, but that was also where T'ang and danger lay. She hated the thought of him in any more danger.

"I cannot grovel for your affection, Han-lin. Or for you to keep me with you," she said after a while in a calm, unemotional voice. "You know I love you, yet you ask me to leave."

Han-lin looked at her, almost reeling from the words she spoke. "Ruth, I'm so sorry. But there will be danger—"

"I know!" she cried. "The tong! The rivalries! The fights! I hate all that! I hate it!"

"That means you hate the thing that has kept me and many of my friends alive."

Finally, she sighed, unable fight him any longer. "All right, I'll do as you ask. I'll return to my parents' home, and wait for you there. And I will spend the rest of my life waiting, if that is what you want."

In silence, they walked back to Madam Leong's house, their arms around each other. At the house, Han-lin met with Lao-she, whose face beamed with pleasure and tears of joy at seeing him again. They hugged, and he spoke with her a long while. In parting, he planted a brief kiss on her old, wrinkled forehead.

He then took Ruth in his arms one last time, kissed her, held her, and then turned away and was gone.

CHAPTER 28

RUTH AND LAO-SHE soon left Chinese Camp for Stockton in Brett's buckboard. They rode silently until they reached the outskirts of the city when Brett spoke.

"Things didn't quite work out as everyone had planned."

"I guess not," Ruth replied wearily.

"I don't mean you, Ruth, I mean your father and that Li fellow."

Ruth looked at him questioningly, "My father?" she asked.

"Yes," Brett responded, with a little cough. "You see, I work for him. My name is Ronald Benson. I'm a manager in the scheduling department. I've kicked around a lot, and your old man knew that. When he heard you were going off to the mining camps he was sick with worry. He asked me to tag along to make sure you stayed out of harm's way."

"I see," Ruth said, thinking back to her father. "I was surprised that he put up such a small fight about my going. Now I know why."

"Neither of us thought you'd ever find Li—and as it turned out, he found you. He had seen us ride into town that day, and at the gambling parlor he approached me. I told him who I was and why I was there, and he thoroughly approved of your father's plan. He had planned to stay hidden until we left the area. But then you showed up."

Ruth nodded, and said nothing.

CHAPTER 29

*I*N SAN FRANCISCO, the days rolled into weeks as Ruth waited, hoped and prayed for some word from Han-lin. Life in the city slowly returned to normal.

Ruth passed her time working at the shipping company, but even there things were different. She knew that her father was hiding something from her, but she couldn't find out what. Some of the books were missing, and although she asked, threatened, ranted and raged to find them, her father met her threat for threat and she did not get her request. Other than that mystery, however, things were running smoothly and profitably, and she could take some pleasure in that. Ronald Benson was a constant visitor and escorted her to a few functions she absolutely had to attend, but he knew there was no hope for him to find a place as anything but a friend in Ruth's heart.

As one month went by and then another, Ruth found something new to occupy her mind, and even went to a doctor to confirm what she could not believe had happened. He confirmed it; she was pregnant. She told no one about this, and knew that for only another month or two, it would be her secret alone. A happy secret, for she had no doubt of how much she wanted this baby, despite what her father's reaction would be, or even society's.

Greer raised Ruth to be tough, gave her a man's education and strength in a time when her women friends learned to value soft helplessness. As a result, she was very much the outsider, and the rejection she would face upon this child's birth gave her no qualms.

One Sunday Ruth sat in the parlor leafing through a magazine when she heard a knock on the front door. She listened without moving, expecting Smitty to see to the caller, but she did not. Instead the light tapping sounded again.

Ruth opened the door and was surprised to see a small Chinese man standing there. He bowed silently to her and held out a white envelope. Ruth took it as the man turned and quickly scampered away.

She entered the house and tore the envelope open. Inside was a note, neatly printed:

38 Waverly — 11 a.m.
    —L

For an instant she wondered at Han-lin signing "L" for Li rather than the "H" she would have expected, but she gave it no further thought as she was far too elated at the thought of seeing him again. It was almost eleven o'clock now, so she fairly flew to her bedroom to get ready to go.

The morning fog was still thick as Ruth got off the cable car. The last few days it had not burnt off until one or two in the afternoon.

Nevertheless, Ruth pulled her shawl more closely around her as she headed up Dupont Gai (she would never call it Grant Avenue) towards Waverly.

She reached Waverly Place and began to look at the newly numbered buildings, trying to find the meeting place. The buildings were all different from the ones formerly on Waverly, yet the street seemed remarkably similar to the way it had been. As she walked deeper into Waverly, it seemed number 38 would be right about where Han-lin's former house was. He couldn't have rebuilt on that property, not after the memories he had of it, Ruth thought. But there it was, another house where the old one had been. Number 38.

She knocked on the door, half expecting Lao-she to open it. Upon their return to the city, Lao-she went to live with friends in Chinatown; she had apparently found the atmosphere at the Greer household too stifling and too sad.

No one answered Ruth's knock. Hesitating only a moment, she reached for the doorknob and turned it. The latch rolled out of the way and the door opened.

"Han-lin?" Ruth called. No answer.

She entered the house. She had to admit to being curious about it, and wondered how it was set up compared to the old days.

There was a long staircase just inside the door, as formerly, plus a door on the first landing. Although the outside was finished, there was still a considerable amount of work needed inside.

Ruth slowly walked up the stairs. She called for Han-lin another two times, but to no avail.

The top floor was much smaller than it had been, with only three rooms—a kitchen, parlor and what would probably be a bedroom.

An eerie feeling came over Ruth as she stood there; something seemed desperately wrong. She stepped out of the parlor and hurried down the stairs. None of this made sense. Why would Han-lin want to meet in this place? Why wasn't he there?

Something was definitely wrong. Han-lin would not do this to her.

Her feet reached the bottom step and as she hurried to the front door to leave, a hand grabbed her arm. "Han-lin," she prayed, and spun towards him with a smile.

Her smile froze in mid-expression as she found herself looking into the sneering face of a Chinese she had never seen before.

"Let go of me!" She tried to free her arm as she lunged towards the door. He jerked her towards him and pushed her back against a wall as he clamped his free hand tight over her mouth.

She was terrified. Who was this man? Her brain racked to find the answer as she struggled to free herself.

Her struggles only served to make him more determined to hold her, and he dragged her into the room on the ground floor. Once there, he opened a door at the far end of the room, which led to another staircase, this one going down below ground level, as if into the bowels of the earth.

Ruth attempts to free herself or to scream were futile. He was strong and carried her half-way down the stairs. Then, he not only let go, but pushed her so that she fell the rest of the way, landing in a heap on the earthen floor below.

He was beside her in a second, rolling her over onto her back and studying her face.

"Whore!" he sneered in Chinese, nearly spitting the word at her, then threw a stream of vile words at her.

She did not know what to do, but lay there, dazed and shocked, staring at him.

"Do you understand me, bitch?" he asked.

"I don't understand," she replied in his language.

He switched to English. "He taught you well, my brother-in-law! What else did he teach you?" T'ang leered. "Maybe we'll find out."

Brother-in-law! Mrs. Li's brother—the man who had nearly killed Han-lin. Han-lin had warned her of his brother-in-law's madness. She knew she must get away.

"You are an attractive woman," he said, running his hand over her neck and breasts. "But not beautiful like my sister was. Your hair is too red, your eyes too big, and your nose…it is altogether disgusting! But the combination comes together in a way that a man might find pleasing. I can see why Li took you. It would be almost a pity to just kill you and not make use of you one last time."

"Leave me alone! You have no reason to kill me!" Ruth exclaimed. She tried to get up, but he clasped his hand onto her neck, his fingers like steel as he began to squeeze.

"No reason? But of course I have a reason. Revenge. My brother-in-law's negligence killed my sister, and now it will kill you. I suffer, he suffers. Eventually, though, I will be kind. I will kill him and end his torment."

He was a little man, no bigger than Ruth herself, yet his grasp was strong as iron. The madness in his eyes seemed to add to that strength, if only because it added to her fear of him. His expression turned from pure hatred to something else as he looked at her again. A wicked leer came into his eyes as he let go of her neck and slid his hand under the neckline of her dress, and rubbed his calloused fingers over her skin.

"You worm! You vile slug!" Ruth gasped, trying to get her breath back. Finally, she spit at him, and when he recoiled, she shoved him, twisting her body trying to get away. "You are not fit to lick Han-lin's boots! You think you can harm him? He will have you roasted like the pig that you are. You will be skinned alive! Do you know the things that will be done to you?"

He could barely hold onto her. At first he laughed, but then his fury grew. She was strong, but he managed once again to force her onto her back. Holding each wrist, he pinned them to the floor near her head. On his hands and knees he straddled her.

"You'll never succeed with any of this so-called revenge," she shrieked. "What happened to your sister was tragic, but it was no man's fault. Take your revenge and your sorrow and leave here, before you start something you can't stop."

"Well spoken. You have a glib tongue, whore, like your father. He's my partner, you know, in opium and whores like you. You should be friendlier to me. Your father would approve!"

She pulled one wrist free, then swiveled around and bit his arm hard enough to draw blood, freeing the other wrist he held. She tried to crawl away as he grabbed and pawed at her on the floor, her fight only serving to arouse him even further. Finally one hand around her neck, strangling her, he tore open the front of her dress, then rose his body off her as he reached down to lift her skirts.

Her knee shot straight upward and struck him full force in the groin area. He couldn't cry out, couldn't do a thing as he convulsed in pain. Ruth knew he would have killed her in a second if he could.

She jumped up, but saw that even in pain T'ang was crawling into position to block the stairway to freedom. Her eyes quickly swept the room looking for something to use to defend herself, but it was empty except for one small table. In the corner there was a door. Perhaps a closet, she thought, with something she could grab for protection. She rushed to the door and flung it open.

Much to her surprise it was not a closet, but a passageway. T'ang was stumbling to his feet behind her. Without hesitation, she plunged into darkness.

She was in a tunnel, narrow and damp, and ran until the light from the room could no longer be seen. She gave no thought to where she was going, but only knew she had to put as much distance as possible between herself and T'ang. Hand over hand she hurried along the wall, following wherever the passageway lead her.

Where will this end? she thought, as she stumbled along despite the filth that clung to her hands from the walls, or the rats she heard scurrying away and occasionally running over her feet or jumping onto her skirts in their blind, neurotic, dash to get away.

The underground tunnel—it really does exist, she thought. There were so many tales of people disappearing off the streets of China-town, it was always suggested that they had been bought under-ground and from there carried to the waterfront where they would be transported to some far away land to be sold as a slave, or worse. Many scoffed at such a network, but here it was. Either it had not collapsed during the earthquake, or someone or some group found it so valuable that it had been immediately rebuilt.

A light! Finally she saw a light in the distance. Safety at last. She ran towards it, hoping against hope that it would provide a safe exit from the tunnel and T'ang. Where was he, she wondered? Had he given up the chase so easily?

She turned a corner in the passageway and saw a lantern on the ground. It must have been left there to help guide people along the way, she thought. She would borrow it to help her navigate the black maze even more quickly than she had been doing.

She took several hurried steps towards the lantern when a move-ment in the shadows beyond her caught her eye. She looked up, and froze. "No!" she sobbed, then screamed, praying someone, some-where would hear her.

T'ang stood ahead of her, his face contorted into a leering smirk.

No wonder she hadn't heard him behind her, she thought. Obvi-ously the tunnel was more of a maze than she had suspected, and T'ang knew the way through it.

How foolish she had been to think she could escape so easily!

"No one will hear you down here," he said. As he stepped closer, she saw that in his hand was the hatchet of the tongs.

More than anything, that scared her. She had seen what one could do; saw how it could remove a man's head, slice through bone and sinew. She knew T'ang would show her no mercy. Her life and that of an innocent, unborn babe's would end here in this miserable tunnel, never again to see the one she loved so much. Should she turn and run? Could she reach the lantern before T'ang and then throw it at him? Without trying either she knew both ideas were hopeless. With his superior speed and knowledge of the tunnel she could not match him. And so, she stood frozen, her eyes unable to leave the shafts of light bouncing off the blade of the ax.

T'ang raised his arm and slowly stepped towards her.

Her breathing stopped and her knees felt about to buckle beneath her as a fear more total and overwhelming than anything she ever imagined flooded through her. She watched, mesmerized, as he raised the hatchet even higher in preparation for its final, terrible descent.

Suddenly, the air was shattered by a loud explosion. The hatchet flew high in the air, but instead of coming down towards Ruth in a death blow, its handle shattered and the head flew off to clatter harmlessly in a corner.

T'ang spun around, away from her, and peered into the darkness.

Han-lin stepped towards him, a number of Yuen-li close behind him. Han-lin's entire being shook with rage. "Your miserable life would be ended now, except for one thing, T'ang. My children."

"I will never let you have them," T'ang raged. "You are unfit to be a father. Murderer! You abandoned them to run off with that white devil. Only by my intervention are they alive today. They are well hidden. I won't tell you where they are."

"I can make it worth your while to do so."

"I doubt it. Even if you murder me the way you did your wife, you will not have them. They will be killed first! I have it all arranged. Word of my death is their death sentence."

Han-lin sucked in his breath. Ruth realized he had suspected as much, that he well realized the full extent of T'ang's cruelty. Calmly he spoke, "We will have a battle. Your tong, the Wang Shao, against my tong, the Yuen-li. We had such a battle once before, and you almost won. This time, to the victor, goes the children and the Yuen-li, its territory and its gold. Is that bait enough for you?"

God, no! Ruth cried inside, but she didn't dare speak, didn't dare move or do anything that might cause the tense stand-off to erupt in gunfire.

T'ang smirked as his eyes lit up with greed. "That is a good prize for the winner. But how can I be sure you will give up your tong?"

"Two things must be done. First, I will make a document to sign over to you those things I possess upon my death in this battle. Second, you must bring the children to a place known and agreed upon by all of us, where they will be held for the victor. Upon this battle, all will rest."

T'ang's eyes narrowed as he thought this over. Ruth could all but see his brain working, thinking that he had beaten Han-lin once, and if she hadn't found him, he might be dead now. T'ang probably thought he could do it again. T'ang's face suddenly broke into a smile. "It is agreed," he said.

"We will make arrangements the next two days. On the morning of the third day, at dawn, we will meet in Ross Alley."

T'ang nodded, then slowly, without taking his eyes off Han-lin, backed away until he was lost in the darkness of the tunnel, then he turned and ran.

At the sound of his departure, the shock and fear Ruth had felt began to take its toll, and she dropped to her knees. Blood surged through her temples, as if to make up for the time it seemed to stand still in her veins from sheer fright.

The world started to spin and blacken, and she shut her eyes when strong arms reached for her. She had no need to open her eyes, she knew those arms, those hands, so well, perhaps better than her own. He helped her to her feet, and she lay her head against his, feeling the warmth and safety of his body envelope hers.

He put his jacket on her to hide her ripped dress, and then said, "Let's leave this evil place."

They quickly made their way out of the tunnel where Soo Chen-gai, Wong Lon-po and several others from Yuen-li waited.

The tong walked with Han-lin, ready to fight and protect him if necessary since none of them trusted T'ang or his Wang Shao. When they reached a small, two-room apartment on Washington Street, the tong left. But Ruth knew they would not be far away.

Han-lin no sooner shut the apartment door than he held her close. "This is what I feared," he whispered. "I will kill him for touching you! You can be sure of that."

She clung to him, her face chalky with cold beads of perspiration on her forehead as she felt her insides spasm and convulse. Her eyes widened with fear of the irreversible damage T'ang might have done. "Let me lie down a moment," she said haltingly, trying to keep the panic within her.

He carried her to his bed. "What's wrong?"

"Nothing," she said. She couldn't tell him. Not yet. "I need to rest."

He covered her with a blanket and darkness soon overtook her, a faint more than sleep, as her body could no longer cope with the assaults upon it. She slept many hours, well into the evening, while

Han-lin sat and watched, growing ever more concerned about her health. When she awoke the first thing she did was feel her belly, worried about any spasms. There were none; no unnatural pain. She could have cried with gratitude, but instead grabbed Han-lin's hand and kissed it.

"Are you all right?" he asked, gently brushing the hair back from her forehead and looking into her luminous eyes, his voice full of the worry he had felt. She just nodded and smiled.

She looked long at him before she spoke. "T'ang said something about ... about my father, about some activities ..." Han-lin said nothing.

Ruth understood his silence, "You knew?"

He nodded.

"Thank you for not telling me." She sighed deeply and shut her eyes in shame that her own father could have stooped so low. She knew why he did it—love of money, the fatal flaw of a man who might have been great, but wasn't. She sat lost in thought for a while.

"However did you come to find me, Han-lin, in that terrible place?"

He smiled. "That's a rather long story with a beginning that I fear you will not like."

"Not like? Why?"

His face was a mixture of embarrassment and pride. "I had one of my men watch you."

"What! Like my father did when I went to Chinese Camp? How could you do such a thing? All this time I have wanted to see you so badly I could barely stand it, but instead of seeing me yourself you sent some spy. How could you?"

"I'm sorry Ruth," Han-lin said softly. "Sorry for failing you, for not being with you myself; but I am not sorry someone was there. I have been in the city some eight weeks now, looking at what could be done to rebuild what I ... what we ... had. I feared for your safety. You never have realized the extent of my position or my enemies. I was afraid they might try to get back at me through you. It turns out my fear was well-founded."

"Well, perhaps, on this occasion ..." Ruth said, her irritation quickly placated remembering T'ang and her terrifying experience.

Han-lin continued, "My man saw the fellow bring you a note.

When you left the house, he sneaked in, hoping to find the message. Luckily, you left it on your desk, and he brought it to me.

"Of course I recognized the address. T'ang had bought that property from the broker I had sold it to. The first thing I thought of was to call on my old tong members to help. A group was here in a matter of minutes. It made me realize how much we still need each other. Perhaps the new Chinatown is not so very different from the old.

"In any case, half of them went to T'ang's house by way of the street, and the other half came with me to the tunnel, which I thought would be a good alternate approach to the house.

"We had not gone far in the tunnel when I heard you scream. We ran to you, but T'ang found you before we did. You know the rest. This episode is coming to its inevitable conclusion."

A shadow of sadness crossed Han-lin's face. "All that began one year ago must now be concluded. It was unfinished, you see. A blood battle with no clear results leaves everything out of balance. And now, the stakes are much higher.

"Back then, at that first battle with T'ang, I would have died easily, almost willingly. I had nothing to live for except a certain pleasure I felt when a rich, young woman masquerading as an English teacher would come to call at my house and intrigue me with her big green eyes and curiosity about things foreign to her. You alone were special in my life, and so far out of my reach I didn't dare to think about you. I purposefully stayed away after that first, wonderful day we spent together, trying to keep you out of my thoughts. Not that I succeeded. So I would have died without a care.

"But now I have much to live for. Much is at stake in this battle."

She reached out to touch his face, his dark, exotic eyes, his beautiful jet black hair. She didn't think she could bear it if she lost him again. "Must it be a tong battle? Is there no other way?"

"Perhaps there is; but it would not be our way. This is known to us. T'ang will uphold his part of the bargain with the children, and I will uphold mine.

"Ruth, if I lose, you will have nothing left from me, no material goods. But if you need them, the men of Yuen-li will always help you. Soo Chen-gai will care for you and do all he can for you. In that, at least, you will not be totally dependent on Winston Greer."

"I will never be dependent on my father again, not after what he has done. But that isn't important now. What is important is to stop this fight! There must be a way, some way to find those children without risking your life. We need to find them and steal them back, bribe someone, anything! I have plenty of my own money. We can use it to get the children. I will not let you fight. I'll have T'ang killed first myself! I won't let you die!"

Han-lin looked at her, his eyes softening, knowing she could never really understand, "There is the matter of face."

"Face? What do you mean face?" she sounded indignant. "Where is the honor in a hatchet fight? It's barbaric!" She had learned enough about the tongs to know her words weren't exactly true, but she would say or do anything to cut through the cold determination he felt about the battle.

"Do the implements of the duel really matter so much Ruth?" he asked. "My wife fought with me over the last battle, and then she was so afraid I would hurt her precious brother that she tricked an innocent girl into a life of misery trying to prevent it. Women want to interfere. They fear harm to those they love, and don't realize that to live without one's honor is unbearable as well. Do not interfere in this. It is necessary, and has been for over a year, since the last battle was unfinished."

"No," she insisted. "I can't let you do this Han-lin. There's more to it now, there's ..." she stopped short.

"What do you mean? What else is there?"

Ruth gave up. "Nothing." It crossed her mind to tell him her own news, but then decided not to. She would do nothing that might make him see their child as a weapon she could hold over him.

"Ruth?" he asked.

"There's love. I love you. I can't bear the thought I might lose you."

He smiled, and then stood and held out his hand to her. "For that reason, I will succeed. For you, and for my children. Come, I will take you to your father's house. Wait there until the battle is over. Word will be sent to you of the outcome."

She looked at the determination in his eyes and, as a cold numbness came over her, she understood. He must do this. It was his way, the way of the tong. All of Chinatown had wondered over his recovery from the last battle, and, as he said, they all knew the fight had not been concluded. Things were out of balance, which was unacceptable in the Chinese way. This duel must be fought.

She nodded. "This is hard for me, but I accept your way."

oOo

Han-lin rode with Ruth back to her father's house. They sat in silence the entire distance, unable to face the words that must be spoken. He knew what it cost Ruth to accept the fight that must take place. He knew that she, like all women, could not understand why the tongs would do battle, and he knew that he had to be strong against her emotions and convince her of his need to fight when called upon. But deep down, he wished she could somehow stop the battle, could convince him to do other than to fight. He loved his men, his friends, and the thought of any of their deaths in this was agony to him.

The carriage stopped at the entrance to the Greer home. Ruth turned to look at him, perhaps for the last time. Feeling her eyes upon him, he faced her.

"We must say good-bye here," he murmured.

"I know." Her voice, too, was little more than a whisper. "Is there any chance I can see you again before ..." She couldn't speak the words.

"I must remain with my men and prepare. It is necessary to prepare mentally as well as physically. We are not wanton murderers who do battle with ease. Prayers and meditation are all necessary to a successful outcome."

"That's how I imagined it would be," Ruth whispered, her eyes cast downward. "There is so much I would say to you, but now, no words come except to say I love you and I will pray every moment that you are brought safely back to me."

"Trust that I will be back, Ruth. But if I am not, if I do not return, I want you to remember that my life ended one year ago in Sullivan's Alley at that first battle. I was given a second chance, a second life if you will, when you saved me. The time I spent with you on Macondray Lane was the happiest I have ever known. If it is not allowed to continue, remember my joy at having had it at all. I have no regrets, Ruth, only thanks."

She would not allow herself to cry. She didn't want his memory of her to be one of weakness. "It was the same for me," she whispered.

"Go now. Always remember how much you are loved." He took her hands in his and held them a moment, then reached across her to open the carriage door.

Ruth straightened her shoulders and held her head high as she descended the carriage, the proud lady once again. Before turning to the house she faced Han-lin one last time, and then, placing her hands on her thighs, bowed to him in a perfect imitation of the Chinese gesture, which showed him the obedience, respect and honor she felt for him. Then she stood upright, turned and with dignity walked into the house, quietly shutting the door behind her.

CHAPTER 30

THE NEXT NIGHT Han-lin met with six members of his tong in Soo Chen-gai's apartment. They were the men chosen to meet the Wang Shao in little more than twenty-four hours. This battle would not be a show of strength as some were, where many hundreds of tong members would show up to fight. This was a battle of skill, the best seven of Yuen-li against the best seven of Wang Shao: a fight to the death for T'ang and Han-lin. Both of their honors were at stake. The American law, even were they to trust it, had no recourse to pursue a suit of revenge. Matters had to be taken into the tongs' own hands.

Now was the time to prepare. With Han-lin were Soo Chen-gai; Wong Lon-po; Pu-yin, who helped with Chang's escape; Lo Ying, an outstanding fighter; Lee Sung, a hulking Chinese, six foot six and two-hundred forty pounds of pure muscle; and Ah Ling, small but well-trained in the martial arts in China before coming to the U.S.

Soo Chen-gai's rooms were empty except for bedrolls and a few books. From the time the men entered the apartment, they would fast, except for water. At first it would be painful, they would feel hunger, but after a while the feeling would pass and what was left was an almost euphoric feeling of lightness and speed, as if they could accomplish anything they wanted to.

Along with fasting, they would read passages from the *Tao Te Ching*, the ancient Chinese book that spoke of following one's destiny, and separating oneself from the pleasures of this world. Reading the *Tao*, one could face death with peace.

But most important was the time they spent together, knowing what they were to face and why. Under the brotherhood, when one member needed help he had others to turn to. Each man was willing to give up his life for his friend; they could ask no more of each other. If one died, there would be sorrow at the death, but no regrets, for each knew the risk, and faced it willingly. If death met a man's brother one day, it could call on him the next.

Han-lin had risked his life numerous times for each of them and for others. They could do no less for him, and felt joy at being called to aid him in his dark time. Never had the stakes been so high in a battle, for this would determine the life of the tong, and possibly the lives of three innocent children.

All Chinatown was aware of the terms that the Wang Shao and Yuen-li had agreed upon; the terms were unbelievable, but the people understood why they were made, and the people would see that they were carried out, no more and no less, to the victor.

The next evening, and throughout the long night before the final battle, the men of Yuen-li did not sleep. Those who would not be in the battle went to Soo Chen-gai's apartment to await the dawn with their brethren. They knew they could be seeing each other for the last time, and although prepared for death, their hearts were heavy.

That night, Ruth, too, could not rest. It was impossible for her to try to sleep peacefully in her bed knowing that the battle would be fought in the morning. Finally, unable to stay away a moment longer, she left her parents' home and went to Chinatown. She was afraid to be near Ross Alley, the battle site. If by chance Han-lin should see her, it might disrupt his concentration. She knew enough about tong battles to understand the importance of proper preparation before, and total concentration during, the battle.

To the outside observer a tong battle took but seconds and was completed with haphazard whacks of a hatchet. To the participant, due to the complete mastery of the mind, the battle slowed to the point where milliseconds felt like minutes. Each movement was as clear and sharp as if in slow motion.

Lao-she had learned that Han-lin's children would be taken to a Christian mission on Sacramento Street run by Donaldina Cameron. Miss Cameron was trusted to be unbiased in the outcome of the battle. She could not be bribed to support one side or the other, and would protect the children until a guardian came for them.

At the moment, the mission was no more than a hastily erected structure that housed those displaced by the earthquake and fire, but already the idea of creating a permanent building was being spoken of, particularly because of the way the mission helped the women and children of Chinatown.

Ruth entered the building, and saw a surprisingly young woman, tall, heavy-boned and of rather plain demeanor. "Miss Cameron?" she asked.

"Yes." Donaldina stood, her expression registering surprise to see an elegantly dressed white woman enter her mission on such a night.

"My name is Ruth Greer. I'm a friend of Li Han-lin." Ruth paused, knowing the announcement would have meaning. "If I may, I would like to see Mr. Li's children. They know me. It's been a long time since I've seen them."

"Of course," Donaldina replied. "I can't see where that would do any harm."

Ruth nodded as she studied the New Zealander who had done so much to help Chinese women. Most San Franciscans heard the story of how Donaldina Cameron led policemen armed with axes and sledgehammers on nighttime raids to rescue girls brought from China and sold into prostitution. Donaldina was a master at finding girls hidden under floors and behind false walls, and was said to know how to make her way through the tunnels under Chinatown in her searches. Donaldina and the mission house were under constant threat, legal as well as physical, from the tongs whose women she rescued. They called her *fang quai,* the white devil. The girls, however, called her *lo mo,* or little mother.

"Miss Cameron," Ruth began, "although we've never met, I've heard of and admired your work in this community for some time. I know a young, unhappy girl, little more than a child, really, who was wickedly tricked into going to the Wang Shao tong. Her name is Mai-ching, and T'ang Tsu-shao considers her his woman. Do you think there is anything that can be done to help her?"

Donaldina raised an eyebrow in surprise at Ruth's words, then looked at the woman with some compassion, for the first time looking beyond the fancy dress to the luminous green eyes that held so much concern and grief over all that was going on around her. She patted Ruth's arm briefly before she spoke. "I knew Mai-ching. She came here to play many times when she was a child. But she is beyond our help. Her trials and sorrow are over."

Ruth stared at Donaldina in stunned silence, not wanting to believe what she was hearing.

"Mai was found dead last week. I'm very sorry. It's said she took her own life."

"My God. Do you think she really did? Or did T'ang kill her?"

Donaldina shook her head. "We'll never know for sure."

Ruth bowed her head, remembering the unhappy young woman she had met only once, but who had helped her so much. Another senseless, wasteful death, she thought. When would it end? She walked in silence to sit with the children. They didn't really under-stand what was going on, and Ruth was glad of that. The less they knew about this terrible night, the better.

In a short while, everyone in the mission bedded down, until only Ruth and Donaldina remained awake. They sat in the main room and talked long into the night. Donaldina, too, like most of Chinatown, would not sleep this night, wondering what the morning light might bring to her mission in the wake of the battle.

At one point when Donaldina seemed to doze off, Ruth quietly reached into her handbag to pull out the snub-nosed pistol she had purchased for her trip to the Sierra foothills. She placed it on her lap and covered it with her shawl. T'ang had done so much evil—to Han-lin, herself, the children, and Mai-ching—that if he were the one to walk through the door of the mission after the battle, he would find that he was not the only person who could be moved to take vengeance into his own hands over the death of a loved one.

And so Ruth, too, awaited the dawn.

CHAPTER 31

AS THE FIRST LIGHT from the morning sun lit the horizon, the seven Yuen-li fighters chosen to meet the Wang Shao donned pure white ceremonial tunics with vermilion sashes at the waist. Their sleeves were wide, and tucked within them lay their hatchets, the blades honed to sharp, strong edges. The men folded their arms within the sleeves, gripping the hatchet handles. They bowed to their friends, who stood and bowed low in return, keeping their backs bent and heads downward until the seven had left the room.

Abreast they walked down Grant Avenue to Washington Street, turning west for a half-block to Ross Alley. Shop doors and windows were locked, the streets unnaturally quiet. Even gaming parlors were shut tight. Chinatown did not sleep; it waited.

Standing at the end of Ross Alley, the men looked down the street. The Wang Shao had not yet arrived. They took their positions: Ah Ling, Pu-yin, Soo Chen-gai, Han-lin in the middle, Lee Sung, Wong Lon-po and Lo Ying. They knew T'ang's instructions to the Wang Shao were to kill Han-lin at all costs. The bulk of Lee Sung and the fearless devotion of Soo Chen-gai would provide the best and deadliest defense for him.

The Yuen-li tong's mission, besides protecting Han-lin, was to kill T'ang. Nothing less would do.

The entry to the alley at far end soon became filled with the seven

Wang Shao fighters. T'ang's men were the lowest of the *boo how doy*, literally, "hatchet boys." They were huge and ugly, and killed with guiltless, efficient ease.

The Yuen-li knew who they would face. Nonetheless, they trembled inside at the sight of these *boo how doy* and the memory of their last battle.

The Wang Shao got into position. T'ang was in the protected middle like Han-lin. Slowly, never taking an eye off the other, the two tongs walked into the alley along opposite walls. They continued until T'ang and Han-lin were aligned directly opposite each other. Both sides stopped, and all men turned to face their opponents.

They silently removed the hatchets from their sleeves, and then stood absolutely still. This was a test of nervous endurance. Each side waited for the opponent's defenses to waver. The flicker of an eye away from an opponent could trigger the attack; a split-second advantage could give a foe the edge to win. As soon as one person moved, all the others immediately sprang into battle, ready to kill or be killed.

A shift of weight or twitch of the arm had triggered battles in the past. Everyone knew it.

And so they waited.

oOo

Around the corner from Ross Alley, hidden on Washington Street, stood about a hundred additional men of Yuen-li. They were there to ensure that the Wang Shao played by the rules. If more than seven Wang Shao rushed their leader, they would be ready to protect him. On the far side of Ross Alley, on Jackson Street, an equal number of Wang Shao held the same grim vigil.

The fighters stood on both sides of Ross Alley, hatchets poised, ready to strike. Time meant nothing to them; there was only the now, only the waiting. The tension grew as every passing moment meant one of them was that much closer to making a move, or losing his guard.

Watching his opponent intently, daringly, with a blood-curdling yell, Wong Lon-po suddenly sprang forward, hatchet raised. The first move of Wong's foot sent his opponent's hatchet into the air as the two rushed at each other. Wong spun to the side and around to avoid the ax, then swung his hatchet once more. It came down, but the Wang Shao fighter was fast. The ax only slashed the air.

With Wong's initial movement, a roar filled the alley as both sides attacked the other. Like flying wedges, they left the protection of the alley walls to meet each other in the center of the street.

The two *boo how doy* who had positioned themselves next to T'ang treacherously ignored their direct opponents and instead rushed Han-lin. He would have been killed, unable to ward off blows from two directions at once were it not for Lee Sung and Soo Chen-gai who selflessly stepped in front of him. In doing so they knew they not only faced danger from the Wang Shao hatchet men, but could be stepping into a blow from behind as Han-lin's hatchet had been ready to strike. Han-lin checked his swing in time, as his men's hatchets clanged against those of the Wang Shao.

Lee Sung's hatchet hooked onto his opponent's and the two men became locked together. Lee Sung grabbed the Wang Shao with his free hand and pushed him down. As he hit the ground the Wang Shao desperately swiped with his ax, catching Lee Sung slightly off balance, and slicing a gash in his lower leg. Lee slashed at the Wang Shao, who, having regained his footing, faced the wounded Lee. It was a stand-off.

Soo Chen-gai stopped the other *boo hoy doy* rushing Li by a more direct means. He swung hard, and his hatchet sliced through flesh and bone. Chen-gai's opponent froze in horror as his arm fell to the ground, leaving only a bloody stump dangling from his shoulder. Blood shot out as the Wang Shao fighter screamed in pain and terror. He turned to run from the alley, but fell as Lo Ying's hatchet landed on his back.

Pu-yin swiped at his opponent too soon. His opponent's timing was better and his hatchet came down on Pu-yin's shoulder. The Yuen-li shuddered as they heard the shoulder blade crack loudly. Pu-yin went to the ground. The Wang Shao considered his job done and backed off when Ah Ling made it clear that he would protect the maimed Pu-yin as well as himself.

After Soo Chen-gai and Lee Sung held off the two men charging Han-lin, Han-lin expected T'ang to immediately step into their place to fight him directly. But T'ang was no longer facing him. T'ang had seemed ready to duel when the *boo how doy* first attacked; but now T'ang was gone. Han-lin felt frenzied disbelief. His eyes quickly scanned the alley, and he spotted T'ang creeping along the wall towards Jackson Street, confident that his men would dispatch Han-lin and he would be victorious. Han-lin started in pursuit.

At the end of the row of combatants nearest Jackson, Ah Ling saw T'ang heading in his direction. He knew that his main duty was to kill T'ang, regardless of his own safety. He turned from the Wang Shao he was fighting to follow T'ang. The Wang Shao wildly swung his ax, hitting Ah Ling's arm, stopping him from reaching T'ang. Despite his painful wound, Ah Ling leaped and turned in fury at his attacker, coming down with a death blow. A forceful stream of blood gushed out of the gaping hole where the Wang Shao's neck and shoulder had once joined.

T'ang slackened his step for one instant as the blood from his ally splashed out at him. That instinctive reaction caused him to see Han-lin's approach. He swung his ax at Han-lin, but swung too soon, missing his foe. The instant T'ang's blade swiped past him, Han-lin took a step forward and swung hard, waist level, at Tang. The blade caught T'ang in mid-belly.

T'ang gazed in astonishment at Han-lin, then watched in frozen horror as his entrails and other gore began to spill from the deep wound. He grabbed at his stomach, trying to hold himself together as he staggered a few more steps towards the end of the alley. He dropped onto his knees, his eyes open, his expression etched in with pain and terror, as his insides slid out of him and he fell to the ground mortally wounded. The sickly sweet smell of blood and death filled the street.

The death of T'ang was a signal for the other Wang Shao to back off from the fight. As soon as they took their first, cautious steps backwards, the Yuen-li men stopped all pursuit. They knew their victory was complete.

Han-lin watched the fleeing Wang Shao disappear. He turned to survey the alley. T'ang and two of his *boo how doy* lay dead. Pu-yin was badly bleeding; Soo Chen-gai, Lee Sung, and Ah Ling were wounded.

Han-lin threw down his hatchet in disgust and walked to the side of the fallen Pu-yin. Wong Lon-Po came to the other side and together they carried Pu-yin out of the alley to the cheers of the Yuen-li men waiting on the next street.

Chinatown now knew who was victorious in the battle, and soon the word began to spread.

A doctor was waiting at Soo Chen-gai's apartment as the men arrived. Han-lin sat with each man as the doctor tended the wounds until he knew every man, with time, would recover.

Only then did he remove the blood-stained clothes he wore and cleanse himself from the filth of the battle.

Although exhausted, he had more to do before he could rest that day. He quickly wrote out a note and gave it to a driver to take to the house in Pacific Heights. As he handed it to the man, he heard a familiar voice behind him, "May I have the honor of carrying that message for you?"

He turned quickly, recognizing the voice, but not believing it. "Chang!" He put his arms around his old servant and hugged him.

Chang bowed, overjoyed at Han-lin's reception of him. "I didn't like Los Angeles, my lord. I thought, with all the other troubles up here, the police wouldn't be after me anymore. If you will have me, I'd like to come back to work for you."

"You heard about the battle." Han-lin spoke of the real reason Chang had chosen to return.

The older man nodded. "Yes, I wanted to be near in case I could help in any way."

"You are always welcome in my house, Chang." With that, he gave Chang the message for Ruth.

Li gathered some men with him and, with fondness, bade the others farewell. They got in coaches for the ride up the steep side of Sacramento Street to the mission site.

Things were stirring in the mission already. At the crack of dawn many of the children began to awaken, and were soon up and about, playing and waking everyone else.

The three Li children sat in the office with Ruth and Donaldina Cameron. They had not been told what had happened, so they sat and waited. Finally, there was a noise outside, the sound of horses and carriages approaching. Ruth sat bolt upright as Donaldina walked to open the front door.

She stood expressionless with the door open, looking out of it, as two unrecognized Chinese men approached the building first. They entered the office, looked about, then turned and signaled to the others.

Donaldina turned to smile at Ruth while she opened the door wider. Ruth knew then who she would see enter the room. In walked Han-lin.

"Father!" the children yelled as they rushed towards him.

Han-lin dropped to his knees to better hold them and look at them. He gathered them to him and kissed them, thankful that they were with him again.

Donaldina approached Ruth and whispered to her, "You can put the gun away now."

Ruth looked at the woman in surprise. "You knew?"

"Oh yes, I knew. But, could you have actually used it?"

Ruth paused a moment, her mind reflecting on the thought of T'ang walking through the door, knowing that would have meant Han-lin lay dead. "Yes," she whispered.

Donaldina just nodded her head and studied the younger woman. "You have guts, Ruth. If you ever want to channel some of that, I could use a little help. I expect I'll be here a long, long time, so keep me in mind."

"I'll never forget you," Ruth said, then hugged the other woman for her kindness and for helping her through the long night. "Thank you, Donaldina, for everything. I'll be back one day, I promise."

Han-lin had risen and looked at Ruth. Because the men of his tong watched, he only nodded briefly to her, and then thanked Donaldina for watching his children, placing a very large donation in the tray as Ruth took the hands of the younger children and followed Han-lin to the awaiting coach.

As soon as the carriage door shut Ruth was in Han-lin's arms. "Thank God," she cried, kissing him, touching his head, his face, his arms and holding him to her the while. "How did it go? Your men, your friends—are they all right?"

"We were lucky, no Yuen-li was killed. T'ang is dead, and two of his men. It was all quite senseless."

"But T'ang is dead! It's over. We can have peace."

"No, there will always be another T'ang—someone else who wants to fight for whatever reason, real or imaginary, he may find."

Ruth knew the truth of his words and shuddered inwardly. All of a sudden, all the pieces fell together, and she understood all he had been saying to her for so long. "So many deaths, and yet there will be more to come. That's what you've been trying to tell to me for a long time now, isn't it, Han-lin? That tongs exist to protect their members, but that protection means that everyone is also vulnerable. One man's cause becomes everyone's cause; one man's wrong act means revenge can be taken on anyone. It is a constant struggle, isn't it, to protect others as well as oneself and one's family; to have the security of the group, but also the insecurity of being part of that same group."

He nodded. "That is what I've wanted you to understand, so that you can better decide if you want to come with me, knowing the life I offer. I have men working on rebuilding the house on Macondray Lane, making it bigger and stronger than it was. It's not quite finished, but it is livable. The foundation was strong so it went up quickly. I can't help but think I am being selfish, and unfair to you, knowing you could have a much brighter, easier future with some rich American. But if you will come there to live with me and my three children, I'll spend my life doing all I can to make sure you never regret it."

"Four," she said shyly.

"Four?" Han-lin repeated looking confused until he realized what she was telling him and then looked simultaneously stunned and elated. But almost as quickly his expression changed, and he looked at her intently, "How do you feel about it?"

She smiled. "That it's wonderful, and that I am truly fortunate. Are you sorry this has happened, Han-lin?"

"Sorry? No, never! But I'm afraid this child will have a difficult life —never quite in your world or in mine; never quite accepted anywhere."

"Maybe someday, the world will change and see that good can come from a child like ours."

He drew her close. "For the sake of the child and your honor, we should marry. Since we can't in California, there are other countries we can go to. China, Hong Kong, or maybe Singapore or islands in the South Pacific."

She smiled and hugged him. "Only if we can get an attorney to find a loophole in the Chinese Exclusion Act so that you'll be able to return home with me! And while we're there, we can make contacts for our new shipping business."

He shook his head. "You are truly the ever practical one."

"Someone has to be," she teased. But then her smile vanished and she became serious again. "If it's important to you, Han-lin, we'll find some way to marry and to deal with the strange laws of this country. And maybe someday, there will no longer be such laws. But in my heart, know that you are my husband, and no law can ever say otherwise."

"Until death do us part, Ruth," he said and kissed her gently.

"Until death do us part," she repeated softly.

Fear of that death coming far too soon was something she would carry all the days of their life together. She wrapped her arms around him as if to protect him with her body if need be, and nestled her head on his shoulder. To be leader of the tong was his life, and so it was now her life as well.

Soon, involuntarily, she found herself shutting her eyes as the fatigue from the night before swept over her, and she was finally able to relax, knowing Han-lin was beside her and would not leave her again.

He watched with admiration as she controlled her fears and accepted the life he offered. The coach rolled slowly towards their new home. Tong leader, murderous hatchet man, he held his woman by his side, and smiled at the three children in the coach. He looked forward to a life with them of peace and safety, and could only pray that it would be so. The tong gave him this, and to it, he would give his all.

EPILOGUE

*L*ATER THAT DAY a white passerby saw a suspicious bulk in an alleyway in Chinatown and called the police. Upon investigation the police found three Chinese men, mid-to-late thirties, who had apparently died of hatchet blows. The newspapers had a field day with cries and howls that the Chinatown fire had not managed to burn out the pestilence known as tongs, and that the bodies were a sure sign that the tongs were as strong, and perhaps even stronger, than ever.

Politicians raged that every member of every tong should be rounded up by the police and summarily executed, or at least deported, for their violent, inhuman ways.

After about three days of questioning people to no avail, the police set aside their investigation of the deaths. They quickly and simply decided the matter probably meant nothing, a random act of violence for no reason, with no forethought, and no justification.

The incident became simply another of the many meaningless, unsolved killings in Chinatown, a mysterious part of the city that no one of any importance cared about or understood.

As for Han-lin and Ruth, soon after they moved into their new home on Macondray Lane, they began to work on establishing a shipping business. It quickly grew into one of the largest and most respected in the Pacific trade. They traveled many times to ports throughout Asia, including to Hong Kong where they were married, but were always happy to return home to San Francisco. They had three children, two girls and a boy. Their son, Jacob, took over the business with his half-brother, Pao-yang, when their parents grew too old to run it. Their oldest daughter, May, became a doctor and worked in Chinatown, and their youngest daughter, Elizabeth, became an attorney heavily involved in Chinese immigration law.

Of Han-lin and Li Jun's other two children, their son died in 1919 during the world-wide flu epidemic, and their daughter moved to Singapore with her husband.

To Han-lin's amazement, given the struggles of his early years and the battles he had been in, he lived to be age 81 and died peacefully in his bed. His funeral was one of the largest Chinatown had ever seen, causing the white population of the city to wonder why so many people turned out for the quiet businessman.

Ruth spent much of her life, particularly her later years, supporting the woman who had become her best friend, Donaldina Cameron. She was one of the most generous benefactors to the Presbyterian Mission that did so much over the years to help Chinese immigrants, and she was there when the Chinese community honored Donaldina by renaming the mission building Cameron House.

Ruth died at age 92, surrounded by children, grandchildren, and great-grandchildren. She had lived a full life, filled with more adventure and love than she had ever imagined possible. But throughout all of it, she never forgot that everything came about only because, one day, she decided to help a sad little boy return to his home in the intriguing part of the city known as Chinatown.

- The End -

The Chinese Exclusion Act was signed into law on May 6, 1882. It effectively halted Chinese immigration and prohibited Chinese from becoming US citizens. The law was repealed in 1943 during World War II, when China was an ally in the war against imperial Japan, however, the 1943 act allowed only 105 Chinese immigrants per year. Not until the Immigration Act of 1965, which eliminated previous national-origins policy, did that large-scale Chinese immigration to the United States begin again after a hiatus of over 80 years.

California's Anti-Miscegenation Law was first enacted in 1850, and expanded in 1905 to declare "illegal and void" all marriages between whites and "Mongolians" (the term used by the legislature for people of Asian descent). The California Supreme Court declared the law unconstitutional in 1948 (*Perez v. Sharp*). In 1967, the U.S. Supreme Court declared all state laws that limited, based on race, who one could marry violated constitutional guarantees of equal protection (*Loving v. Virginia*).

Those who wish to learn more about the behind-the-scenes struggle over the rebuilding of Chinatown, might wish to look at my short study of it entitled "The Battle for Chinatown." A number of maps of the area in 1900 are included. More information on Donaldina Cameron can be found at www.cameronhouse.org, and in biographical studies of her life. For photos of Chinatown just before and after the 1906 San Francisco Earthquake, you could do no better than to turn to the fabulous photographs of Arnold Genthe which can be found in numerous books and museums.

PLUS ...

To find out more about Joanne Pence's books, visit her website at www.joannepence.com and be sure to sign up for her newsletter.

If you enjoyed this historical romance by Joanne Pence, you might also enjoy her emotional historical romance set in Arizona. *Dance with a Gunfighter* is the story of a young woman forced by tragedy to grow up far too soon. It is a Willa Cather Literary Award finalist for Best Historical Novel. Here's the first chapter:

DANCE WITH A GUNFIGHTER

Jackson City, Arizona Territory, 1876

Disappointment rolled over her like dark thunderclouds, but sixteen-year old Gabriella Devere refused to acknowledge it. The same stiff smile that had been fixed to her sun-bronzed face throughout the music-playing remained, even as she stood alone at the edge of the outdoor dance area and watched Johnny Anderson, the handsomest boy in school, kick up his heels with Molly Pritchard.

Gabe squeezed her arms tight against her waist and thrust out her bottom lip.

Johnny Anderson was nothing but a scrawny turkey, and she

didn't give a darn who he danced with. Yet she couldn't tear her gaze from him, and every skip he took vibrated in the pit of her stomach.

Two weeks and five hours ago she had begun to count the minutes until this dance. She had returned home from riding her gray, Maggie, and was walking her into the stables, just as she'd done day after day, year after year.

She had been looking back at Maggie, pulling the mare's head around, and giving her a tug as she'd reached out blindly to open the stable door, only to find that it had been opened for her. Standing inside, smiling at her, was Johnny Anderson. He was tall and thin with light brown hair. The sleeves of his shirt seemed to have too much material in width and too little in length because skinny brown arms jutted out from the ends of the cuff.

"Hi, there," he said.

Her eyebrows popped up high in surprise, and her heart fluttered strangely. His eyes had a sparkle to them, and his teeth, she noticed when he smiled, were pearly white. "Nice mare, you got," he added. She felt herself go hot and cold, and her tongue seemed to choose that very moment to attach itself securely to the roof of her mouth.

"I'm all set, Johnny!" Her brother Chad barreled out of the stable leading his gelding. Chad's hair was black, his skin tanned a golden hue. Gabe knew the older girls whispered about his being handsome. She couldn't see it. Especially not when he stood beside Johnny Anderson. "Gabe, get out of the way!"

She stepped back. "Where're you going?"

"Quail-hunting." They mounted their horses and started toward the road. "Be back at dinner."

"Can I come?" She chased after them, unsure where she found the boldness to ask to go anywhere with Johnny Anderson.

Her brother laughed and waved her off as he broke into a canter. Johnny smiled and shrugged. She watched until the two boys disappeared at the bend in the road.

Her breath was short, her head giddy, all because of Johnny Anderson's smile.

Now, she stood at a section of the dusty street just past the church where the edge of the town met the desert had been roped off for the dance. Tables filled with canned peach and custard pies, prickly pear candy, plum preserves, molasses and sugar cookies, lemon punch, and apple cider were set up along one edge, and near them, on a raised platform, four fiddlers played. Paper lanterns ringed the area, casting a warm, festive glow into the summer night.

Gabe was certain Johnny would ask her to dance soon. The excitement, the anticipation that had seized her when she awoke that morning continued to course through her. Finally, Jackson City was holding a dance she had looked forward to instead of wanting to avoid. Finally, she would have a chance to talk to, and dance with, Johnny Anderson.

oOo

Jess McLowry pushed open the slatted wooden half-doors of the Red Lizard. He needed a bottle of Jim Beam, a high-stakes game of five-card stud, and an accommodating woman. Eventually he might eat, but he was a man who kept his priorities straight.

A plank oak bar stretched along one wall, gleaming like a snake caught in a hailstorm. A white-haired, ruddy-faced prospector stood at one end, his clothes baggy and his skin powdered with rock dust. Shaky hands gripped a shot glass, and the old codger seemed to be concentrating hard to aim it at his mouth. Behind the bar, over rows of liquor bottles and beer kegs, a gilt-framed portrait of a bare-assed woman smiled onto the room. She was the liveliest thing in it.

Wooden tables with empty chairs filled the space between the bar and the opposite wall. No hurdy-gurdy music. No cards. No women. Not even a raucous crew of drunken cowhands.

The barkeep, a balding man with reddened skin and a bulbous stomach squared his shoulders and nodded a quick, cautious greeting. His gaze darted from McLowry's tied down holster, to his black satin vest, to his butter smooth black walking boots.

McLowry moved with a deceptively slow and easy stride. He plunked a gold dollar on the bar. Hard blue eyes scanned the liquor bottles. There wasn't a label in sight. "Whiskey." He watched as it was poured. The moonshine was raw and harsh, but he drank it down fast, needing to wash away the sour taste of his last job. He was a hired gun. He had learned one thing long ago about his kind of work, the men hiring him were every bit as bad as the ones he was paid to fight against. The only difference was that they were rich bastards instead of poor ones.

The barkeep wiped down the bar over and over with a blue-checkered cloth, not that it was wet or dirty, but as a means to give him something to do while keeping an eye on McLowry.

"This place looks like a morgue." McLowry pushed his empty glass forward.

"Town dance down the street. Regular customers are all there." Tossing the cloth over his shoulder, the barkeep poured another drink. "This isn't the kind of town you'd be interested in anyway, gunfighter. You might think about moving on." He stepped back quickly, as if ready to duck if the man before him took offense at the suggestion.

Instead, McLowry ignored him. He took a sip, then put one elbow on the bar, easing against it as he scoured the place. The old man hunched over the bar nodded at him, then picked up his drink, one-handed this time. The hand shook and some rye sloshed onto his fingers. From the shadows, a dance-hall woman slowly strolled toward McLowry, swinging her hips. She stopped a little ways from him, answering his bored gaze with a feigned smile.

Her face was heavily powdered, her eyelids covered with kohl, and the thick orange cream on her lips had smeared and run down along the corners of her mouth, giving her the appearance of a sad-faced clown.

McLowry pushed aside his drink and slapped more money on the bar. Holding the barkeep's eye, he pointed at the rye bottle then the old man. As the barkeep nodded, McLowry cleared out of there. He'd come to town for action, not a wake.

With his thumbs hooked on the heavy cartridge belt that held the greased open holster the barkeep had found so fascinating, he surveyed Main Street from one end to the other. The town was smaller than most. General store. Barber. Tobacconist. Saddle shop. Tin shop. Livery stable. Hotel. But there wasn't another saloon in sight. What kind of shit hole town was this, anyway? The only commotion along the entire street was at the far end, near the church.

A town dance. They were too damn sissified for him. Still, he was sick of doing nothing but counting stars at night. His empty hotel room was uninviting, its smell musty and dank from stale sex and rotgut liquor of patrons past. Maybe at the dance he would get lucky and find a woman wise enough not to take him to heart when he whispered the sort of words women liked to hear. Right now, he didn't care if she looked like a schoolmarm, as long as she was warm and willing.

He spun the cylinder of a snub-nosed Remington single-action pistol to make sure it was fully loaded, then tucked it into the small, flat shoulder holster he wore hidden under his black satin vest. He might be asked to check his six-shooter at the dance, but that didn't mean he would let himself go unarmed.

His boot heels made a hollow sound on the empty boardwalk as he turned down the street, toward the dance.

oOo

From the time Gabe had sprung out of bed early that morning she had done her best to hide her excitement from her father and brothers. Chad was seventeen, and Henry was already nineteen. Being the only female in the family wasn't easy, and with two older brothers who enjoyed nothing quite so much as teasing her, Gabe had learned to do all she could to give them as few chances for ridicule as possible.

She had been cool as a night breeze in the desert as she fired up the cookstove, ground some coffee, and then fried eggs, sausage and cornmeal mush to have hot on the table when the men came in from tending to the horses and milking the cows. As soon as she finished cleaning up the kitchen after breakfast, she ran into her small back bedroom and changed to the new dress she'd worked on from the time she decided to attend the dance. Her pa knew what she was up to, but so far she had managed to keep the dress a secret from her prying older brothers.

The house had four rooms--a kitchen, a bedroom for Pa, one shared by Chad and Henry, and a tiny room, scarcely bigger than a closet, for her. Long ago her pa had planned to add a parlor and maybe even a dining room, but after her ma had died, his heart went out of the idea. Instead, he focused his attention away from homey things, and put all his energy into running the ranch and growing his stock each year. Household chores were left to Gabe.

As had happened each of the past two years since Jackson City was founded, the celebration would start with the mayor and councilmen giving speeches, followed by games, a picnic supper, and finally, the town dance. Gabe would need to somehow keep her dress nice for the dance throughout the long, hot afternoon. Normally, she didn't much care how she looked, and would join in on the fun and games. Last year, she had surprised everyone--including herself--by winning the long rifle shooting competition. This year, though, she decided not to enter. She had better things on her mind than shooting cow pies.

The day was already warm and the buckboard loaded with the supper basket when time came to leave the ranch for the five-mile ride to Jackson City. She knew her pa and brothers were waiting for her. Usually, she was the first one ready to go. Usually, she wore denim trousers and a chambray shirt. But then, other girls wore dresses--especially to dances--so why shouldn't she?

When she awkwardly stepped out of the house onto the front porch wearing her new yellow dress, thin-soled brown leather shoes, and with a yellow ribbon in her hair, her brothers gawked at her in silence. That was a real bad sign. As she suspected, when they got over being speechless, they pointed and catcalled, and Chad laughed so hard he tumbled right off the buckboard. Her cheeks flushed red and she gave serious thought to running inside and hiding under the bed when she heard her pa shout, "Stop it, you two!"

Then he climbed down off the buckboard, and walked to the bottom step of the porch. He looked at her a long moment and then held out his hand. The proud beam in his eyes made her throat tighten. "My baby's growing into a beautiful young lady," he said softly. "Just like your ma was."

She smiled, and clutched his hand tight as he led her to the buckboard. Her brothers simply gaped from her to their pa. She was sure they were trying to decide which was the more addled.

Her pa hied the horses and they were off. The anticipation that had crackled through her and filled the morning air swelled even more. She felt like a cat whose back had been rubbed over and over with velvet until the fur stood on end. Tonight something special was going to happen, she just knew it. Something new and exciting. Something like—if she was very, very lucky—Johnny Anderson asking her to dance.

Her father had been the first to comment on her grown-up looks, and she had been touched and even a little overwhelmed by his compliment. Her heart had filled with love, as it always did, for the hard-working man who had been both father and mother to her almost as long as she could remember, and who always knew the right word to say.

Her pa's words and a sense of expectation stayed with her throughout the afternoon ceremonies dedicating Jackson City's new town hall and through the games and picnic afterward. She could hardly wait for the dance, for Johnny Anderson to take notice of her. Her tumult over what was to come grew into a full-fledged uproar as the day wore on.

Until the day of Johnny's smile, no boy had ever bothered to take notice of her unless his horse was ailing. The whole town knew she had the touch with horses and often came to her for help. She hadn't cared if the boys were mindful of her or not. That is, not until Johnny noticed her that day.

Would Preacher Carson be angry if he were to learn she'd prayed to dance with Johnny Anderson? How could emotions like Johnny stirred in her be sinful when they felt so divine?

But now, as she stood alone at the dance, she wondered if such passions had been wicked, because she surely was facing retribution. So far, Johnny hadn't even glanced her way.

Even worse, her pa had been the only person to ask her to dance. Dancing with one of her brothers, Henry or Chad, was the only thing that would have been more humiliating. Her worst enemy in school, Louisa Zilpher, must have been as pleased by this embarrassment as a donkey with a bucket of fresh oats.

Not that she cared a hoot what a prissy fluff like Louisa Zilpher thought anyway.

The music ended and Johnny Anderson gripped Molly Pritchard's elbow as he escorted her back to her mother's side. He was such a gentleman! He spun on the heel of his polished boots, surprisingly free of dust despite whirling about on the dirt dance floor. Even *dust* knew better than to grime up Johnny Anderson.

To her astonishment, he started walking toward her.

She felt her breath rush into her lungs, but it didn't come back out again. Her heart hammered against her ribs and she leapfrogged between blushing and shivering with each approaching step he took.

He was so close she could almost see the chip on his otherwise perfect front teeth. She was sure she would keel over in a dead faint. All the witty words and gentile mannerisms she had planned for their meeting flew from her head. What should she do? What should she say?

"Hiya," he said, and continued right past her to the refreshment tables behind her. There, two girls rushed to his side.

Her breath came out all at once. The crowded dance floor shimmered and blurred. When it cleared, she saw Molly Pritchard staring at her. Then Molly's whole body began to shake with laughter.

Gabe's cheeks blazed. She turned around and ran from the dance before Molly or anyone else saw the tears that fell.

oOo

Near the dance, lit by lanterns, a proud banner stretched across the dust of Main Street, from the peaked roof of the tobacconist to the false-front roof of the dry goods store. "Jackson City, Arizona Territory, September 5, 1876."

McLowry gave a snort of ridicule. He'd seen a number of two-bit towns come and go in this barren wilderness. Mostly go. The foolish optimism of men never ceased to amaze him.

As he neared the dance, he noticed some movement near the livery stable. He eased from the moonlight into the darkness of a doorway, his palm against the ivory handle of his six-shooter.

The silhouette of a dress came into view. A woman, out here alone. She stood at the entrance to the stables. He mused as to whether she had come out here to meet someone. Stables made great trysting places. He had known a few rolls in the hay himself. Or maybe the woman was just hoping a stranger might come along....

Gabe stood outside the stable door. She wasn't hiding from the revelers at the dance. Not at all. She was simply anxious to go home. The dance had bored her, that was all. No big surprise, there. The past two weeks she had been fooling herself with childish high hopes and bewildering anticipation about tonight. Hah! She would know better next time--if there'd ever be a next time. Her pa and brothers would show up here at the family's buckboard eventually, and she could go back to the ranch where she belonged. At least her pa's horses wouldn't laugh at her, even though everyone else seemed to.

Absent-mindedly, she reached for the pocket where she always carried a few oats for the horses at the ranch, but stopped herself when she felt the thin, cotton material of her dress. When she wore trousers, shirts and vests like her brothers, she could carry all the things she needed. She despised this dress and she hated herself for bothering to get gussied up like one of those town girls with all their lady-like airs. She felt like a roadrunner sporting eagle feathers.

Tears stung her eyes, but she wouldn't let them fall. The thought of how she had run, crying, from the dance made her mad enough to spit. She would never demean herself that way again. Never!

She yanked the yellow ribbon from her hair and threw it on the ground, then ran her fingers through her short, curly strands, letting them loose to cap her head the way they usually did. She didn't care if her hair was ugly--or if she was ugly. She didn't care at all.

She blinked hard. She would *not* let herself cry any more. Still, she couldn't help but remember how time and again Louisa Zilpher's mother, among other busy-bodies, had told her pa to make her grow her hair long, to force her to wear dresses like a "proper" young lady, to stop swearing like her brothers and to stop running wild like some tomboy. Just because her mother was dead, the town biddies thought her pa needed their advice in raising her. They didn't consider it ladylike for her to doctor horses either, although they surely hotfooted it to her door for help when all else failed.

She had nearly burst with pride, love and gratitude the day she overheard her pa telling Mrs. Zilpher he would find Gabe proper even if she were bald and dressed in sackcloth. Battle-ax Zilpher left in a snit.

Her older brother Henry's interest in Louisa Zilpher was nothing less than the worst sort of familial betrayal.

With a loud sigh, Gabe leaned against the outside wall of the stable. The scrap of yellow ribbon she had thrown away lay at her feet and beside it was a cigarette. It looked like someone had rolled it, taken a puff or two, and then tamped it out before going into the stable.

Proper ladies never smoked. Mrs. Zilpher turned green at the mere smell of tobacco. Gabe picked up the cigarette and tore off the charred tip. Just holding it made her think of Preacher Carson's warnings about the road to damnation.

She should toss it away. Her pa and Henry smoked every evening after supper. She would clear the table and make coffee, then they'd all go out and sit on the porch. Her pa would lean back in his rocking chair and look at the stars while talking to her and her brothers about all kinds of things, but particularly about the ranch and his plans for building the few head of cattle they owned into a thriving business. To sit on the porch on warm evenings, watching brilliant desert sunsets, listening to the security and promise of her pa's voice, were the happiest minutes of her day.

She had always wondered, though, watching her pa and older brother's obvious pleasure, how a cigarette would taste. Louisa Zilpher didn't know and never would. The same for Molly Pritchard. Maybe not even Johnny Anderson …

Just the thought of him made her heart ache once more.

Inside the door of the stable a tin match holder hung on the wall. She plucked out one of the matches and hurried clear of the building. Shoving her skirt to one side, she balanced on one foot and struck the match against the bottom of her shoe, nearly toppling over as she did.

The match burst into flame. Holding the cigarette to her lips, she slowly brought the match closer. As it touched the tip, she sucked on the cigarette as if it were a straw. A hot, ragged, burning sensation filled her mouth and lungs.

Shaking out the match was all she could do before she dropped the cigarette and doubled over in a spasm of coughing. Her eyes, nose and throat burned so badly she was sure she was dying.

A man's laughter broke through her coughing and gasping, and at the same time someone took hold of her arm and whacked her hard on the back.

"Damn it!" she yelled. She tried to pull free, groping blindly, her eyes tearing too heavily to open them.

"Smoke's got to get out so you can breathe." The man had a pleasant Southern accent and voice she couldn't place. He slapped her back a few more times. Finally, her eyes began to clear.

"Enough!" she cried.

"Are you all right?" he asked, still holding her arm.

His words were kind, but Gabe heard the laughter in his inflection. Now, even strangers mocked her! She was sick of being laughed at. "Get your filthy hands off me or you'll be sorry!"

Raising his hands in mock horror, the man backed away from her. He shimmered in a teary-eyed haze. She coughed, blinking hard, until she could make him out in the moonlight. He was tall, with a rangy slimness and broad shoulders. A black, flat-crowned Stetson worn low on his brow shadowed eyes that were no more than a hard gleam.

His hair was long in back, fair in color, and wavy as a whittler's chips. A gold-colored mustache spanned the width of his upper lip and curved down along-side deeply tanned cheeks. Noticing it, she noticed, too, that he was still grinning at her discomfort.

She frowned at the cigarette, then stepped on it to put it out. "I must have smoked it wrong."

"I would say so." He stood loose and easy watching her, shoulders sloped, one thumb hooked on his pocket.

Her gaze followed his long, slender hand to his gun-belt and tied-down holster. Holsters were tied down for one reason—so the guns in them could be drawn fast.

Quickly, she raised her eyes, meeting his. "Who are you?"

"Just someone passing though." His mouth curved into a smile, but it didn't reach his eyes. A shiver touched her spine. Instinctively, she knew he wouldn't tell more. He was secretive, this stranger, and had a comfort with the night that gave her pause. She studied him with frank interest.

"Haven't you been taught that young ladies don't smoke?" His accent, with the softness of the South, was mellow and educated sounding, not the quick, nasal slur she was used to hearing around Jackson City.

"Hell," she muttered. "I don't give a cayoot's damn what young ladies do."

His grin widened. "Young ladies don't swear either."

She casually shrugged. "I've never been mistaken for one yet."

He cocked his head. "Your mother'll take a switch to you if she hears you say things like that, miss, especially to a man. In a few years, he just might mistake your meaning."

He jus' maht mistake yoah meanin'. She didn't think sassafras molasses could be any smoother. She folded her arms. "My ma's dead, so I don't have to worry. And as for men, I don't give a fig what they think."

He laughed, but cut it short and caught her eye instead. He seemed to study her, as she did him, but she couldn't imagine why he bothered. He placed a foot on the water trough and leaned forward, resting his elbow on his thigh. With his thumb, he tilted back his hat.

For the first time she could see that his eyes were light blue and that his face was rather pleasing...which surprised her since he didn't at all resemble Johnny Anderson.

"I guess," he said softly, his drawl coating his words, "that's why you're out here swiping cigarettes instead of at the dance."

A pang hit her stomach and twisted. She spun away from him, her arms crossed, and her back stiff. "I do as I please. Not that it's any business of yours, *stranger*."

"Are you waiting for someone?" he asked. "Maybe expecting a beau to come along and give you a kiss?"

Her cheeks flamed. Peering at him over her shoulder, she frowned at him for all she was worth, hoping he would have the decency to go away and leave her alone here at the stables with her father's buckboard and the ranch horses. "Like hell!" she said. "I don't have anything to do with the boys around here."

He lowered his foot to the ground and straightened. She thought she saw his mouth twitch, as if he were thinking about laughing at her again. She turned to face him square on and frowned harder. Just let him try it.

"You fancy yourself a tough little miss, don't you?"

She raised her chin. "I have no fancies about anything."

"Do you dance?"

"Of course I do." She smoothed the skirt of her yellow dress. "But there's no one I wish to dance with." Her chin went up even higher to show him how little the dance mattered to her. She walked a few steps away, hoping that would make it clear to this pesky stranger that any conversation with him was ended.

McLowry watched her go, and only when her back was turned did he allow the grin he had been fighting for the past few minutes, ever since she had first raised that small, defiant chin in a gesture of complete bravado. From the time she had struck the match and it lit up a gamin-like face with huge dark eyes, a bow-shaped mouth and a straight nose dusted with freckles, he had seen she was far too young and innocent for him. Still, he couldn't help but wonder what she was doing out here and what had her so obviously upset.

He had figured it out now. He recognized the symptoms, and remembered enough of his own awkwardness as a youth to grasp the real story here. He had bet anything the right boy hadn't asked her to dance, or maybe nobody had danced with her. He could see where boys her age might ignore this girl.

She was pretty in an offbeat way. Her wide, brown eyes were warm and friendly, eyes that carried her feelings right up front where the world could see them. He guessed she was only fourteen, fifteen or so. Her body was slender, but he could discern a budding woman's figure. She carried herself with a bold, sassy assurance that probably scared the boys she knew half to death. Young men usually thought delicate, doll-like creatures were the only girls worth pursuing. They had a lot to learn.

He had learned plenty about women and other equally dangerous things in his twenty-three, or so, years. He had stopped counting a long time ago. With all he had seen and done in life, he felt he should be about a hundred.

He took out his tobacco and began to build a cigarette. "What's your name?" he asked.

"Gabe."

"Gabe?" He couldn't stop the grin this time. "I can't see calling a girl by a boy's name."

"Nobody's asked you to."

Well, that put him in his place all right. "That's true."

"My full name's Gabriella," she announced.

"That's pretty." He lit his cigarette.

Her mouth tightened. "I gave a fat lip to the last person who called me by it."

"I'll keep that in mind, *Gabe*," he replied with great seriousness.

Slowly, her mouth spread into a grin.

Fiddlers began playing a fast-paced quadrille. She clutched one elbow and turned toward the music, a wistful expression flickering across her face before she faced him once more. "Do you have a name?" she asked.

"This week it's Jess McLowry."

One eyebrow rose. "And next?"

"Depends on how much trouble Jess McLowry gets into."

He watched her initial incredulity turn into amusement as she gave him a sidelong glance, one that would have been flirtatious if it were given by a woman a little older, a little more experienced. "I see." Her voice was almost a whisper and sounded suddenly knowing in a way that jarred him.

She was at that age where girls are an odd mixture of child and woman, and changed from one to the other quicker than the colors change in a desert sunset.

McLowry tore his gaze from her and looked up at the clear night sky. He had been at a mining camp on his last job. Clearly, he had spent too long there if a slip of a girl like this could give him pause.

The moon was full tonight and the stars bright. Night fell suddenly in the desert. One minute the mountains and rocks were orange, gold and red, and the next, the sun was gone and starlight turned the land a glistening silver. People said desert nights could drive a man a little crazy. McLowry figured maybe they were right.

He gazed in the direction of the music, then dropped the cigarette and crushed it with his heel. It was time to head for the dance and find himself a full-fledged, no-doubt-about-it woman, instead of wasting time with this saucy-mouthed kid.

"Go ahead," Gabe said. "I don't need a chaperone."

His eyes snapped back at her. Had he heard right? Chaperone? Up until now, he had always prided himself as being a reason for a young lady's chaperone, not as being one. The thought gave him a chill, as if he had been poked in the gut by the finger of Old Age.

He cleared his throat and turned to leave, but as he did, he noticed the yellow hair ribbon lying in the dust. She had tried to make herself look pretty for these pudding heads, and ended up standing alone by the stables. He stared at it a little too long before he glanced back at her—at her firm chin and the defiant flare of her nostrils, at the hint of hurt and loneliness in her eyes. Hell, she wasn't his problem. He straightened his Stetson. What did he know or care about young girls anyway?

The expression on her face as she gazed toward the dance captured him. She wore the look of the outsider—the one who longed to be included, but was too awkward, or too poor, or had spent too much time on the wrong side of the law, to ever be accepted. He knew all about that feeling.

For some foolish reason he didn't want this girl to see herself that way. He didn't want her to face that kind of isolation.

"Gabe," he said, sure he had lost his mind, "would you walk back to the dance with me?"

Her eyes widened with astonishment. "What?"

He held out his hand. "May I escort you to the dance?"

She stared at his slender, fine-boned hand—not the hand of a working man or a cowboy. Temptation flickered across her face, but also hesitation. "You're just playing with me," she said finally.

He smiled, thinking about her tender age. "Not likely."

Cautiously, she reached her hand toward his. He took hold of it and could almost feel her let go of the breath she had held. The smile she gave him dazzled, and he felt himself rocked by its force.

He stood absolutely still as he held her soft, slim hand in his. He couldn't remember the last time a young, innocent girl held his hand. Her open, good-natured trust in him as she stepped closer touched something deep within him. Something he had thought had died many, many years before.

Using the manners he had been taught in another time, another world, he shifted her hand to the crook of his arm and escorted her down Main Street to the dance as if she were an elegant lady, and he, a most proper gentleman.

Continue with Dance with a Gunfighter wherever fine books and e-books are sold.

ABOUT THE AUTHOR

Joanne Pence was born and raised in northern California. She has been an award-winning, *USA Today* best-selling author of mysteries for many years, but she has also written historical fiction, contemporary romance, romantic suspense, a fantasy, and supernatural suspense. All of her books are now available as ebooks, and most are also in print. Joanne hopes you'll enjoy her books, which present a variety of times, places, and reading experiences, from mysterious to thrilling, emotional to lightly humorous, as well as powerful tales of times long past.

Visit her at www.joannepence.com and be sure to sign up for Joanne's mailing list to hear about new books.

The Rebecca Mayfield Mysteries

Rebecca is a by-the-book detective, who walks the straight and narrow in her work, and in her life. Richie, on the other hand, is not at all by-the-book. But opposites can and do attract, and there are few mystery two-somes quite as opposite as Rebecca and Richie.

ONE O'CLOCK HUSTLE – North American Book Award winner in Mystery

TWO O'CLOCK HEIST

THREE O'CLOCK SÉANCE

FOUR O'CLOCK SIZZLE

FIVE O'CLOCK TWIST

SIX O'CLOCK SILENCE

Plus a Christmas Novella: The Thirteenth Santa

The Angie & Friends Food & Spirits Mysteries

Angie Amalfi and Homicide Inspector Paavo Smith are soon to be married in this latest mystery series. Crime and calories plus a new "twist" in Angie's life in the form of a ghostly family inhabiting the house she and Paavo buy, create a mystery series with a "spirited" sense of fun and adventure.

COOKING SPIRITS
ADD A PINCH OF MURDER
COOK'S BIG DAY
MURDER BY DEVIL'S FOOD
Plus a Christmas mystery-fantasy: COOK'S CURIOUS CHRISTMAS
And a cookbook: COOK'S DESSERT COOKBOOK

The early "Angie Amalfi mystery series" began when Angie first met San Francisco Homicide Inspector Paavo Smith. Here are those mysteries in the order written:

SOMETHING'S COOKING
TOO MANY COOKS
COOKING UP TROUBLE
COOKING MOST DEADLY
COOK'S NIGHT OUT
COOKS OVERBOARD
A COOK IN TIME
TO CATCH A COOK
BELL, COOK, AND CANDLE
IF COOKS COULD KILL
TWO COOKS A-KILLING
COURTING DISASTER
RED HOT MURDER
THE DA VINCI COOK

Supernatural Suspense

Ancient Echoes
Top Idaho Fiction Book Award Winner
Over two hundred years ago, a covert expedition shadowing Lewis and Clark disappeared in the wilderness of Central Idaho. Now, seven anthropology students and their professor vanish in the same area. The key to finding them lies in an ancient secret, one that men throughout history have sought to unveil.

Michael Rempart is a brilliant archeologist with a colorful and controversial career, but he is plagued by a sense of the supernatural and a spiritual intuitiveness. Joining Michael are a CIA consultant on paranormal phenomena, a washed-up local sheriff, and a former scholar of Egyptology. All must overcome their personal demons as they attempt to save the students and learn the expedition's terrible secret....

Ancient Shadows

One by one, a horror film director, a judge, and a newspaper publisher meet brutal deaths. A link exists between them, and the deaths have only begun ....

Archeologist Michael Rempart finds himself pitted against ancient demons and modern conspirators when a dying priest gives him a powerful artifact—a pearl said to have granted Genghis Khan the power, eight centuries ago, to lead his Mongol warriors across the steppes to the gates of Vienna.

The artifact has set off centuries of war and destruction as it conjures demons to play upon men's strongest ambitions and cruelest desires. Michael realizes the so-called pearl is a philosopher's stone, the prime agent of alchemy. As much as he would like to ignore the artifact, when he sees horrific deaths and experiences, first-hand, diabolical possession and affliction, he has no choice but to act, to follow a path along the Old Silk Road to a land that time forgot, and to somehow find a place that may no longer exist in the world as he knows it.

Historical, Contemporary & Fantasy Romance

Dance with a Gunfighter

Gabriella Devere wants vengeance. She grows up quickly when she witnesses the murder of her family by a gang of outlaws, and vows to make them pay for their crime. When the law won't help her, she takes matters into her own hands.

Jess McLowry left his war-torn Southern home to head West, where he hired out his gun. When he learns what happened to Gabriella's family, and what she plans, he knows a young woman like her will have no chance against the outlaws, and vows to save her the way he couldn't save his own family.

But the price of vengeance is high and Gabriella's willingness to sacrifice everything ultimately leads to the book's deadly and startling conclusion.

Willa Cather Literary Award finalist for Best Historical Novel.

The Dragon's Lady

Turn-of-the-century San Francisco comes to life in this romance of star-crossed lovers whose love is forbidden by both society and the laws of the time.

Ruth Greer, wealthy daughter of a shipping magnate, finds a young boy who has run away from his home in Chinatown—an area of gambling parlors, opium dens, and sing-song girls, as well as families trying to eke out a living. It is also home to the infamous and deadly "hatchet men" of Chinese lore.

There, Ruth meets Li Han-lin, a handsome, enigmatic leader of one such tong, and discovers he is neither as frightening cruel, or wanton as reputation would have her believe. As Ruth's fascination with the lawless area grows, she finds herself pulled deeper into its intrigue and dangers, particularly those surrounding Han-lin. But the two are from completely different worlds, and when both worlds are shattered by the Great Earthquake and Fire of 1906 that destroyed most of San Francisco, they face their ultimate test.

Seems Like Old Times

When Lee Reynolds, nationally known television news anchor, returns to the small town where she was born to sell her now-vacant childhood home, little does she expect to find that her first love has moved back to town. Nor does she expect that her feelings for him are still so strong.

Tony Santos had been a major league baseball player, but now finds his days of glory gone. He's gone back home to raise his young son as a single dad.

Both Tony and Lee have changed a lot. Yet, being with him, she finds that in her heart, it seems like old times...

The Ghost of Squire House

For decades, the home built by reclusive artist, Paul Squire, has stood empty on a windswept cliff overlooking the ocean. Those who attempted to live in the home soon fled in terror. Jennifer Barrett knows nothing of the history of the house she inherited. All she knows is she's glad for the chance to make a new life for herself.

It's Paul Squire's duty to rid his home of intruders, but something about this latest newcomer's vulnerable status ... and resemblance of someone from his past ... dulls his resolve. Jennifer would like to find a real flesh-and-blood man to liven her days and nights—someone to share her life with—but living in the artist's house, studying his paintings, she is surprised at how close she feels to him.

A compelling, prickly ghost with a tortured, guilt-ridden past, and a lonely heroine determined to start fresh, find themselves in a battle of wills and emotion in this ghostly fantasy of love, time, and chance.

Dangerous Journey

C.J. Perkins is trying to find her brother who went missing while on a Peace Corps assignment in Asia. All she knows is that the disappearance has something to do with a "White Dragon." Darius Kane, adventurer and bounty hunter, seems to be her only hope, and she practically shanghais him into helping her.

With a touch of the romantic adventure film Romancing the Stone, C.J. and Darius follow a trail that takes them through the narrow streets of Hong Kong, the backrooms of San Francisco's Chinatown, and the wild jungles of Borneo as they pursue both her brother and the White Dragon. The closer C.J. gets to them, the more danger she finds herself in—and it's not just danger of losing her life, but also of losing her heart.